IMAGES

Maisie Mosco, author of two highly acclaimed trilogies, now turns to the contemporary scene, and with insight and humour recounts a year in the lives of three couples.

It began as a joke: 'At my age a face-lift would come in handy!' she said. 'And I could probably get you one cut-price,' he answered. But the ripples spread, setting in train a series of events which force the Ridgeways and their friends, the Sangers and the Newtons, to re-examine themselves, their marriages and their friendship.

The Ridgeways didn't even realise they had a problem until the Sangers tried to persuade them that all problems have a sexual cause and a sexual solution. Julie Newton, successful QC, and her barrister husband, Neil, on the other hand, are convinced that brains are the key to success. Anna Ridgeway is forced to consider whether she really does want – or need – cosmetic surgery. James is made aware of his own insecurity and the Sangers and the Newtons discover you can't involve yourself in other people's difficulties without uncovering problems of your own . . .

Also by the same author, and available from NEL:

Almonds And Raisins
Scattered Seed
Children's Children
Between Two Worlds
A Sense Of Place
The Price Of Fame

About the Author

Maisie Mosco is a Mancunian now living in London. A former journalist, she turned to fiction in the sixties. Her early work was for the theatre, and she is also the author of fourteen radio plays. She began writing novels in the late seventies and her compassionate, human sagas were an immediate success.

For Harvey Unna

Images

Maisie Mosco

NEW ENGLISH LIBRARY
Hodder and Stoughton

Copyright © 1986 by Maisie Mosco Manuscripts Ltd

First published in Great Britain in 1986 by
New English Library

NEL Paperback edition 1987

British Library C.I.P.

Mosco, Maisie
  Images.
  I. Title
  823'.914[F]   PR6063.0819

ISBN 0 450 40789 6

Printed and bound in Great Britain for
Hodder and Stoughton Paperbacks, a
division of Hodder and Stoughton Ltd.,
Mill Road, Dunton Green, Sevenoaks,
Kent (Editorial Office: 47 Bedford
Square, London, WC1B 3DP) by
Cox & Wyman Ltd., Reading.

PART ONE: Before . . .

CHAPTER ONE

IT BEGAN as a joke.

They were dressing for a dinner date, he on his side of the bed, she on hers, a tall, balding man who was losing the battle with middle-age spread, and a petite woman with a few threads of silver in her dark hair. Before taking her bath, she had selected what she would wear. While she put on her make-up, he had showered. Now he was stepping into his trousers, and she into her skirt, like the well timed double-act they sometimes appeared to be.

They were due at the restaurant in forty-five minutes, but were unlikely to be late. Punctuality was important to him, and he practised it like a fine art. It had not mattered to her before she married him. Nor had he, before he married her, been the paragon of neatness she required him to be. Neither had found it easy to adapt to living with the other, but, in the name of love, each had adjusted to the other's foibles. Suffice it to say that, among other things, she had trained herself to watch the clock, and he to leave the lavatory seat in the position in which a lady expects to find it.

Some might call it voluntary subjugation in the name of marriage, but this would not have occurred to the peace-loving Ridgeways. Coming home at the end of a hectic day's work was, for him, like returning to a quiet cocoon, where a sympathetic ear and a cordon bleu meal awaited him. And for her, the nightly sound of his key in the lock was the moment around which her day revolved.

They were a devoted couple and had never been known to air marital differences in public. It was rare for them to exchange a cross word in private, since there was little for them to differ about.

Nobody was surprised that they had raised a model

daughter. While other parents of their acquaintance were blaming each other when their offspring dropped out of college, smoked grass, and behaved promiscuously, Kim Ridgeway had completed her education, got a job at the BBC, and married the young director whose secretary she was.

The Ridgeways were accustomed to being told by their contemporaries how lucky they were on all counts. It is perhaps understandable that they had become a trifle smug.

They exchanged a smile across the king-size, Laura Ashley duvet cover their daughter had given them for Christmas, while she tucked in her blouse and he his shirt.

'You'd better clue me up about this new client we're having dinner with,' she said.

'He's a doctor, Anna.'

'Why would a doctor need an advertising agency?'

'You'd be surprised,' he said with a grin.

She added a silk scarf to her simple outfit. 'What's he selling, James? Vasectomies? Or black-market babies?'

'According to him, what he's selling is a second chance for women.'

'Now you've really got me guessing.'

'Well, you're still a down-to-earth provincial, aren't you, love? Like me. Even though by now we've lived in London longer than we did up north.'

'What's that got to do with it?'

'I was thinking that some of the women you mix with nowadays wouldn't need telling what a second chance for women means. Myrna Sanger, for instance, would tumble to it in less time than it takes her to toss one of those endless salads she feeds to Irving, in an oil-free dressing. And Julie Newton would have known immediately.'

'They're more with-it than me.'

'If by "with-it" you mean worldly, that's what I was trying to say, love. But I'd rather be married to you than to either of them.'

Anna laughed. 'They'd make mincemeat of you.'

'Exactly. And heaven help their husbands now Myrna and Julie have reached the menopausal age!'

'So have I,' she reminded him.

4

'But you're not exhibiting the symptoms that poor Neil Newton is having to put up with. Irving is going through the mill, too.'

Anna defended her friends. 'It's women who have to put up with the symptoms, not their husbands, James. And you still haven't explained what your new client needs the agency for.'

'To promote the London counterpart of his Swiss clinic. He's a cosmetic surgeon.'

It was then that she made the joke.

'At my age, a face-lift would come in handy!'

'Maybe we could get you one cut-price, like we got the new dishwasher.'

'Are you telling me I need a new face?'

'I was being funny, like you were. And I love you the way you are,' he said diplomatically.

'Ageing face and all!' She hurled a shoe at him and rushed to the mirror.

'Ouch!' he winced. The shoe had hit him full in the eye. 'I seem to've spoken too soon about you not exhibiting symptoms.'

He joined her at the mirror to examine his injury and recoiled from her reflection. She had pinched the fleshy part of her face between her fingers and was pulling it into a taut and hideous mask.

'I hope my new client can do better than that!' he exclaimed. 'And if you're going to make a habit of sending menopausal missiles flying in my directon, *I* shall need cosmetic surgery.'

She dropped her hands to her sides, and said miserably, 'Losing her looks isn't easy for a woman.'

'I'm sure it isn't,' he said, mustering the sympathy they usually showed each other.

'Then you do think I'm losing mine!'

He could feel a painful throbbing in his eye – and she had not so much as apologised for hurting him. 'Do you want me to lie to you, and say you still look twenty-one?' he was stung to reply. 'There's nothing terrible about looking middle-aged.'

'Tell yourself that when you buy your next bottle of

hair-restorer,' she retorted. 'And you may as well go and wait for me downstairs. I'm not ready yet.'

'What are you going to do? Put another layer of that liquid camouflage on your face? You'd better get a move on, it's almost half-past-seven.'

'If nobody had invented the clock, we'd be living with sundials all over the house,' she told him. 'The one in the garden wouldn't be enough for you.'

He picked up his jacket and left the room, cut to the quick. He was accustomed to being ribbed by his colleagues at the agency, who seemed to have no sense of time. But his wife had never made that kind of crack.

She kept him waiting for a full ten minutes, and said when she joined him in the hall, 'How would you like it if you said you could use a hair transplant, and I didn't deny it?'

'I wouldn't say it.'

'But as a matter of fact you could use one,' she enjoyed telling him.

He managed to smile. 'They say a receding hairline signifies increased virility.'

'Then you must be the exception that proves the rule, James.'

'What the hell's got into you?' he exploded. She was behaving like Myrna Sanger and Julie Newton rolled into one; suddenly displaying both feminine vanity and a witty abrasiveness fit to emasculate a man. That last jab had really been one below the belt. But his performance in bed wasn't what it used to be; he had left himself wide open for it.

'What's got into me,' she said cuttingly, 'is it's taken me twenty-odd years to find out that I'm married to a man who's totally insensitive to my feelings.'

He refrained from verbal retaliation. Irving and Neil had warned him that a chap must be careful what he said to his menopausal wife, and James was learning fast. Instead, he escaped to the cloakroom before leaving the house and made a point of not replacing the lavatory seat.

CHAPTER TWO

THE SANGERS were eating dinner in the Park Lane penthouse Irving had rashly rented when an escalation in his career brought them from New York to London. He had initially thought of the apartment as a brief extravagance while Myrna looked around for something less plushy. But that was five years ago, when their marriage was still in its infancy and Irving had not known his wife as he did now.

'I see you went shopping again,' he said, noting that she had on yet another expensive leisure outfit.

'I gave away my old favourites to the synagogue good-as-new charity shop. They're having a special sale.'

Good as new is right! thought Irving. Myrna's idea of an old favourite was something she had worn twice.

'Did you find out what's bugging James?' she asked while they ate their salad.

'Yes. And you're not going to believe it — '

'If it's agency business, spare me the details,' Myrna interrupted.

'It isn't. James never lets business get him down. The guys at the office call him Cheerful Charlie. It's a pleasure to have him on the team.'

'Take off your managing-director's hat and tell me what you found out,' Myrna said impatiently.

'He's quarrelled with Anna.'

Myrna put down her fork. 'The Ridgeways have actually fallen out?'

'That's what I said, didn't I, babe?'

'Maybe that too-perfect marriage of theirs had to go up in flames sooner or later,' Myrna said after a thoughtful silence.

'What you mean is it's healthier to let off a little steam than wait to blow a gasket – and ordinarily I'd agree with that,' Irving replied. 'But I never once got the feeling that the Ridgeways, with regard to each other, had anything to let off steam about.'

'They seem to have now.'

'Don't sound so pleased! And I didn't tell you yet that it was Anna who blacked James's eye.'

'He must have done something to deserve it,' Myrna declared. 'I'd like to know what.'

'Then why not go visit her and she'll probably tell you. All I could get from James was that she has some crazy bee in her bonnet.'

'Hm,' said Myrna ominously.

'Me, I blame the menopause for whatever it is,' Irving dared to say.

'Don't even mention that word to me!'

Myrna went to the kitchen and returned with the grilled steak that was their staple diet.

'What I wouldn't give for a plateful of fries,' Irving sighed.

'Including your waistline,' Myrna replied, 'which you didn't have when I married you. Even your mother, who loves your first wife and hates me, admitted that you now look ten years younger than you did. If you ever got sloppy-looking again, I wouldn't stay with you, Irv.'

'I'll bear that in mind, babe. If you see me with a candy bar, you'll know I want us to call it quits.'

'Just so long as I don't see you with another broad. Could that be the reason Anna is gunning for James?' Myrna added.

'Are you kidding? James is the archetypal staid married man.'

'That's what I thought my ex was,' Myrna answered. 'Also what your ex probably thought you were, honey.'

'It was true about me. Until you happened along.'

'What's the betting the same goes for James?' Myrna warmed to her theme. 'In France they say *cherchez la femme* – so who is the femme James is now two-timing Anna with? How did she happen along? And how did Anna find out?'

'You sound like a script meeting for *Dallas*,' Irving said

scathingly, 'or one of those format, between-the-sheets bestsellers.'

'If you'd lived for most of your life in Beverly Hills, like I did, Irv, you wouldn't think them so far-fetched.'

'But you're living in the real world now, babe. It's time you got your feet on the ground.'

'You might not find me such fun with my feet on the ground.'

Irving had not known a dull moment since he married Myrna, but he would welcome a lull now and then. Not just in the constant partying with people Myrna picked up here and there, but in the non-stop, one-woman show Myrna herself was. When they socialised with the suburban Ridgeways and the top-drawer Newtons, Myrna sometimes embarrassed the pants off Irving, and all he could do was cap her wisecracks with a few of his own. He tried to recall when he and she had last had an ordinary, everyday conversation, minus the double-talk, and came to the conclusion that they never had.

'Believe it or not, Myrna,' he said brusquely, 'marriages can totter and fall apart for reasons other than infidelity.'

'You mean like if the husband doesn't give his wife enough money?'

'How much is that little number you're wearing going to cost me?'

'If you'd care to change your mind about not letting me take an allowance from my father — '

'Forget it.'

She came to sit on his lap. 'Okay. You're the boss, honey.'

'Is this my dessert?'

'The only dessert you're getting,' she said, inserting her tongue in his mouth.

Irving would rather have had some ice cream, or a slice of his first wife's memorable strawberry shortcake. There was a time and place for everything. But a guy couldn't *have* everything. You make your bed, you have to lie in it – and Myrna was no hardship in that department. She was also the kind of wife whose looks enhanced an executive's image: blonde and willowy. Sleek was the word for her. With Myrna beside him, Irving came over as a high-flier. He sometimes thought she had recreated him to suit her own image, but what the hell? It was the new Irving Sanger who'd been imported to head one of London's top ad agencies. The sloppy-Joe he'd looked before Myrna got her tape-measure around him wouldn't have been in the running.

Myrna unwound her tongue from his and said, 'Did you enjoy that?' as though she had served him with a piece of pecan pie.

'Sure,' he lied.

'Then why haven't you got a hard-on?'

Fortunately, he was not given time to reply.

'You're worried about the Ridgeways, I guess. Me, too,' she said.

'Then drop in on Anna, like I asked you to,' Irving answered. 'Go comfort her with chicken soup, like you told me your girlfriend did you, when your ex walked out.'

'Is James thinking of walking?'

'He didn't say that. But a guy can only take so much. It's been a week since the flare-up, and one miserable week in a marriage like the Ridgeways' would seem like a year of marital hell would to most couples. That black eye James kidded everyone he'd got colliding with a door is lightening up, but his gloom sure isn't.'

'Poor Anna,' Myrna said.

'From where I'm sitting, babe, it seems like it's poor James.'

'Then why did you tell me to go comfort her?'

'She's giving my buddy a hard time. Some girl-talk could help her ease up on him. The next thing it will affect his work – I have to think of that also. You'll prod Anna out of her blues. I know you.'

Myrna got off his lap to pour their coffee, and mentally replied: That's what you think! What Irving knew about her was what she had allowed him to know. There were times when she felt guilty about it, then she'd tell herself to stay wise. She'd been like an open book to her ex. Honest and trusting, and where had it got her? Into the alimony club was where, and she hadn't even known the bastard was playing around. On the nights they didn't have sex, she had

10

thought he was worn out from staying late at the office – an all-too-correct assumption, since her replacement turned out to be a girl on his staff. Myrna had been too busy baking his favourite cookies to smell a rat, and had learned too late that there were better ways to hold your man. Also that marriage was a male versus female set-up in which only a clever woman could come off best.

What a *shlemiel* I used to be, but I'll never be one again, she was thinking when Irving returned her to the present.

'So when will you drop in on Anna, babe?'

'If London were like New York or LA, I could take her to a singles bar.'

'That's your prescription for healing the breach? I doubt that James would agree with you.'

'James can have your loyalty. Anna gets mine.'

'Oh yes?'

'And there's no better tonic for a woman past her prime than to get given the eye by a bunch of guys on the make.'

Irving prickled with disquiet. What sort of talk was this from his loving wife? Was it another product of the change of life, in addition to her growing urge to spend, spend, spend? Or had she got the seven-year itch? Whichever, Myrna might be the wrong emissary to send on a peace mission to Anna Ridgeway. He clapped a hand to his face, contemplating the damage she could do.

'What's the matter?' she asked him.

'Never mind. Just stick to the chicken soup, the tea and sympathy. Or there'll be trouble between you and me.'

Neil and Julie Newton were also discussing the Ridgeways. Neil had brought the news of the quarrel home with him, and it had monopolised their dinner-time conversation, as it had the Sangers'. All that differed was the style. Both Newtons were barristers, and carefully chewing a topic to the bone was second nature to them. Irving had once said to James that after dining with them he felt as if he had spent the evening at the Old Bailey.

They were still considering the Ridgeways' quarrel at bedtime.

'A one-off after all those equable years together has to be serious,' Neil opined.

As usual, the Newtons had retired early and were now sitting up in their twin divans, with thoughtful expressions on their handsome faces. Julie had just put on her half-moon reading glasses, and Neil was tapping his beautifully crowned teeth with a pencil.

On the wide bedtable they shared were two piles of legal notes – his and hers – a motley collection of ballpoint pens, and the briefs each was currently reading. A shelf of law books occupied the wall where one might have expected to see a television set.

'When did we begin bringing our work to bed with us?' Julie digressed.

'Which of us did it first would be a better question.'

'But purely academic, darling, since we've both done it for years.'

'Are you going to work tonight?'

'Aren't you?'

'My mind is glued to the Ridgeways' sudden debacle.'

'Mine, too.'

'And what one has to ask oneself is, are they having trouble adjusting to being a twosome again, since their daughter left the nest?'

'That could be one aspect of it. But Kim's departure would've affected Anna more than James, wouldn't it? Kim was always bringing her chums home for meals, and generally messing up the house. Maybe Anna now has too much time on her hands, and has turned in on herself,' Julie conjectured.

'Which could never happen to you, my love.'

'There's no comparison between Anna and me. We're close friends, but different kinds of women.'

Too true, thought Neil, who had often envied James his placid, domesticated wife. 'It wouldn't be unusual for *you* to throw something at *me*,' he said. 'But it's valid to bracket you with Anna in one respect – you're both in the throes of that certain age.'

Julie replied with a snort. 'If that's what James thinks is the matter with Anna, you may tell him from me that he's

12

clutching at a straw. A convenient masculine one, with which middle-aged husbands are all too eager to taunt their wives. And that includes you, Neil.'

'If you say so, dear.'

'And if you go on humouring me, as you've been doing lately, and never used to do, I shall begin airing my views on the male menopause.'

'There's no such thing.'

'Technically speaking. But what's in a name? Call it what you will. And I learned from Myrna Sanger that someone has published a book about it.'

'She'll give it to Irving for his next birthday, if I know Myrna.'

'You don't. She puts on a show for people like you and me.'

Neil grinned. 'It's called being the right wife for Irving.'

'There are times when you're more perceptive than I thought.'

Julie got out of bed to pace the room, thoughtfully – a habit Neil had found disconcerting when they first married.

'Why are you staring at me?' she asked, noticing that he was, and with a faraway look in his eyes.

'I was recalling our honeymoon.'

'How very irrelevant.'

'The moment I was remembering isn't. What kind of female have I married? I thought, when you leapt from my embrace and began striding around the nuptial suite.'

'But now you know.'

Neil was not sure that he did. In some ways, his wife remained an enigma to him. He had soon grown accustomed to the restless energy that kept her on the move when she was trying to crystallise her thoughts – the number of hearthrugs Julie had worn threadbare with her pacing was a laugh to their friends – but Neil doubted that she herself knew what fuelled the dynamo within her.

'I didn't leap from your embrace tonight,' she said with a wry smile, 'since it isn't Saturday. And, if my memory serves me correctly, the honeymoon suite was just about big enough to take a double bed.'

'There was a rug at the foot of it, and that was where you

strode back and forth,' Neil reminded her. 'Two paces one way and two the other — '

'That was all there was room for.'

'And watching your quick about-turns made me feel dizzy. Then you suddenly stopped, and asked me to lend you my pen. You'd forgotten to bring yours. Some honeymoon! I thought.'

'I do seem to get some of my shrewdest legal thoughts at inconvenient moments,' Julie conceded. 'Remember the one that came to me when I was in labour with the twins?'

Since their sons were not exactly a source of pleasure to them, a moment of silence followed, then Julie went on, 'But that concerned a case you were involved in, while I devoted myself to the domestic scene.'

'Devoted is hardly the word. If it hadn't been for Anna, chaos would have reigned in our household.'

'And how odd it seems,' said Julie, 'that in a different way I'm now called upon to sort things out for her. We can't just leave the Ridgeways to flounder amid their problems, can we, Neil?'

'That's what Irving and I decided, when he rang my chambers to tell me they've now *got* problems. He said he was going to ask Myrna to give Anna a spot of good advice.'

Julie laughed disparagingly. 'No prizes for guessing the sort of advice it'll be. Myrna will hand Anna the "hang on to your guy at all costs" line. It's how she functions. She's been trying for ages to get Anna to dye the grey out of her hair — '

'I wouldn't want you to do that,' Neil cut in.

'I don't care if you would or not, darling. I don't have Myrna's stay-young mentality, or I'd already have done it. Nor, unlike Myrna — Anna too — am I just a shadow of my husband.'

Neil responded with a smile which hid his resentment that, professionally, with him and Julie it was the opposite way round. She had taken a lengthy sabbatical from her career when their boys were born. In those days, the Newtons and Ridgeways had lived in adjoining terraced cottages in Hampstead Garden Suburb. Julie and Anna had shared the trials of pregnancy, and the raising of their children to school age. Then Julie had told Neil that enough was enough. He would not have expected a woman like her to abandon her profession, and had not been surprised when the head of chambers where she had been a junior welcomed her back. That was fifteen years ago, and she was now a QC which Neil had yet to achieve.

'The time when the Ridgeways were our neighbours seems to me now like another life,' he capped his thoughts.

'James was always ringing our doorbell, to make sure we weren't murdering each other!' Julie recalled.

'That's what's so astonishing about them having this big bust-up now. The pots and pans were sent flying on our side of the dividing wall, never on theirs.'

'Even more astonishing,' said Julie, coming to hug him, 'is that two decades later you and I are still friends.'

'That's just as well,' he answered ruefully, as she got into her bed and switched off the lamp. 'For once-a-week lovers – and those two decades account for it – without friendship what is there left?'

CHAPTER THREE

THERE WAS more than a grain of truth in Julie's belief that Anna was her husband's shadow, but they had always seen themselves as a couple with one mind. This enviable harmony had deprived them of the mental distancing, even from one's intimates, which people need to retain their individuality.

Both were products of close-knit marriages like their own. When Anna's father died, some years before, her mother had said, 'Now I'm only half a person,' and she was still saying it. Anna would have thought of herself that way, bereft of James. Nevertheless, she had barely spoken a word to him since they quarrelled, and had spent a painful week delving into why she was behaving the way she was.

If she could be funny about her face, why couldn't he? was the crucial question. It had taken her three days to admit to herself that her ageing appearance was not a joke to her, but something she did not want to accept. Her small build and short hairstyle were a youthful combination, and it did not seem too long since she and her daughter had been taken for sisters.

Not any more, she told her reflection in the dressing-table mirror. Well, not from close up. But why did it matter to her? She couldn't imagine her own mother having been prey to such vanity. Was it only vanity? No. It was something else, too. A feeling of uncertainty. Like getting lost and not being able to find your way back, that had nothing to do with her face.

Impulsively, she went downstairs and telephoned her mother, though she had not sought that sensible woman's advice since she herself became a wife. Until now, there'd been nothing she felt that James wouldn't understand.

'Whatever're you doing ringing me up now, love, when

16

it's cheaper to mek trunk calls at night?' the reassuring North-country voice responded to Anna's mid-morning call.

Anna managed to laugh. 'They haven't been called trunk calls for donkey's years, Mam.'

'An' if that's my daughter's way of calling me old-fashioned, I've never denied it. All this progress that's gone on since I were a lass'll like as not finish up blowing us all off the face of the earth. An' that reminds me, our Anna, I do wish you'd tek back that there pressure cooker you gave me. It were a waste of your husband's hard-earned brass. My next-door-neighbour says the jiggly bit on top keeps blowing off of hers. But I wouldn't've used it anyroad. Who have I to cook for, now your dad's dead'n gone?'

'Don't you cook for yourself, Mam?'

'After a fashion, love. But it were your dad I used to put myself out for, not me. What's this expensive phone call for, our Anna? You've not rung up just to hear your mam's voice.'

In a way, Anna had been seeking motherly comfort. But there was something she wanted to ask, too. 'I'm having a bit of a difficult time,' was her preamble.

'Has something gone wrong between you and James?'

'Sort of. But everything'll be all right when I've sorted myself out, and I'm over the you-know-what.'

'Oh. It's that, is it?'

It has to be that, Anna thought.

'I'm a God-fearing person,' said her mother, 'as you know, our Anna. But I've often wondered why, in His mercy, He afflicted us women not just with having periods every month, but also with the change of life when we're getting shut of 'em.'

Anna finally got her question out. 'How did the change affect you?'

'Mine were thirty years ago, love. I shall have to think back.'

'Were you upset about looking middle-aged?'

'I don't remember that one. But women do get some right queer feelings at that time of life. They have to be careful they don't get caught on the change, as well. An' don't get worried if you pour with sweat. It's Nature's way of getting what's left of your juices out of your system — '

Anna listened dejectedly while her mother rambled on about menopausal headaches and vaginal discharges.

'Never tek a cold drink while you're having a hot flush,' was the final piece of old-wives' advice, which matched Anna's girlhood memories of not being allowed to wash her hair while she was menstruating.

'It was nice talking to you, Mam,' she said before she rang off. But no help at all.

A recollection of James's attractive young women colleagues rose briefly before her, and with it came the first tinge of insecurity she had ever experienced. Would James go on loving her once her looks had gone? But they already had, hadn't they?

Tonight, she would give him an extra-special dinner, to make up for the pot-luck meals she'd been plonking in front of him all week, and for how she'd been treating him. She thought of serving it by candlelight, but he'd think the candlelight was intended to be kind to her face. Well, wasn't it? Come on, admit it! It was the sort of thing Myrna Sanger would do, except that Myrna didn't yet need to. Her age still didn't show – which Julie said was because she had no kids to age her.

Anna was still in the hall, and confronted by the telltale mirror above the telephone bench. A moment later she had fetched a tea-cloth from the kitchen and was covering the spitefully gleaming glass that had become her enemy. Was she going mad? If so, at least she had the dreaded 'change' to blame it on, she was telling the big china dog that sat staring at her from its corner, when the doorbell rang.

Myrna breezed in on a waft of Chanel No. 5, and stopped in her tracks. 'Who's dead, Anna?'

'I beg your pardon?'

Myrna deposited a bottle of white wine on the telephone bench and pointed to the mirror. 'In my religion, people cover looking-glasses in a house of mourning.'

Anna wanted to quip that she was mourning her lost looks – but how could you say that to a woman who looked like Myrna did? When you still had them you took them for

18

granted, and didn't understand how it felt not to have them any more.

'Is the mirror broken?' Myrna inquired, wondering which of the Ridgeways had thrown what at the other and smashed it in the fray.

Anna shook her head. 'But if I told you why I covered it, you'd tell me not to be daft.'

Myrna took in her wan expression. 'Try me.'

Anna tried to laugh at herself, but burst into tears instead. 'I can't stand the sight of my face, Myrna. And I hate myself for not being able to — '

'So have a good cry, and then we'll have a little talk. You can let your hair down with me, it's all right.'

She picked up the bottle of wine and shepherded Anna into the kitchen.

'You must think me a real fool,' Anna said, drying her eyes, when they were seated at the table. 'And James would tell me that crying is a symptom of the change.'

'That's why I'd never let Irving see me weep,' Myrna answered. 'You're not the only one who has to take that kind of crap from her husband right now. If I'd been you, I wouldn't have given James the satisfaction of blaming the menopause for you blacking his eye.'

Anna bristled. 'He told Irving, did he!'

'And Irv saved him the trouble of having to tell Neil.'

'It *was* an accident, Myrna – well, where my shoe hit him was.'

'All you did was throw a shoe at him? I thought it was a punch-up.'

'James probably made it sound like one – to get Irving's sympathy.'

'Don't worry. *You*'ve got mine.'

'But I wish I didn't need it. And how dare James make me seem violent!' Anna flared. 'He knows I can't bear violence. Whenever one of my son-in-law's cops-and-robbers TV series is on, I sit with my eyes shut half the time. I'd rather not see the films Harry makes, but James thinks it would be disloyal of us not to watch his work.'

'Are we discussing your marriage crisis, Anna? Or your son-in-law's movies? And you don't have to watch

19

'what you'd rather not just because James thinks you should.'

'What marriage crisis? I'm going through some sort of crisis on my own account, Myrna. It's got nothing to do with James and me personally — '

'Are you kidding, Anna? Or just dumb?'

'And about me doing something just because James thinks I should,' – Anna ignored the interruption – 'we happen to have a give-and-take marriage.'

'But when it comes to the crunch, one of you has to let the other win.'

'We don't have contests.'

'There must be times when you're faced with a yea-or-nay situation, and you think one way and he thinks the other,' Myrna persisted.

'No, as a matter of fact.'

Myrna got up and went to lean against the work counter. 'I don't believe this! What you're telling me is you have absolutely no mind of your own. I am never going to accept that a married couple exists who agree about everything.'

'James and I usually do.'

'He's fooled you into seeing it that way,' Myrna replied.

'James isn't that kind.'

'But you, Anna, would be putty in any guy's hands. Like I was with my ex.'

Anna found this hard to relate to the Myrna she knew.

'With him I was a different dish of tea from the one I am now,' Myrna went on. 'A person lives and learns.'

She fell briefly silent. Which isn't like her, Anna thought. Whatever the circumstances, Myrna could be relied upon to rattle on regardless. But Anna had never had an intimate chat with her before, not even when the two of them were alone. It wasn't that kind of friendship, like Anna's with Julie, though Myrna seemed to regard Anna as a close friend.

'I guess we're both letting our hair down this morning,' Myrna said with a smile.

And in Myrna's case, it was as if she had allowed Anna to glimpse the woman behind the frivolous fashion-plate. Anna had never been really at ease with her – how could you, with someone who came over as larger than life? And never stopped being the life and soul of the party. But I don't feel uncomfortable with her now, Anna registered as Myrna came back to sit with her at the table. Nor did she feel embarrassed when Myrna, whose demonstrativeness usually made her cringe, patted her hand.

'But I didn't come here to talk about me,' Myrna said. 'Irv and I are worried about you and James.'

'There's nothing to be worried about.'

'Then why has James been getting the cold shoulder from you all week?'

'Did he tell Irving that?'

'How else would I know?'

'He had no bloody right to!'

'Men tell each other their troubles the way women do.'

Anna had not thought otherwise. James was always passing on to her the grouses about Myrna and Julie that he'd learned of from Irving and Neil. But it came as a shock to find out he was now joining in the grousing sessions.

'Listen, without friends to talk to, where would a person be?' Myrna went on. 'There are always going to be things you can't say to your loving spouse.'

But until now it had never been that way with Anna and James. Why had she thrown that damned shoe at him!

'My first few weeks in England, if it hadn't been for you I'd have jumped into the Thames,' Myrna said. ' "How can you be lonely in a big city?" Irv kept saying to me – then he'd go to the office, and I'd have nothing to do but window-shop by myself all day. Someone should tell my dear husband that big cities can be the loneliest places on earth. When you invited us for dinner, and turned out to be so nice, it was like as if you'd handed me a lifeline, Anna. In the States, I'd have gotten palsy-walsy with the other wives in my apartment building in no time. Britishers are nice and polite, but they sure are hard to get to know.'

'Not the ones where I come from. I didn't find "welcome" written on people's mats, either, when I moved here from Manchester. Londoners take longer about it. But I'm not short of friends now, and nor are you.' Going to one of Myrna's big parties was like getting jammed in a football crowd.

Myrna glanced at her diamond wristwatch.

'Have you got to rush off?'

'There's a ladies' committee brunch today at the synagogue – but for you I'm prepared to miss it.'

'You don't have to, Myrna.'

'All I'd be missing is the bagels and lox. They don't dish the dirt about each other, like goes on back home,' Myrna said with regret. 'I guess in London Jewish circles there isn't much dirt to dish. Let's have some wine.'

Anna eyed the bottle. 'At eleven o'clock in the morning?'

'Why not? If James can cry into his liquor about how you're treating him, with Irv and Neil – the three of them got together after work last night.'

Anna, who had briefly relaxed, felt her hackles rise. 'Is that what he's been doing? I got a whiff of booze on James's breath, and thought he'd had a drink at a late meeting with a client. What an idiot I am!'

'They went to that pub where they have those monthly business lunches of theirs. Personally, I've never believed it was for business.' Myrna added fuel to Anna's fire. 'And especially not since you, me, and Julie started on the change.'

Anna marched to her glassware cupboard and got out a couple of tumblers. 'You'll forgive me for not bothering to fetch proper glasses from the dining-room cabinet, won't you, Myrna? The bottle-opener's in the cutlery drawer.'

'Now you're talking,' said Myrna approvingly.

'What I'm doing is what you'd call wising-up!'

'And just one of the things you need to wise up to is that at a time like this, the guys are going to band together.'

Anna plonked the tumblers on the table and watched Myrna open the bottle. 'Fill mine to the brim.'

'I was going to.'

'How dare my husband tell people I'm treating him badly!' she exploded, after gulping some wine – which went straight to her head. 'And if I am, it's his bloody fault, not mine! How does he expect me to treat him, when he's told me I need my face lifting? I expect he shared *that* little observation with Irving and Neil, too.'

'Irv didn't mention it, and I'm sure he would have if he knew.'

'Then I've told you something I needn't have.'

'So you may as well tell me the rest.'

'James didn't exactly say it, but he didn't deny it when he could've done – should've done – ' Anna said wretchedly. 'A joke at my own expense got me more than I bargained for,' she finished after telling Myrna the whole story.

'I can see how it would upset you.'

'Especially as my face does need lifting.'

'Sooner or later, it happens to all of us.'

'A lot of comfort that is.'

Anna drank some more wine, and they shared a moment of contemplative silence.

'Listen, these days cosmetic surgery is no big deal,' Myrna declared. 'Back home, women who can afford it think nothing of getting it done.'

'But it's not like that over here.'

'It soon will be,' said Myrna confidently. 'Our husbands are busy promoting it, right now, and they're good at their job.'

Anna looked sceptical. 'All the same, I can't imagine any of the women I know resorting to it. Not even the vain ones – which I never thought I was, until now.'

'A woman doesn't have to be vain to want to look attractive,' Myrna answered. 'Do you know any women who don't wear make-up? Even Julie does – though if I were her, I'd put the rouge beneath my cheekbones, now her face has started to get podgy.'

'And what would you advise me to do?' Anna asked sardonically.

'Think seriously about what you made the joke about.'

'It's all very fine for you to say that! You could pass for thirty.'

'Are you sure you don't mean twenty-five?'

'Twenty-eight, maybe.'

'Because I've already had cosmetic surgery, you *schmuck*.' Myrna laughed at Anna's astonished expression. 'But if you ever breathe a word about it to my husband or yours, I'm never going to speak to you again. I had it done before I met Irv, and I'd prefer him to think it's my first time if I ever need a second lift.'

What a crafty devil she is, Anna thought with a smile.

'Like I said, back home it's nothing sensational. When a woman drops out of circulation, you know where she's probably at. If she's gone for more than a couple of weeks, you reckon she has to be having the whole number. Her shape also.'

Anna imagined herself being carved and trimmed like a side of beef, and managed not to shudder.

'I was only thirty-nine,' Myrna told her. 'But I take after my mom's side of the family, and they age early – I already looked like forty-five. After my ex walked, Mom said to me, "Go get your face tailored, Myrna."'

'You must have a very different mother from mine.'

Myrna confirmed that indeed she had. 'After Pop had his prostate trouble fixed, he got kind of raunchy and began chasing young broads. So Mom got herself made young again. You should see her. Seventy-six years old, and she's a real dish. Only it hasn't stopped Pop from chasing, I have to say.'

'Then she was wasting her time, wasn't she?'

'That's what I said to her, but she said her spirits got lifted along with her face, and with that I had to agree. All the women I know who've had the surgery say it has that effect on them – and the same would go for you, Anna.'

To Anna it sounded like a conveyor belt that repackaged women in pursuit of eternal youth. But it was part of the lunch-by-the-pool background Myrna came from. Anna couldn't relate it to herself any more than she could *Dynasty* and *Dallas*. Nor would she want to.

'Did James show you the "before and after" pictures in that Swiss clinic brochure?' Myrna asked.

'He wouldn't dare.'

'I guess not. I saw it when I dropped in at the agency to take a look at the new receptionist.'

'Are you scared she's going to be competition?'

'No. Her hips are too big. Irv likes skinny women.'

Myrna smoothed the skirt of her elegant suit. 'I used to be a big girl, by the way.'

Anna found that as hard to believe as Myrna's ever having been putty in a man's hands.

'Maybe you should ask James to show you that brochure,' Myrna said.

'If you came here to cheer me up, Myrna, you're having the opposite effect!' Anna drank some more wine. 'I have no intention of going within miles of a cosmetic surgeon. Not even though my husband thinks he could get me done cut-price.'

'But if you did decide to do it, cut-price or not, James would have to foot the bill, wouldn't he? And tell me a better place to punish a guy for upsetting you than in his pocket.'

Again Anna was stunned by Myrna's wiliness. Julie, though she found the American woman good company, maintained that she hadn't a brain in her head. But when it came to mental machinations, Julie could take lessons from Myrna.

'If you left now, that brunch you were going to would still be in full swing when you got there,' Anna said glancing at the clock. It was only eleven forty-five – and they'd gone through a bottle of wine! 'I'm feeling sort of woozey, Myrna. I need to lie down.'

'I thought you wanted to get rid of me.'

It was a bit of both. Anna's head was swimming, too, from the thoughts Myrna had planted in it. 'I'm grateful to you for coming,' she said sincerely. But was she?

Myrna rose from her chair, pulled on her French kid gloves, and gave Anna a sisterly kiss. 'Right now, you're sore as hell with James, and who wouldn't be? But that will get you no place. If you want to save your marriage, call me and I'll go with you to see the surgeon,' she said, as if cosmetic surgery was the universal remedy for marital ills.

She was gone from the house before Anna had time to register that until Myrna's visit she had not known that her marriage needed saving.

CHAPTER FOUR

JAMES WAS beset by a feeling that everything was against him. High on the list was the trouble he was having with his new client, who had dismissed, one after another, all the promotion ideas that James had put before him. Since James's function was largely that of a middleman between the client and the agency's creative department, it was he who took the flak from both sides.

He returned to the office on a sweltering summer morning with yet another rejected folio, loosened his tie, and prepared himself for a 'whys and wherefores' session with Irving. The Swiss doctor was not James's first difficult account, but in the past he had never doubted his ability to convince the client that the agency knew best. This time, he wasn't so sure – and had the feeling that Irving was aware of it.

'Mr Sanger has Ronnie with him at the moment,' Irving's secretary said, as James was about to enter his friend's office. 'I know things are very informal round here,' she added, 'but barging in on the boss without checking with me isn't on. Ronnie doesn't do it.'

'Who the heck do you think you're ticking off!' James let her have it. 'Ronnie isn't the agency's number two.'

'But everyone thinks he's number three.'

The girl resumed the typing James had interrupted. He felt like heaving her out of the chair and kicking her behind. She gave him a glance over the top of her owlish glasses that told him she knew it. And what had she meant by everyone thinking Ronnie was number three?

Officially, the agency did not have a hierarchy. When Irving took over he had fired the resentful deputy managing director, and had not appointed another to breathe down his neck. Irving's shrewdness in that respect had not escaped

James, whose experience and seniority singled him out to take the helm in Irving's absence.

James's account-exec colleagues were all in their twenties and thirties. James had seen them come and go – and Ronnie was one of the brightest. Irving had once remarked that he would go far. What were the two of them discussing? And why was James recalling that, now?

Ronnie emerged from Irving's office and gave him a friendly smile – or was it an ambiguous one?

'Landed your slippery fish yet, James?'

'Not quite. But I will.'

'I hear the art department are tearing their hair out.'

So would I be, if I had any hair to spare, James thought, entering Irving's office and tossing the unsuccessful folio on his desk.

'Not another no-no, James? This is getting to be a habit!'

'But not my habit,' said James defensively.

'Where's your sense of humour?'

'I seem to've lost it.'

'Let me know when you get it back. I won't make any more cracks till you do.'

'When I tell the art department, they'll want to lynch me.'

'But before we meet with them, you and I had better have a re-think, James.' Irving took off his spectacles, revealing myopic blue eyes that made him appear a good deal milder than he was. 'What it boils down to, I guess, is we're faced here with a twofold problem. We've never had to promote such a touchy product before – the guys who first promoted tampons would've come up against the same consumer prejudice. Your average British lady would've recoiled from the mere idea, like she still does about cosmetic surgery —'

'And it's Mrs Average we're going for,' James cut in.

'So we're making with the discreet approach,' Irving went on with his assessment, 'and that brings us head-on to why our problem is twofold. From subtlety the client doesn't want to know.'

'Our real problem,' said James, 'is if we do it his way, the campaign might fail. But if we don't agree with him, we could lose him to another agency. This isn't a problem, it's

27

a bloody dilemma! Why did you have to lumber me with a twentieth-century Frankenstein!'

'I'm too busy to handle the account myself. And so far, in this agency you're the next best thing.'

James noted the 'so far'. 'Thanks,' he said edgily. 'But I've had to juggle all my other work to cope with it. And – this is going to sound irrational to you – if you hadn't given me this client, I wouldn't have been in the doghouse with Anna.'

'What are you talking about, James?'

'Never mind.'

'Anna threw the shoe at you before she met the guy.'

'But he was indirectly responsible.' James cast discretion to the winds and told Irving why.

'How can a guy who's been married as long as you have not know that women are touchy about their looks?' was Irving's reaction.

'Anna never has been.'

'All the same, you shouldn't have said what you did, James.'

'How was I to know she'd suddenly get touchy and take it the way she did?'

'She's menopausal, isn't she? And when did you last take a good look at her face?'

'After twenty-odd years, you don't sit looking at each other's faces. You and Myrna are newly-weds, compared to us.'

But you're the ones who've always behaved like newly-weds, Irving thought. Maybe that lovey-dovey way they had in public was only a habit they hadn't bothered dropping as the years passed by?

James confirmed Irving's conjecture. 'When a couple have been together as long as Anna and me, and they hit it off like we do – did! – well, their relationship is what you'd call the comfortable kind, if you know what I mean — '

Irving did – all too well. 'Their looks become like part of the furnishing; you don't have to say any more.'

'But I will, if you don't mind listening.'

'I'm your friend. Why would I mind?' But I also have the agency to run, and time is ticking away – which James is usually more aware of than anyone else. London isn't like New York, where everyone raced through today as if there might not be a tomorrow.

'What I'm really trying to say,' James went on, 'is when you've had a comfy armchair, or a hearthrug, for years, you don't notice it's starting to look worn until something, or someone, draws your attention to it. It wasn't till after Anna got mad with me that I saw how she's aged, Irving — '

'But I'd advise you not to make that speech you just made to me, to her, James. Especially not the bit about the hearthrug.'

'It wasn't an insult. I'm as fond of the flower prints on our living-room wall now they've begun looking faded as I've always been.'

'Another unfortunate analogy! And let me tell you something, boychik: comfortable is a dangerous word applied to marriage. In that context, what it means is boredom, and I'm here to prove it. In London, I mean. Married to Myrna.'

'Are you telling me you're bored with her?'

'I sometimes wish I was, but there's no danger,' Irving said wryly. 'What I'm telling you is my first marriage was the same as yours and Anna's. My family blamed the break-up on Myrna, but she couldn't have hooked me if I hadn't been ready for some action.'

'If you think I am, you're wrong.'

'I'd have said the same about myself.' Irving gazed into space for a moment. 'I used to think a childless marriage could be wiped out as if it never existed, but once or twice lately, I've thought about my ex. Married to a guy who couldn't give her kids – mumps got me where it counts. She didn't let it sour her. Then what does the guy do? Walk out, when she's past the age to start a family with someone else. She'd have made a terrific mother. That's something I'm always going to have to live with, James. But what the hell am I doing unloading this on you, and in office time?' Irving said, collecting himself.

'Maybe you needed to get it off your chest. I didn't tell you yet that Anna has soaped over every mirror in the house. This face thing is getting to be a phobia, Irving.'

'Blame the menopause. Like I do for my wife's spending mania. Myrna's always had expensive tastes. With a father who made a fortune from real estate, why wouldn't she have? But not like right now. A day never passes that she doesn't make with the credit cards. What's the latest on Julie?'

'They're eating at our house tonight, so I'll probably find out. Has it struck you, Irving, that all the married men we know in our age group must be going through the sort of nonsense we are at the moment? Only they don't talk about it.'

'How did you, me, and Neil get to talking about it?'

'I don't know. But I'm damn glad we did – or I'd be more sick and sorry for myself than I am, thinking it's only happening to me.'

'What's happening to you doesn't affect your bank balance.'

'And that penthouse you live in must cost you a bomb,' said James.

'Tell me about it! But Myrna's Pop would be happy to pay the rent. That's the ace she has up her sleeve. She also thinks our swanky address is the right setting for her, needless to say.'

James eyed Irving's pinstripe suit, the Brooks Brothers shirt and tie, the well-barbered black hair – that he suspected had to be dyed – and the manicured fingernails. After five years in London, Irving still had Madison Avenue written all over him. 'It's the right setting for you, too.'

Irving rested his folded arms where his belly was in his pre-Myrna days and gave James a wistful smile. 'Believe it or not, boychik, a home like yours, or Neil's, would suit me fine.'

'You're a bit of a split personality, aren't you?' James said with a grin.

And who made me into one? thought Irving. Myrna.

James was thinking that the man who had become his friend was a different one from the agency's high-powered managing director.

Irving stepped briskly back into his role. 'So let's get down to business; we don't have all day, James.'

Part of James's mind had never left it. He had a record of holding on to an account once the agency had landed it. Was this going to be the one that got away? 'What were you and Ronnie closeted together about?' he asked Irving – without meaning to.

'What has that to do with this?'

Nothing – James hoped. But failure now would be put down to his age, and could set him on the downhill path. Whereas Ronnie . . . Pull yourself together! James ordered himself. Irving's your friend, he isn't going to do you down. But it was Irving the boss who was eyeing him impatiently.

After they had discussed the tricky new account, Irving ended the meeting with a final word of personal comfort – or tried to, he thought, when it led to another spate of grumbling.

'I found a wine bottle in the dustbin,' James said. 'After Myrna had dropped in to see Anna.'

'You're blaming the contents of your garbage can on my wife?'

'Anna said Myrna brought the wine — '

'So they had a sip of Chablis, or whatever, together,' Irving replied with a shrug.

'Some sip! My wife was in bed sleeping it off, when I got home from work – but she didn't tell me wine was the reason till I found the bottle, later. Yours was able to drive herself home!'

'That doesn't make Myrna a wino.' But it did confirm Irving's fears about her methods of helping to heal a marital breach.

'And whoever heard of a burst waterpipe in midsummer!' James exclaimed irrelevantly. 'Our bathroom was flooded this morning. Who knows if the plumber has been to fix it yet? It could only happen to me!'

'If you're going to get paranoid, I'll find you a good shrink,' Irving answered. 'Meanwhile, go back to your office and ask Marj to make you a nice cup of tea.'

On the secretary front, James was envied by all his male colleagues, Irving included. Marj had just had her fiftieth birthday, and was no less efficient now than when James engaged her, seven years ago. How did Marj go through the menopause without me even noticing it? he asked himself as he made his way to her comforting presence. Maybe it was only their husbands they let have it? But he couldn't imagine Marj letting anyone have it.

'Any calls, Marj?' he asked, pausing by her desk. He didn't need to ask for some tea; the kettle was steaming, and a teabag was waiting in his mug.

'Several,' she replied. 'But I dealt with them, don't worry.'

'Of course you did, Marj.' What a treasure she was.

'There's something I have to tell you, Mr Ridgeway,' she said.

'And what might that be?'

'My husband thinks it's time I packed it in.'

James blanched at the thought of losing her. It would have been a blow at any time, but just now, what with how things were at home, and everything, it was as if the ground was really starting to slip from under his feet. 'I see,' he said quietly.

'I feel as if I'm letting you down, Mr Ridgeway, especially since you haven't been yourself, lately — '

'Who says I haven't?'

'Nobody has to. I can tell.'

What? That I'm slipping? thought James. Was it becoming as apparent to others – especially Irving – as it was to himself? 'Everyone has bad patches of one kind or another,' he said stiffly.

'But I've not noticed yours showing before,' said Marj. 'Coping with this and that doesn't get easier as we get older,' she added philosophically.

James was coming to see that for himself! 'Are you going to take notice of your husband, Marj?' It wasn't for James to tell her not to – though a pipsqueak like Ronnie certainly would.

'I was coming round to the idea myself, when Arthur said it,' Marj replied. 'Now the kids are off our hands we can get by on what Arthur earns. I might as well move over and make room for someone younger,' she said with a self-deprecating laugh.

'There's plenty of life left in you yet, Marj,' James said, feeling as if he was also saying it to himself.

'Thanks, but I've made up my mind, Mr Ridgeway. I'll stay till we find you a replacement, of course.'

'She won't be like you, though.'

'But she'll probably fit in around here a lot better than I do nowadays.'

James knew what she meant, but saw no point in prolonging the discussion. Marj was deserting him – he felt like a sinking ship. Who wouldn't, with one thing and another?

That evening his car stalled on the journey home, and held up the heavy traffic on the North Circular Road. The cacophony of honking horns would have unnerved anyone. To a man in James's present mood, it was as if everything was indeed conspiring against him.

The irate driver of the lorry directly behind him came to shake a beefy fist under his nose.

'Get this bleedin' jalopy movin', will yer, mate?'

'What makes you think I haven't tried to?'

'Try again!'

This time, the engine started immediately – galvanised into action, as James was, by the lorry driver's belligerence!

'Yer don't know yer clutch from yer balls!' shouted the beetle-browed, sweaty-faced individual as he stomped off.

James almost got out of the car to chase after him and sock him one. But the man was built like a bruiser, and the black eye James already had was not fully faded. He comforted himself by buying a rich gateau from his local pastry shop, to take home. Anna hadn't bothered serving a sweet course since she threw the shoe at him, and there was no guarantee she'd have made a dessert just because the Newtons were coming for dinner. They'd be lucky if she took her mind off her face long enough to boil them an egg.

Julie's Rover was already parked in the drive. And Neil's Honda on the street, where James was obliged to leave his car, since his garage was blocked. By a woman who considered nobody but herself, he thought peevishly, as he entered the house.

'You're late, James!' Julie called, in her best prosecuting-counsel voice.

'This is the first time I've ever known you get here on time!' he hit back.

The Newtons were notorious late-arrivers, especially when they came directly from their respective chambers as they had this evening. No hostess who was expecting them for dinner would risk including a soufflé in the menu, and they were liable to be served casseroled this or that wherever they dined. The reason would not have occurred to either of them.

James washed his hands in the cloakroom, combed what remained of his hair before a soaped-over mirror, took the gateau into the kitchen, and stopped in his tracks. Julie was frying onions on the stove – the room reeked of it. But James's gaze was riveted to his wife, who was seated in the Windsor chair by the window, wearing her dressing-gown, her face hidden by a stiff white mask with slits where her eyes and mouth should be.

By now, it would not have surprised him to come home and find her groping blindly around with a sack over her head. But where the Ridgeways came from, you only sat around in your dressing-gown if you were ill.

He found his voice and looked at Julie. 'What's the matter with Anna?'

'You're a fine one to ask! And don't try to talk to her, James. She can't speak.'

James prickled with alarm. 'Why can't she?'

'She's got a face-pack on, you dimwit! It gets mixed with water and then it hardens.'

James let the insult pass. He was getting used to being told, directly or indirectly, that he had something lacking. 'I thought she'd had an accident,' he said. 'That it was plaster-of-Paris.'

'It's a wonder he didn't say my face needs propping up with splints,' Anna managed to hiss without moving her lips.

She sounded like a bad ventriloquist and James could not help laughing.

'You cruel devil!' Julie exclaimed.

'Thanks for telling him,' Anna burst forth. Then the face-mask cracked and crumbled onto her lap.

Neil, who had made himself scarce before James's arrival, chose that moment to enter from the living-room, carrying the glass of whisky with which he had fortified himself, and another that he had anticipated James would need.

'Take your partner-in-crime out of here!' Julie flashed to him. 'Anna and I can do without you two exchanging self-pitying glances over our heads.'

'I'm not being driven out of my own kitchen,' James retorted.

'Then why not ask me why I'm cooking dinner?'

'Probably because Anna didn't bother to. I've been living on snacks since the menopause went to her head — '

'Snacks are more than you deserve,' Julie declared. 'You've upset Anna so much, she called my chambers and left a message cancelling tonight. I didn't like the sound of that, so I ignored the message.'

'Well you can stop frying onions on my account,' said James. 'I never eat them – as Anna could have reminded you.'

'Too bad.' Julie snatched the cake box, which James was still clutching. 'Did it never occur to you that women have other things to think about than their husbands' fads?' She dumped the cake box on a stool behind Neil, who promptly sat on it. 'Now look what you've done!' she yelled when he got up again.

'I'm sure it will still taste delicious, dear.'

'Why do I get the feeling you're humouring me again?'

'That's what James has been doing with me,' Anna said to her.

James lost his temper. 'Maybe you *should* get your face seen to, then there'd be nothing to humour you about! Anything for a normal married life again!'

'What makes you think yours was normal?' Julie put her oar in.

'Stay out of it,' Neil warned her.

'I'm already in it. I didn't come here to cook a meal for poor, starving James. I came to help my friend sort herself out.'

'But your idea of a normal married life doesn't happen to be hers,' said James. 'You and Neil have gone at it hammer

35

and tongs since the day we met you – and it isn't Neil I put it down to.'

'Well, you're a bloody male chauvinist, aren't you?' Julie said sweetly. 'Fortunately, Neil isn't. And he and I, may I point out, are still together.'

What was Julie hinting at? Had Anna told her she was thinking of leaving him?

'Since James and Anna fell out,' Julie said to Neil, 'it's crossed my mind that the reason for their extraordinary record of rapport could be that neither of them has ever said or done anything to upset the other – not even on the most trivial level. And if that's a normal marriage, count me out.'

'It's called consideration. And it beats the hell out of a cat-and-dog life,' James said pointedly. 'When Anna gets over this momentary madness, we'll be just like we were before.'

'That isn't possible,' said Julie.

'Are you trying to stir things up?'

'They're already stirred up, aren't they? And if you've ever stood on a beach and thrown a handful of pebbles in the air, you'll surely know that they're not going to settle back where they were before you disturbed them, James.'

'Spare me your courtroom analogies,' said James crossly. 'And if you don't mind, I'm ready to eat.'

Julie gave him a withering glance. 'How can you think of food, when your wife is going to pieces?'

'Maybe I will get my face lifted,' Anna said quietly.

'Don't be ridiculous,' said Julie. 'Your daughter would have a fit.'

'Kim won't be back from Australia till Harry's finished the film he's making there. By then, the deed could be done — '

'I'm coming to think you've been housebound for so long, your brain has rusted up,' Julie told her.

'Being a housewife doesn't mean being housebound,' James interposed.

'Housebound, my dear James, can be a state of mind.'

Anna rinsed the white debris from her face at the sink.

36

'You'll excuse me if I don't bother to change into my party frock, won't you!'

'Our social life has gone for a Burton,' James said to Neil.

'Would you like all our other friends to know I can't stand the sight of myself?' Anna said tersely. 'It's bad enough that the Newtons and Sangers do.'

'And Lord knows what you'll present me with from your new repertoire tomorrow night.'

'It isn't every man who can go home to a cabaret after his day's work,' said Neil with a smile.

Julie was serving the fry-up she had hastily concocted, and gave one of the sausages a lethal stab. 'That sums up the male attitude towards what the change of life can do to a woman, doesn't it?'

'But what it's mainly doing to you, dear,' said Neil snidely, 'is you're putting on weight.'

'Frankly, I don't give a shit if I turn into a fat pig. I'll still be a QC who's hard to get.'

From Neil's expression it was clear that she had touched him on a sore spot.

'I don't have to concern myself with looking attractive to men,' Julie went on airily. 'That, I leave to the Myrna Sangers of this world, who perpetuate the old myth that with a woman what you see is all there is.'

'I used to think that about Myrna. But not any more,' Anna said.

'Then I'd advise you not to confuse guile with grey matter. If you must have a guru, Anna, better me than her. Any woman who could tell a friend that a face-lift will save her marriage — '

'If I did it, it wouldn't be for that reason. It'd be for me.'

'At least you have your priorities right.'

CHAPTER FIVE

A PERIOD of contrition followed Anna's brief show of bravado – James had almost choked on a fried potato when she said that if she had her face lifted it wouldn't be to save her marriage – and she made a supreme effort to set right their disrupted homelife.

What she could not bring herself to do was remove the coating of soap from the mirrors. The day I do that, I'll know I'm back to normal, she thought one morning while she was cleaning the cloakroom basin. But would she ever feel quite the same way again about James – or him about her, after some of the things they'd said to each other? At the moment, they were both doing a good job of pretending her face-phobia – though she didn't like him calling it that – had stopped coming between them. James never mentioned it. But why was he still deliberately leaving the lavatory seat up? Anna put it where it should be, as she'd been doing since the night he'd first made what she now knew was a defiant gesture. A couple of weeks ago she'd have slammed it down – but that was before she'd told herself that a man who'd always been a good husband didn't deserve what her vanity was doing to his life.

Left to herself, Anna would probably have found the resigned philosophy most women adopt when their looks blur into middle age. She had always been a private person, and would not have chosen to have her innermost feelings mulled over by others. Once that had happened, there was no going back, and Julie and Myrna continued pulling her their two ways.

'It's nice of you to keep dropping in to see how I am, but it isn't necessary,' she said when Myrna interrupted her housework.

Myrna gave her the sisterly kiss that was now habitual. 'How're you doing, Anna?'

38

'Fine. All right, I'm not but I'm trying to be,' she admitted when Myrna glanced pointedly at the hall mirror. 'Where are you on your way to today? You look even more toffed-up than usual.'

'It's Wimbledon fortnight, isn't it? The big-boss's wife has invited me to join her party. Between you and me, she's a pain in the ass – and what do I care about tennis? – but I have to run when she beckons, for Irv's sake.' Myrna twirled around to show Anna the full effect of her cunningly pleated, lilac silk dress, and tilted her matching straw hat yet more fetchingly over her brow. 'This is one outfit Irv daren't say he minds paying for,' she said with a smile. 'Did you get the invitation to my cocktail party yet?'

'Yes, thanks, and James will probably come. You must excuse me if I don't. We haven't seen anyone but you and the Newtons for ages.'

'That must be why your husband told mine that you're living like hermits. James won't go on like that for ever, and the sooner you take my advice the better is how I see it. I have to fly now, Anna, but my thoughts will still be with you.'

'And you don't know how grateful I am, Myrna, for how you and Julie are trying to help me through this,' Anna said warmly.

Even though, between them, they had caused her to open up what sometimes seemed like a can of worms. One of which was that if James had got the managing-director job when it fell vacant, it would be Anna, not Myrna, who had to make the right impression on the big-boss's wife, whom everyone said was the power behind the throne.

The agency had changed hands shortly before Irving was brought in to run it, and was now owned by a man who spent his winters in Bermuda and rarely appeared at the offices in spring or summer. Might James have been running it now, if he'd been married to a different sort of woman from me? Anna wondered, inhaling the sophisticated perfume that lingered wherever Myrna had been. Someone who would have pushed and helped him to get where he had the ability to be? Could that be a private grudge their marriage crisis had caused him to dwell on?

If so, he wasn't showing it. But nor was she showing her resentment that he had failed to understand her, she was thinking when Julie rang up.

'Have you unsoaped the mirrors yet, Anna?'

'No.'

'Then kindly stop bleating that there's no need for me to keep calling you. And unless you and James intend going to Myrna's cocktail party, I think Neil and I will give it a miss.'

'That isn't very nice of you, Julie.'

'Possibly not – but you know how I feel about Myrna. If it weren't for Neil getting consultancy work from the agency – which James was kind enough to ask Irving to suggest to their solicitor — '

'Neil and Irving are personal friends, now,' Anna cut in.

'But I don't count Myrna among *my* intimates, push for it though she does,' said Julie. 'Nor did you use to feel that close to her, Anna.'

'She's being very kind to me.'

'And she'll have you on a cosmetic surgeon's table if you're not careful. I was going to say, when you interrupted me, that it's only for Neil's sake that I'm socially embroiled with the Sangers.'

'Don't you like Irving, either?'

'I do, as a matter of fact, but I prefer him in small doses, taken not too frequently. The same applies to a lot of people Neil and I mix with. But even those it doesn't apply to, like you and James, we don't have time to see as often as we'd like to. Though Neil remarked last night that you, we, and the Sangers are getting to be a regular sixsome.'

'But I don't expect you to go on rallying around me like you're doing.'

'As both the Sangers are fond of saying: What are friends for?' Julie replied. 'Especially when they're the only ones who know what a mess you're in – and I'm damned if I'll leave you in Myrna's clutches,' she said before ringing off.

Julie's socialising with the Sangers solely on Neil's account confirmed Anna's sudden perception that she had somehow failed James, and he was now letting it matter.

'Why have you stopped putting the loo seat down?' she asked when he came home that evening.

'Oh, have I started leaving it up?'

Why had she hoped for a straight answer? Fencing was preferable to fighting – but how long could they go on doing it?

James was asking himself the same question. If this was still going on when Kim got back from Australia, she'd think both her parents had gone potty – Anna about her face, and James for not knocking some sense into her. But knocking sense into each other had never been their way, nor had it ever been necessary before.

'Ready to do some gardening, love?' he asked after dinner. He was getting decent meals again, and should be thankful for that.

'Aren't I always on a summer evening?' Anna replied pleasantly.

'But this isn't any old summer, is it?'

Was he referring to the hot, dry weather? Or to how things were – or weren't – with them? Anna held her breath. 'Nor was last year's,' she added, when he said no more. Once, each had known what the other was thinking. Or had they? Hadn't there been times when she'd stopped herself from saying this or that to James? What made her think that he'd always spoken his mind to her? Maybe Julie was right – but when wasn't she! – when she'd said Anna and James had got on so well only because they'd tried never to upset each other.

The summery sound of busy mowers greeted them on all sides when they went into the garden, and the heady scent of the jasmine they had planted together years ago. James had dug the hole and Anna had put in the shrub. She glanced at it poignantly. Kim had tugged at her skirt, while they watched James digging. Was it really that long ago? She hadn't noticed the time slip by. Only Kim growing up, and the jasmine continuing to bloom, year in, year out. If ever it didn't, she would think something had got at its roots. Like she was coming to think about her marriage. But how could a good relationship wither and die, just because the wife had suddenly got a thing about her face?

At the moment, it's only wilting, Anna stemmed her anxiety, while she did the watering and James clipped the hedge.

So is my willie, James might have said to her if their relationship had still been good, and he able to divine her thoughts. Trying to prove in bed that all was now well between them had served only to convince James that he was losing his grip in every department. He had failed to maintain his erection.

What the hell is happening to me? James kept asking himself. The so-called 'male menopause' had been taken no more seriously by him than it was by Neil, when Julie made cracks about it. Neil had once called it the modern woman's way of trying to establish equality in reverse, and he and James had had a good laugh. Had they compared notes about themselves, instead of about their wives – Irving, too – they could not but have concluded that a 'change of life', when one is prey to one kind of uncertainty or another, is not confined to women.

Instead, James continued to think it was happening only to him. Nor was he as unconcerned with his own ageing appearance as he had once thought.

'I was pleased to hear you've finally landed that fish,' Ronnie said, waylaying James in the corridor one morning. 'Excuse me doing this while we chat — ' He took a comb from his pocket and ran it through his already well-groomed fair hair, then straightened his already-straight tie. 'Irving wants me in his office at the double.'

'Then don't let me delay you.'

'Actually, he said in ten minutes.'

But Ronnie would be there ahead of time. An 'eager beaver' described him. 'If you were referring to my Swiss client just now, Ronnie, the account isn't just a fish, it's a whale,' James said, hoping he didn't sound as defensive as he felt. Why had Irving sent for Ronnie? His accounts were mere tiddlers, compared with the ones James handled. They'd been closeted together too often lately. Too often for what? James's good?

'A prize one, I gather,' Ronnie replied, with a boyish smile James was beginning to think was part of his career equipment. As was his air of there being nothing he couldn't pull off, given the chance. The chance was what he was after. Him and the rest of them, James thought, watching a couple of young colleagues pass by at the end of the corridor – probably on their way out to see clients. One of them was female, and her briefcase was made of crocodile. If you look successful you will be, was how all their minds worked.

But I've never felt threatened by them before. Why do I now? Because the picture's changed since I was their age. Advertising has always been something of a shifting-sands terrain – but not the way it is now, when a man heading all too fast for his fifties could feel himself being jostled by those impatient to step into his shoes. And Ronnie is at the head of the queue!

'Whether or not the whale turns out to be a prize one is down to the art department, now,' James said to him.

Ronnie didn't let him get away with it. 'That wasn't the way I heard it, James.'

'Since it isn't your account, Ronnie, you can't be expected to be *au fait* with every stage of the campaign. It's still in its infancy.' Don't worry about the next stage – who am I kidding! – be thankful to have got it off the ground.

'Whatever, James, you're not the one to let a whale slip out of the net.'

'Thanks for the compliment, Ronnie.'

'Well, you're a bit of a legend around here, aren't you?'

What he meant was an old-timer – but who ever said what they meant any more? If they did, it might not match their image, or could slow them down in getting where they intended to get. Years ago, what mattered was what you were made of and James had had no trouble proving his worth – or he wouldn't be where he was now. But staying there, in the new climate, was something else.

When he and Ronnie went their separate ways, James felt as if he had spent a few minutes discussing fish with a barracuda. Boyishly bland though Ronnie's office image was to his elders, he wouldn't think twice about gobbling up James, so he could move up one. I'd better sharpen my own image, instead of coming over as a legend whose time is running out. When did I last buy myself a new suit? What with his bit of a paunch, he thought, it might be best to get one tailormade. Not one; two or three: if he was going into competition with the snappy dressers he spent his days with, he must do it properly. Get some new shirts and ties, as well. Was this why Irving and Neil took such care with their appearances? If so, I've wakened late to the need for it. But I draw the line at having my teeth crowned, like Neil did. Ought I to think seriously about a hair transplant? I'm getting as bad as Anna! – but the reason isn't vanity, it's bloody survival.

Later, on his way to keep the monthly lunch date he had with Irving and Neil, appointments permitting, he went into a store that sold toupées and tried one on.

'It takes years off you, if you don't mind my saying so,' said the attractive brunette who was giving him her undivided attention.

James agreed – though she was paid to say that. Why else would a chap on the wrong side of forty-five be buying one? But was he really prepared to go this far to stay in the race?

The girl saw his uncertain expression, met his gaze in the mirror, and said, 'Think what it could do for you.'

She must be working on commission – and taking it for granted that a man's reason for not wanting to look his age had to be the same as a woman's.

'I can show you a better one,' she offered when he took off the toupée.

'No, thanks. I'm late for a date.'

'I hope it's with someone nice.' She replaced the wig on its stand, reminding James, somewhat irrelevantly, of seeing his late grandfather's dentures in a glass of water beside his bed. But Grand-dad had required the dentures to eat with. James's need was not yet that desperate – and to hell with the toupée!

At the wine bar, Irving was tapping his fingers impatiently on the table.

'Neil called to say he can't make it today. I've just come from a terrible meeting with Travelbest. The way the weather is here for the second summer running, you British have gotten cocky about it. The main response from that Spanish vacation campaign we did for the client is a great big raspberry, James.'

'Who sits indoors watching TV commercials on evenings like we've been having?' James answered. Thank God this wasn't one of his accounts.

'The commercials were shown during the winter, weren't they, you *schmuck*? That's when summer holidays get booked.'

'It's been a long time since I booked one, Irving. Anna and I have had a yearly reservation at a hotel in the Lake District since Kim was a school-kid. If you'd ever spent a peaceful couple of weeks at the Langdale Chase, you'd know why we keep going back there.'

'I wouldn't mind trying it some time. But this year we're going to California, needless to say, and Myrna also wants to take in Las Vegas – which I'm shivering in my shoes about in case she turns into a menopausal gambler. How's your marriage crisis, by the way, boychik?'

James had to wait until their order had been taken before replying. 'Apart from the still-soaped-over mirrors, I don't seem to have one any more.'

'That's the kind of line your wife has been handing to mine. "Seem" is a nice useful word, isn't it, James?'

'For what?'

'For trying to kid yourself with, is what. And I hate like hell to have to land you with extra responsibility at this time, including my hysterical client. You didn't forget, did you, that Myrna and I always start our vacation at the end of July?'

'I did, as a matter of fact.'

'We'll have a meeting before I go — '

'Don't we always?'

'But maybe I should throw Ronnie in at the deep end, with that client. Getting blamed for the weather, as well as for the things we get blamed for regularly, would be good experience for him, and take some of the load off you.'

James had just helped himself to a breadstick. He snapped it in half. 'If you want to risk it, you're the boss. But I can do

45

without worrying that Ronnie might lose us the account while I'm in charge.'

'I agree.'

'Then why suggest it? Are you trying to test me out, or something?'

'Why would I do that?'

James avoided Irving's eye. 'Forget I said it. I'll make sure the agency doesn't fall apart while you're in America.'

'And let's hope the same applies to yourself.' Irving reached for a bread roll and buttered it. 'I'm cheating on my diet.'

'I won't tell Myrna.'

'You needn't tell her, either, that I ordered a baked potato with sour cream, today.'

'You can trust me not to. Guess what I found on my doormat this morning, Irving?'

'A dog turd,' said Irving facetiously.

'A letter from a tax inspector.'

'Me, I'd rather have the dog turd.'

'Thanks for cheering me up.'

CHAPTER SIX

'IF WE keep on getting summers like this, we'll all have to install air-conditioning in our homes. Myrna says everyone has it in America,' Anna said to James. 'All I've done is cook your breakfast, but I feel like going upstairs and taking another shower.'

James fanned a fly away from the toast rack. 'They have screen windows in the States, as well.'

'Well, you can't have hot sticky weather without flies, can you?'

'No. The two go together.'

What would we do without the weather to discuss? James thought. That and the other bits and bobs it was safe to talk about, like you did with someone you didn't know well. Not that their conversations had ever been what you'd call world-shaking, they weren't that sort. It was just that the ease had gone from them, as if they were wary of each other. Well, weren't they? Lucky their summer holiday was behind them, that they always went away in early June to avoid the crowds and the ear-splitting noise of Lord knew how many speedboats on the lakes. If they had to spend every minute of the day together, right now, James didn't know about Anna, but he would come back a wreck from the strain.

'More tea, love?' she said to him.

'Yes, if you wouldn't mind.'

'There's plenty in the pot.'

James knew there was, since they'd each had only one cup. 'Good.' Had they always been this polite to each other? If they had, it hadn't felt like this.

'This is the first time the Sangers and Newtons have been away on holiday at the same time,' Anna said, bridging the conversational gap.

James wanted to ask her if she was missing her daily

phone calls from Myrna and Julie, but thought better of it. Maybe she thought he didn't know she chatted to them every day? But he'd found out from their husbands, who kept him informed on the face front. In Julie and Myrna's opinion, Anna was getting no better at all.

Talk to me, love, James had to stop himself from saying, as he watched her sip her tea. You mean the world to me, let me help you, Anna. But he didn't know how to help her, did he? That was the bloody trouble, and it'd got so he was scared to put a foot wrong. He'd just have to bide his time till the menopause let her be and he got his sensible wife back, he told himself before rushing off to the office.

Though James was unaware of it, Myrna had called Anna from the States, and Julie had phoned from Cornwall. Both had said they would call her again, but it was not like having a chat with them every day, and made Anna realise how much their supportiveness had meant to her.

There's nothing like having a woman friend you can talk to, she thought while clearing the breakfast table. Myrna had said that to her not long after they met, but Anna hadn't known it herself until after she threw the shoe at James.

If I hadn't made that damn joke, I might never have known there are things you can talk about to another woman that you can't to your husband, she thought as she stacked the dishwasher. What was that long word Julie had used about herself and the few other women barristers in her chambers? Camaraderie. Julie had had to explain to Anna the kind of feeling it was, but she wouldn't have to now.

All my other friends must think that I don't want to know them any more, she thought guiltily, and on an impulse she called one of them.

'How have you been, Maggie?'

'Oh, you're back in circulation, are you, Anna?'

'And I don't blame you for being cool with me because I haven't been in touch.'

'Well, it's certainly been long-time-no-see.'

An awkward silence followed.

'How's your little grandson, Maggie? He'd got measles the last time we spoke.'

'And he's now got chicken pox. I hope he gets over it in time to start school next month. Shirley and her husband have split up and she came home to her mum and dad. Mike and I had forgotten what it's like to have a little kid raising hell around the house.'

'I'm sorry to hear about Shirley's marriage.'

'And you'd think, wouldn't you, the way they live together before they get married, nowadays, that they'd know each other properly by the time they tie the knot? Not that your daughter did that – we'd all have died of shock if she had. She takes after her sensible parents, your Kim does.'

And what would Kim say when she got home from Australia and saw what was going on?

'Nor is it like you,' Maggie remarked bluntly, 'to start giving people the brush-off.'

'You'll have to forgive me. It's just that – well, I haven't been myself.'

'Have you seen a doctor?'

'It's nothing physical, Maggie.'

'And down to your age. Say no more. I'm five years older than you, and over mine, thank the Lord. But I can remember cheering myself up by going to the West End and trying on hats at Selfridge's.'

'I don't think that would work for me.'

'Then it's time you did see the doctor, Anna. There are all sorts of things they can give you nowadays.'

Why hadn't Myrna and Julie suggested it? Because neither of them is a down-to-earth woman, like Maggie is and I used to be, Anna thought when the conversation was over. Cosmetic surgeons were more in Myrna's line than a bottle of tonic. And Julie's idea of a cure was for Anna to re-think her relationship with James. But she would take the advice of a woman like herself.

'I'm afraid Dr Kindersley has left the practice,' Anna was told when she rang the surgery to make an appointment. 'It must be a long time since you last saw him, Mrs Ridgeway. He had a heart attack and retired before I came to work here, and that was four years ago.'

Anna was upset on the doctor's account. Though the Ridgeways had never troubled him about anything with which they could cope themselves, he had seen Kim through her childhood ailments, and it had been good to know he was there if they needed him.

'We've got four doctors, now,' said the brisk female voice at the other end of the line. 'Dr Binns is the one with a surgery this afternoon. I could manage to squeeze you in before he leaves on his rounds. Just before three o'clock.'

It wouldn't be like unburdening herself to her old friend Dr Kindersley – who'd once ticked her off for not troubling him about a sore throat until she knew it must be tonsillitis, she recalled. 'Thanks. I'll make sure I'm there on time,' she replied.

A board outside the house that had been Dr Kindersley's home, as well as his surgery, told Anna that it was now a health centre. The house was on a side avenue off the main road, and Anna's route, when she drove or walked to the shopping precinct, didn't bring her past here. Seeing the clinical-looking board went with Dr Kindersley's not being here any more. In view of what she'd come about, ought she to bother going in?

What was there to lose? But it was a shock when she entered to see that the big, oak-panelled hall, that used to be Mrs Kindersley's pride and joy, now resembled a hospital reception area. Well, a cross between that and a bank, thought Anna, when she had to knock on a window above a counter to speak to one of the girls behind it. Why did they need to be glassed in? To protect them from what Myrna would call a rip-off? Or from patients who kept interrupting the clerking they all seemed to be doing?

Anna rapped on the window a second time.

'Yes?'

'Sorry to disturb you, but where's the waiting-room?' It used to be the hall, but there weren't any chairs here, now.

'It's along that corridor. The room that was the dining-room, or so they tell me. Dr Binns only has one patient still to see apart from you. You *are* Mrs Ridgeway?'

'That's right.'

'I'm the one who squeezed you in – and nearly got shot by

the doctor for doing it,' the girl said with a smile. 'Dr Binns doesn't like it when his surgeries run over time.'

On her way to the waiting-room Anna passed a uni-formed nurse in the corridor. Things had certainly changed around here. When James had once needed his ears syringing, Dr Kindersley had done it himself. Nor had there been a light on the waiting-room wall, to signal that the doctor was ready to see his next patient. Now there were four of them, each with a doctor's name beside it. Oh well, it was all in the cause of efficiency, like a lot of other things that had changed. A nurse could syringe ears and dress boils as well as a doctor, and saved his time by doing it. Health centres like this had sprung up all over the country and everyone had got used to them. But Anna could remember her mother's dismay when her local doctor's practice was suddenly turned into one. Anna had felt the same when the family grocery store on her local shopping parade closed down and she had to start going to a supermarket. As if something warm and comforting had gone from her life.

Dr Binns's other remaining patient was eyeing her over the top of a copy of *Woman's Weekly*.

'I don't know why they bother putting magazines in doctors' waiting rooms,' the woman said, replacing hers on the table. 'Who's in the mood for reading, I ask you, when they're worried about themselves?'

Anna managed to smile. 'You've got a point.'

'Or waiting for the doc to write 'em a prescription for the only thing that puts them right, like I am,' her companion-in-waiting went on. 'If I suddenly burst into tears, dear, you'll have to excuse me.'

'The same goes for me, I'm afraid.' Why had she said that to a stranger? But it was a relief not to pretend she was fine. Not to have to chat, like she did with James – and with her neighbours – about everything but what was uppermost in her mind.

'Say no more,' the woman said, just as Maggie had on the phone, as if something unspoken had passed between herself and Anna. 'But we still have to carry the same load we carried before, don't we, dear? And without my tranks I'm hopeless and helpless. How I let myself run out of 'em,

I'll never know. It was lucky I had an appointment to see the doc for another lot this afternoon.'

She played with the clasp of her red plastic handbag and picked a thread of loose cotton from the floral printed frock she was wearing. 'Before I was on the tranks my husband began calling me "Weeping Winnie".'

It was a wonder Anna's hadn't begun calling her Vanity Vera.

'Winnie's my name. What's yours, dear?'

They chatted companionably, each with her eye on the light bulb beside Dr Binn's name. What we're here for is a bloody obsession to both of us, Anna thought. But if it wasn't one with me, I wouldn't be here.

'I'm not on edge, and burning the breakfast bacon, when I'm on my tranks,' Winnie explained. 'They work like magic and you won't know yourself if the doc puts you on 'em.'

'That's what a friend of mine once said to me about camomile tea,' Anna replied sceptically. Maggie's father was a herbalist, and it was herbs, not drugs, that Maggie relied upon for this minor ailment or that. When Anna once sprained her ankle just before going on holiday, Maggie had rushed round with some comfrey leaves to relieve the swelling. Without them, some walking-holiday it would have been, Anna had to admit now. But camomile tea every night hadn't stopped Maggie from needing to lift her depression by trying on hats. There was no herbal potion for what the menopause could do to you. Nor would a herbalist's daughter have suggested seeing a doctor if she believed there was.

'Oh, there's the doctor's light,' said Winnie. 'Ask him to give you the same as he's given me,' she advised as she got up. 'It's worth a try, dear.'

Her friendly manner and her cheap print frock reminded Anna of the housewives who lived in the back streets where she and James had grown up. James was the only boy from that kind of background in his class at the Manchester Grammar School. It wasn't like that any more, but in James's day it was a real feat for the son of a bus-driver to win a scholarship and go there.

It was James's brain that had elevated him and Anna to

the status they now enjoyed. Nowadays, it was only when she went north for a visit that Anna mixed with women like Winnie. James's parents had let him and his brother move them to a bungalow on a new housing estate, but Anna's mother had stayed put, among the kind of neighbours she was used to.

Winnie was their London equivalent. And so much for Julie's theory that only middle-class women with too much spare time go to pieces on the change! Just one of the things Winnie had told Anna was that she went out cleaning, as well as having to cope with her own household.

Winnie had been gone from the waiting-room for only five minutes when the light summoned Anna. She glanced at her watch. Or was it four?

Her own consultation was destined to last little longer. When she entered the surgery, Dr Binns was reading her medical notes. He gave her a pleasant smile. 'You seem to have a healthy record, Mrs Ridgeway. That's the sort of patient I like to have.'

Anna watched him put down the notes and pick up a pen. 'But lately, I haven't been myself, Doctor.' She could think of no other way to put it.

'What's been the trouble?' he inquired.

How did you tell a lad young enough to be your son that you wished your face didn't announce your age? Anna was dismayed by his youth. Doctor or not, he would think, "What a vain old bird!" which Anna now knew she was. And doctors weren't there to treat vanity. If it had been Dr Kindersley, he'd have said, "Come on, now, Anna. Let's have it," and everything would have come pouring out, while he sat and listened with a kind look in his eyes. But he was one of the old school, wasn't he? Not the sort who thought pills could make up for getting things off your chest to the doctor.

She saw Dr Binns glance at the clock. She'd better get on with it. But how? As best she could. 'It probably has something to do with my time of life, Doctor. My periods have more or less stopped,' she added lamely.

'And feeling a bit hot and bothered at times, are we?'

'Yes. But there's more to it than that.'

'There often is, Mrs Ridgeway. But anxieties are not unusual at your age. Is that what we're talking about?'

'One in particular.' But Anna could not bring herself to tell him what it was. He was already writing a prescription.

'This will take care of it,' he assured her, ripping the paper from the pad as if he had a train to catch. 'You must excuse me if I rush off to visit a patient who is very ill.'

And neurotics like me ought not to come here wasting your time, she silently replied.

Thus it was that Anna Ridgeway embarked upon the tranquilliser path. She left a nearby pharmacy with the quick answer to what ailed her in her handbag, and ran into Winnie who was waiting at a bus stop on the main road.

'Did the doc give you some, dear?'

Anna showed her a large jar of capsules, and a phial of tiny white tablets. 'I seem to have two kinds.'

'Them little ones is for our flushes, and the others is to settle us down,' Winnie said, her smile reminding Anna of Myrna's when she advised opting for cosmetic surgery. Winnie and Myrna were at opposite ends of the pole, but that didn't stop Anna from suddenly feeling like part of a sisterhood who were the only people who understood what she was going through. Julie and Maggie, who had never even met, were in it, too. Anna hadn't told Maggie, and certainly not Winnie, about her face-phobia, but was sure they'd be sympathetic if she did.

'Once you're on the tranks, you won't know yourself, dear,' Winnie repeated before boarding the bus.

Anna, who was already unable to relate to her former self, could not have foreseen the significance of that prophecy.

She decided against taking the tablets prescribed for hot flushes, for the same reason that she had not taken the contraceptive pill. She and James had hoped for a second child, but it had not happened. When Kim was fifteen, James had said, 'It's too late for us now, love. Let's not take chances.' Anna had agreed. Who wanted to start again, when they had a teenage daughter, and were getting set in their ways? She had got herself fitted with a Dutch cap. Why was she recalling that, now? Because the cap hadn't been out of its box for some time? The one place where she and James couldn't try to kid each other they hadn't got a marriage problem was bed. He hadn't wanted to make love since the night he tried to and couldn't.

But what had led her to think of the Dutch cap was that she preferred it to the pill. Anything that does things to your hormones isn't for me, Anna said to herself, eyeing the phial of little tablets. I can live with hot flushes.

But not with an old-bag face. So here goes! she thought, swallowing her first tranquilliser. Maybe the next time I see myself in a mirror it won't seem quite so bad.

She cooked the evening meal, set the table, and went upstairs to lie down, aware of a feeling of well-being that had enabled her to relax. She hadn't felt this good even when she wasn't menopausal.

She had the best sleep she had had for weeks. And a crazy dream about herself and Myrna and Julie in their nineties. Julie was hideously fat, and Anna a crone whose face had caved in. Myrna looked like a girl of sixteen, and kept swallowing a new rejuvenation pill invented by James's Swiss client, who was the only person in the world with the formula and was selling the pills for a million dollars each. Myrna had inherited her father's fortune and offered some of her pills to Anna and Julie, who refused the offer and were then chased by their still middle-aged husbands into a graveyard.

Anna woke up laughing, though yesterday it would not have been a dream, but a nightmare. And so it was to be in her waking hours, while she was taking the tranquillisers. The perspective from which she had seen herself while she slept away the rest of that summer afternoon – as though once removed, and to where nothing could touch her – persisted in her daily life. It began when she rose from the bed, changed her crumpled frock, and sat down at the dressing-table to brush her hair. She had not soaped over her hand-mirror, since it lay face-down and was necessary, like it or not, to make herself look passable for James. When she picked it up, the same ageing face confronted her, but something was between Anna and her reflection, stopping her from caring.

If she had Winnie's phone number, she'd ring up to tell her she was right. Magic was the word for it.

That evening, she asked James to show her the brochure the agency had done for their cosmetic-surgeon client.

'I don't think I've got one here,' he said hastily. 'Why do you want to see it?'

To test my reaction to the 'before and after' pictures. 'I just do, James.'

'Well, I'd rather you didn't!'

'Don't get so worked up, love,' Anna said with a smile. 'What you need is one of my tranks.' His sharpness had not bothered her.

'What the heck are you talking about?' James listened uneasily while she told him about her visit to the doctor, and said when she had finished, 'How long are you supposed to stay on those things?'

'For as long as I need them, I suppose.'

'I don't like the sound of that.'

'Would you rather have me like I was, James? Or like I am this evening, after just one tranquilliser? The soap's gone from the mirrors, hasn't it?'

'How would I know? I've only just set foot in the house.'

'There's one in the hall.'

'But when I walked by it my mind was still at the agency.' Did she think all he had to think about was her face-phobia? And that all he need do was shut the office door and hey-presto! his working day was behind him? Like her shutting the kitchen door after the dinner things were cleared and stacked in the dishwasher, and saying, as she sometimes did when she joined him in the living-room, 'Well, that's me done for today'? Someone should tell women it wasn't like that for a man, that men brought their work home with them, even if it was only in their head. James could be watching telly with his feet up, but things that were happening at work were still niggling at him. The other way round, too, nowadays. He'd be discussing something with a client, and giving it all he'd got, but gnawing away at him all the time was, 'What the hell's gone wrong with me and my marriage?' And now the taxman was after him, as well.

These and similar thoughts occupied James while he and Anna ate dinner. Fortunately, Anna did most of the talking. All he was required to do was appear to be listening and keep a pleasant look on his face.

'It's lovely not to have to pretend to you any more that I'm all right again,' she said later, after they had done their gardening and were sitting on the patio enjoying a cold drink.

'Not that you had me fooled.'

'I didn't think I had. But there's nothing to fool you about now, love.'

James noted her relaxed expression, and thought it too good to be true. The change in her was too sudden, too fast. As though someone had waved a wand over her and said, 'Abracadabra! You're back to normal.'

Anna put down her glass and came to give him a hug. 'Nothing bothers me now, if you know what I mean.'

James stemmed his disquiet. 'Let's hope it lasts.'

As the days passed by, and Anna continued to seem her old self, James was lulled into a state of blessed relief, and did not pause to recall what Irving had said about the word 'seem'. The strain had gone from their relationship. But that was not to say that all was now well with himself. Running the agency during Irving's three-week vacation had always put extra pressure on him – but it had never before afflicted him with the sensation of wearing a tight band around his head.

Anna usually rose earlier than James did, to cook his breakfast, and had just picked up an official-looking envelope from the mat one morning when he came downstairs and snatched it from her hand.

'Are you sure you don't want a trank, love?'

'No, I bloody don't.' Why was the taxman writing to him again? He'd replied to the first letter.

He followed Anna into the kitchen, and joined in the chit-chat while they ate. *She* might not be pretending any more, but he was – or trying to, he thought, fingering his forehead. 'For some reason, I feel as if I'm wearing a hat that's too small for me,' he said, forcing a laugh.

'That sounds like tension, James. When Irving gets back

you won't have so much on at the office. A trank a day would tide you over — '

James leapt from his chair and his cup of tea went flying. 'When I say no, I mean *no*, Anna!'

'All right, love, I won't suggest it again,' she said placidly. 'But I gave you a bad time, on top of your workload, didn't I? It's not surprising that your nerves are in shreds.'

'Who says they're in shreds!'

Anna cleared up the mess he had made on the table without batting an eyelid. She had never made much of something like that, but James had expected her to chide him for staining her new gingham breakfast cloth. Disapprove of them though he did – James wasn't the one to take an aspirin if he could get by without it, nor was Anna – there was no denying what the tranquillisers had done for her. There she was, all smiles, with spilled tea all over the tablecloth – and here he was, shaking like a bloody leaf, just because a tax inspector thought he had something to hide when he hadn't.

The hell with it! He went upstairs, stole one of her magic capsules, and swallowed it down in the bathroom. Which shelf in the cabinet had he grabbed the jar from? The middle one, probably, where Anna kept most of her bits and bobs. If he'd put it back in the wrong place, so be it!

He had, and was in too much of a hurry to realise that the glass, with some water still in it, was an additional clue. Anna had no trouble in putting the clues together. But if James didn't want her to know he'd taken a trank, that was his privilege.

By the time James reached the office the tension around his head had eased, and was gone by mid-morning. But when he chaired a meeting with the art department, it was as if he was watching himself participate. Was this what the tranks did to Anna? It couldn't be, or she'd be scared to take them. It was like being here, but not really being here. One person's reaction to a drug could be different from someone else's – but whatever he'd swallowed this morning wasn't right for James.

The next morning, he was able to understand why so

many people did take tranquillisers. The hat that was too small for him was back on his head.

A week later, his misgivings about Anna taking the drug were re-aroused.

'Let's give the garden a miss tonight, and watch the TV film,' he said to her after dinner.

'Whatever you feel like doing is fine with me, love.'

There was nothing extraordinary about Anna's reply – over the years she must have said it to him a million times. And he to her. But there was something about her acquiescence without a second's thought that rang a warning bell in James's mind. No, it wasn't quite that. Then what the heck was it about her that was different from the old Anna?

'Are you going to read the evening paper while you watch the box, like you usually do?' she said with a smile, as they settled down.

'Probably, with all the repeats they feed us. But here's hoping we haven't seen this film before.'

'We have,' Anna said as the pre-title sequence unrolled. 'A couple of years ago, I think.'

'Do you want to change channels and watch that old sit-com?'

'Not unless you do, since we saw that when it was new.'

'We should have stuck with the gardening!'

'But watching a film with your feet up for a change will do you good, James.'

The kind of good the film did James was probably the same as the effect blue movies had upon dirty old men who sneaked in to see them, he thought. If this movie wasn't exactly a blue one, it didn't fall far short. Mary Whitehouse must be putting through a protest call right now. Though Anna wasn't a prude, in a minute she'd say that films like this ought not to be shown when children were still about. It was only nine-fifteen.

Anna said nothing.

'You didn't make your usual little speech,' James remarked during the commercial break.

'Which little speech?' She offered him a caramel and unwrapped one for herself.

'The one about sex and violence and kids.'

'Oh, that.'

'Doesn't it bother you any more?'

She shook her head. 'Aren't you glad?'

James was not sure if he was or not.

'You'll be able to sit watching the tits and bums without my going on about it distracting you,' she added with a laugh.

A couple of months ago, James had not required this sort of stimulation. Give or take the lessening of frequency that comes with the passing years, all it had needed, on the nights when he wasn't too tired, was holding his wife in his arms. Since the night when he was unable to maintain his erection, there had not been a spark of life in him where it counted. But what the heck did it matter how the flicker he felt there now had come about?

By the second commercial break it was more than a flicker. 'Don't laugh at me,' he said to Anna, 'but I suddenly feel like making love.'

'Why should I laugh at you?' She got up and switched off the television set. 'That film's a load of codswallop anyway. Come on.'

'If you feel like going to bed when it isn't bedtime, like we sometimes did a long while ago,' she said as they went upstairs, 'now Kim's gone and we're on our owney-oh again, there's no reason why we shouldn't.'

Since everything now seemed to her fine between them again, Anna had attributed James's not making love to his being more worn out from work than usual. Thanks to the tranquillisers, she had read nothing more into it and was usually blithely out for the count the minute her head touched the pillow, unaware that her husband tossed and turned all night.

'By the way, we're invited to Maggie and Mike's, on Saturday night,' she said while they were undressing.

James was in bed before she was and wondering how much longer her nightly ritual would take, listening with only half an ear to her prattling.

'I suggested the four of us go out to dinner, but Maggie said they had to baby-sit with their grandchild. Their

Shirley coming back home with a kid has really clipped their wings is how it sounds to me, James — '

'Don't bother brushing your hair, love, it'll only get mussed-up again,' James cut in.

But he still had to wait for her to clean her teeth.

'Wasn't it a lovely letter we got from Kim, today?' she called from the bathroom.

Now, she'd be putting her cap in – if it hadn't rotted from disuse. Another delay.

When she finally switched out the lamp and snuggled up to him, James's burning urgency was down to a flicker again. He tried visualising what he had watched on TV – without effect – and sickened himself by doing so. Apart from where it put him – along with the dirty old men – it was an insult to Anna.

'Come on, I'm here now,' she said playfully.

'And you smell lovely.'

'It's that toilet water you gave me before we went on holiday.'

'I must get you some more of it.'

Now who was doing the delaying? If James couldn't make it this time – well, God help him.

'Don't let it worry you, love,' Anna said, after he had tried and failed.

'Doesn't it bother you?'

'Worse things can happen.'

But not to a man, thought James. He would have been even more mortified had he known that Anna was mentally compiling her grocery list, while he was grinding away to no avail between her legs.

CHAPTER SEVEN

As HAPPENS with even the closest of friends, there are times when, for one reason or another, they do not see much of each other. Anna saw Julie only once after the Newtons returned from Cornwall, before Julie was plunged into an Old Bailey case that was to immerse her until the end of the year. And Myrna had stayed on in California; during the Sangers' vacation, her father had had a stroke.

'Don't keep apologising, I know how busy you are – and you were around when I needed you,' Anna said when Julie called her to cancel a date.

'You certainly seemed to have fully recovered when we last lunched together,' Julie replied.

'I have, Julie. James and I are back in the swim with all the people my daft phobia made me drop. I never liked James calling it that – then I had to accept that it was one. Look how it made me hibernate and not want to be bothered with anyone – I'd have dropped you and Myrna, too, if you hadn't both found out what was going on from your husbands. Like Maggie said, when she suggested I see the doctor, it isn't my way to give folk the brush-off, is it? But she still doesn't know the gory details and there's no need to tell her. My face is just a face to me now. Miraculous, isn't it, Julie?'

But how will you be when you come off those capsules? Julie silently answered. If, now you're on them, you ever do. 'How's Kim?' she asked. 'Still enjoying Australia? When is she coming home?'

'It was to have been December, but the series Harry's making there is taking longer than he expected – one of the stars fell ill, and has to be written out of the rest of the episodes, Kim said in her last letter. It could be next spring before they get back. How are your two lads doing?'

'From my point of view or theirs? If you mean from mine, you should know better than to ask, Anna.'

'Haven't you forgiven Mark yet, for not turning up to your Silver Wedding do?'

'Would you forgive Kim? But she wouldn't do that to you,' Julie said crisply. 'And the state of intoxication Paul was in when he arrived, I'd rather he had stayed away, too! I sometimes wonder what Neil and I have done to deserve the sons we've got. But I didn't ring up to depress you with my parental angst. I'll call you again, and we'll get together soon, Anna.'

Julie's "soon" stretched through autumn into winter. In the interim, James held on to his Swiss client precariously and got in deeper with the taxman, while Anna knitted him a Fair Isle sweater, content in her fool's paradise.

Myrna returned to England in time to invite the Ridgeways and Newtons to Thanksgiving Dinner, as she did each year.

'Have you four ever wondered why you're the only ones I invite?' she asked, while Irving was pouring their first round of drinks.

'Given the scale on which you usually entertain, I must say it had crossed my mind,' Julie replied.

'But on Thanksgiving, I always keep things homey and simple, don't I?'

Irving laughed. 'You don't know what keeping things simple means, babe.'

'Just because I put the Stars and Stripes on the table, next to the pumpkin pie?'

'Simple would be sticking a little paper flag in a bud vase, or whatever. Nobody but my wife,' Irving said to the others, 'would have sent to New York for a real silk one in a silver holder.'

'If you think it was to show off, Irv, you're wrong. When I sent for it was my first year in England. I had to show how important Thanksgiving is to us — '

'Haven't we digressed from what Myrna started out to tell us?' said Neil.

Julie said, 'Bravo, m'learned friend!'

But why did she have to say it sarcastically? thought James.

'Anyways,' said Myrna, handing round some hot hors d'oeuvres, 'Thanksgiving is a family occasion and, since Irv and I don't have family over here, I picked on you to share it with us.'

'That's a nice compliment,' said Anna.

'Like the one you pay us, also Julie and Neil, by having us spend Christmas Day with you. I guess, in a way, we're all exiled from our family, aren't we?'

'James and I used to go up north for Christmas but it got too much for the old folks,' Anna said. 'My mother and James's are past the age of putting on a big spread.'

'Neil's parents always spend Christmas at a hotel. Before they started doing it, we used to trek to Weston-super-Mare for the festivities,' Julie reminisced.

'That was when the boys were still honouring us with their company,' Neil added.

'And when I think of the trouble I went to when they were little, giving them the kind of family Christmas I never had myself —' said Julie, who had been raised by a maiden aunt after her parents died in a boating accident. 'Oh well. Kids will be kids.'

'I'm surprised you can look at it like that,' said Myrna. 'With Mark squatting in that commune, and Paul doing what he's doing.'

'How did we get talking about Christmas, on Thanksgiving?' Irving intervened hastily. Didn't Myrna know what a sore subject their sons were to the Newtons? Not that that stopped them from giving Paul a handout whenever he asked for one – which Irving would not have done. Mark, on the other hand, preferred to get his handouts from the social services.

'We got on to Christmas when I said that in a way we're all exiles,' Myrna harked back.

'A lot of people who live in London are,' said James. 'And the same would go for any capital city.'

'Everyone wants to be where it's at,' said Irving. 'But only the ones who pull up their roots and go there know how a person can miss what they left behind.'

And Thanksgiving is our yearly reminder that the Sangers

are exiled from their own country, thought James. It was an evening when Myrna got sentimental about the folks back home, and Irving sang 'God Bless America', and drank too much, which Anna and James always found rather touching. If the Newtons found it embarrassing – James was sure they did – too bad. But anyone could be forgiven for scratching their head about how we three couples got together, James said to himself, listening to the easy chatter going on around him.

'Have another vol-au-vent, James. I made them myself.'

'In that case I will.'

The food Myrna served at dinner parties was more often than not supplied by a caterer, but that was far from the only difference between Myrna and Anna. Julie did her own cooking – James sometimes wished she didn't – yet she was no more Anna's sort than she was Myrna's. The same went for James and the other two men. But they'd all come from very different backgrounds, hadn't they? Neil's was old-school-tie, though the way he dressed for social occasions – well, Irving had thought him too much of a dandy, when he saw Neil's brocade waistcoat the first time they met. He was wearing one tonight, but Irving thought nothing of it by now, and had once remarked, about Neil, that everyone was entitled to their own image.

Had Irving made up his mind to project the image he did? James wondered, watching him play host in his luxury apartment. Success was the name for it, but it didn't sit comfortably on him, and if it *felt* comfortable, he wouldn't have let slip to James that he wished he had a homelier place. The trouble was, once you adopted an image for yourself you had to keep it up. Unless you were the sort who wore it like a second skin and forgot it wasn't really you. As he, James, probably did, except that he hadn't known he'd got one till Ronnie called him a legend, and made him feel it was slipping. Why else had he tried on a toupée and ordered some new suits, if not to smarten his image?

It's what people get judged by, he thought, taking another vol-au-vent. And with folk you met casually, the impression they got of you then was the one that counted. If the three couples in this room had encountered each other for the first time at a party, with no reason to meet again, an encounter was all it would've been. Fancy us living next door to toffs like that, was his and Anna's initial reaction to the Newtons, James recalled with a grin. And heaven knows how the Newtons had reacted to them. As for the Sangers and Newtons, well, they wouldn't have found themselves at the same party. Yet the six of us have had some good times together. James returned full-circle to what had set his mind on this track. So much for snap judgements.

Irving came to top up his glass. 'Why the pensive expression, boychik?'

'I was thinking about how us lot had got together. When Anna and I were a courting couple, if anyone had said that we'd end up with barristers and rich Americans for friends, we'd have thought they'd had one over the eight.'

'If I'm your idea of a rich American, James, you should see how Myrna's parents live! Did you tell your girlfriends yet, babe, what your mother did while your father was hospitalised?'

'So Mom bought her Pekinese a diamond collar for its birthday – what of it?'

'Not that. The other.'

'Mom got herself a retroussé nose,' Myrna told them with a smile. 'She's always wanted one. And she had to get even with Pop somehow for having his stroke in compromising circumstances.'

'Our Swiss client should only have customers like her lining up,' Irving said to James.

'But where does getting even with your father come into it?' Neil asked Myrna.

'He doesn't like retroussé noses.'

The Ridgeways and Newtons managed not to laugh. The more they learned about Myrna's parents, the more outrageous the old couple seemed.

'But I'd like you to know my ma- and pa-in-law are not the archetypal American senior citizens,' Irving felt constrained to say. 'If my mom, or her next-door-neighbour in Queens, wanted to get even with their husbands for whatever, they would probably serve them with mashed potato instead of fries.'

'What would you do to get even with James?' Julie asked Anna.

'She isn't the getting-even kind,' he said.

'Why don't you let her speak for herself?'

'I don't mind James answering for me.'

'That's always been your trouble.'

'Hey, you guys, this is supposed to be the Happy Hour!' said Myrna, piling everyone's plates with chopped liver.

'Do Americans always have the first course with the drinks, like you do?' Neil asked her. 'It's a nice idea.'

'At informal dinner parties, yes. That's why hostess aprons are so fashionable. Could you imagine me flitting about the living-room in one of those big butcher's aprons Julie wears and sometimes forgets to take off when her guests arrive?'

Myrna never lost an opportunity to express her disapproval of Julie's disinterest in her appearance – and Julie's getting worse, Neil thought, noting her two-year-old, clingy blue velvet dress, that emphasised her increased girth. 'I couldn't imagine Julie in one of your teeny-weeny aprons, either, Myrna. And I must say you look very sexy in them,' he added, giving her a wink.

'Anyone who tells Myrna she looks sexy is her buddy for life,' said Irving. 'You just ensured yourself a double helping of turkey, Neil.'

'And you, you'll get the neck, Irv!'

'The diet you feed me, babe, even that would be a welcome change.'

'Do you go hungry?'

'You bet I do.'

The Ridgeways and Newtons settled back to listen to the habitual crack-for-crack exchange. Neil had once said to James that he sometimes had the feeling that the Sangers' non-stop wisecracking was the only way they were able to talk to each other.

Myrna had the last word. 'But your babe knows best, doesn't she? And on Thanksgiving, fighting is forbidden.'

She went to give Irving a kiss, and an embrace that glued their bodies together. The Sangers often behaved that way in public, but when Irving's hand strayed to Myrna's bottom, Julie thought it time to remind them with a cough that they were not alone.

'That was my wife's way of saying that she compensates me for my diet in other ways,' Irving said with a laugh.

I bloody bet she does, thought James. But it would take more than even Myrna's skills to put right what was wrong with *him*.

Neil felt like saying to Irving: Wait till you've been married as long as the rest of us.

'I was thinking of recommending Irv's diet to Julie,' Myrna said to him.

'Since I've no intention of dieting, it would be more useful if you wiped the lipstick off your husband's chin.'

Irving took out a handkerchief and did so himself. 'Fortunately Myrna doesn't wear lipstick in bed, or it would be all over the place.'

'Lucky old you,' said Neil.

Julie gave him a sweet smile. 'It takes two to tango, doesn't it, darling? When do we get to eat the turkey, Myrna?'

'I timed it for eight.'

Irving switched on the television set. 'Then we may as well catch what's left of the seven-o'clock news.'

'Now we can really say goodbye to the Happy Hour!' Myrna exclaimed. 'Even on Thanksgiving, my husband has to have his nightly dose of doom and gloom.' She sat down beside Anna to finish her hors d'oeuvres. 'Oh my God, why do they have to keep on showing us this?'

Channel Four was presenting an in-depth report of the Ethiopian famine and the far-away misery filled the screen.

Myrna's fork clattered to her plate. 'I can't bear it.'

'Me, neither,' said Julie. 'And what price the birthday present your mother gave her dog, now!'

'My parents have sent a big cheque to the relief fund.'

'I'm sure they have. But it makes you think.'

Myrna and Julie averted their eyes from the sight of some emaciated children dying in a hospital tent.

'It's terrible, but I've stopped letting it affect me,' Anna said to them.

No, you haven't, thought Irving. It's those capsules your husband has let you take, doing their job too well. 'How in the hell will we bring ourselves to eat our dinner, after watching this?' he said.

Myrna got up and switched off the TV.

'But it's still happening, isn't it?' Julie said hotly.

'Who are you angry with?' Neil wanted to know.

'Myself! And anyone else the cap fits – which wouldn't leave many people minus a cap. I feel just like Irving does, but of course we'll eat our bloody dinner, just like we always do. By the time we get to the pumpkin pie, what we saw on the box will've gone from our minds.'

'That's human nature, dear.'

'And there's no need to tell me you can't change that. But plenty for some and next-to-nothing for others *can* be changed.'

Was Julie turning into a menopausal revolutionary? Irving wondered.

Myrna led the way to the dining alcove, though she felt like putting the turkey on a plane to Ethiopia, and said, when she brought it to the table, 'Giving thanks to God for all we have is what Thanksgiving Day is about. It isn't any old public holiday.'

'And we've sure been reminded of its meaning, tonight,' said Irving, watching Anna pop a grape from the fruit bowl into her mouth.

The following morning, he asked James to come to his office.

'Can whatever you want me for wait?' James said when he got there. 'I'm up to my ears, and also trying to break in my new secretary.'

'You're also up to your ears at home, but you don't seem to know it – or I wouldn't be wasting *my* valuable working time.'

James wriggled his brow to try to loosen the ever-present restriction. 'What the heck're you on about, Irving? My marriage crisis is over – and I don't want to resurrect it.'

'So you finally admit to a marriage crisis? Well, that's something. Did you think if you denied it, it would go away? Maybe you did. But I have to tell you that it's still with you. It doesn't require resurrecting. All that's happened, James, is something has been added. Your wife has turned into a zombie.'

'I beg your pardon, Irving?'

'What else would you call a person who can sit there calmly noshing chopped liver, while they're watching something like we saw on TV last night? Everyone else stopped eating, didn't they? Even Julie did.'

'The drug Anna's on stops her from getting upset. That's what it's bloody for.'

'You're doing a lot of swearing these days, boychik. It isn't a good sign. And since you've mentioned drugs, the only time there was a spark of life in Anna was when Myrna told us over coffee she was offered coke to sniff at a party in LA.'

'Do you think Myrna sniffed some?'

'My wife, thank God, doesn't need to get her kicks that way. But it's drugs and *your* wife we're talking about. Anna has learned their magic power, James, first-hand.'

'You're making her sound like a junkie!' James flashed.

'Well, she's sure learned what drugs can do for her, hasn't she?'

'I'm thankful they can.'

'Also on your own account, no doubt. She's stopped giving you a hard time, which may be fine for you, James. It isn't fine for her. I'm not saying that tranks don't have their place for short-term treatment. But they ought to be monitored — '

'She sees the doctor each time she renews her prescription,' James cut in.

'And my guess is that he just says, "How are you, Mrs Ridgeway?" and gives her what she's come for.'

James knew this to be true, and avoided Irving's eye.

'If she were his wife, he'd notice the change in her,' Irving declared. 'And don't tell me you haven't. Anna isn't the woman I've known for enough years to care about her like I do. The sparkle has gone from her, and that's the least of it.'

'She'll get it back, Irving. You just said that tranks had

their place for short-term treatment, and they're tiding her over the menopause.'

'Which with some women lasts longer than for others. And Anna's already been on those things long enough for the effect they have on her to seem like her norm. Some norm! By short-term, I meant like after a sudden bereavement, to help someone put themselves together when they're reeling from the blow.'

Irving took off his spectacles and polished them. 'Wouldn't you say, James, that it's better for a person to, one way or another, live through their bad times, than be cushioned from all the painful emotions we humans are prey to?'

James could use some cushioning right now.

'And there's more to it than just that,' Irving went on, without waiting for an answer. 'What happened to a buddy of mine back home, who went on tranks, would make you think.'

'If you're going to put the fear of God into me about Anna taking tranks, like you did with that tale you told me about your other buddy back home and the taxman, I'd rather you didn't.'

'You're still getting letters from *your* taxman?'

'Yes. And I don't want to talk about it.'

'It's Neil you should talk to about it, not me. He could recommend you a good tax counsel.'

'Who needs a tax counsel for something they haven't done?'

'Without one, my buddy could have gone to jail, and he hadn't done anything, either. He's a salesman, in the lingerie business. My buddy who got in trouble with the tranks is a writer.'

James had no option but to listen to Irving tell how his writer friend had written a drama while taking tranquillisers, and had it rejected by a film company because it lacked the emotion usually present in his work.

'Since the writer has to feel everything his characters feel, or they'll be cardboard, not flesh-and-blood, it was the tranks not letting my buddy feel anything that was responsible,' Irving finished his tale.

'No prizes for guessing who told him so,' said James.

71

'You can bet your ass I did. Or he would probably be on the skids by now, instead of being a top Hollywood screenwriter. And don't ask me his name, it's irrelevant.'

'If he ever gets an Oscar, I'm sure you'll feel responsible.'

'But the one who has to be responsible for doing the necessary with Anna is you. Take the advice of someone who cares about you both. Get rid of those capsules down the john.'

'What does the oracle suggest I do when she's back the way she was?'

Irving replaced his spectacles and gave James a look that reminded him of his late grandfather, when that irascible old gentleman was about to put someone in their place.

'Practise not being sarcastic,' he replied. 'How about starting right now? And prepare for the possibility of living with a woman who doesn't look her age, when *you* do.'

Irving waited for James to digest the implication of what he had said, then went on, 'It isn't funny, I can tell you. Especially the times when someone who needs their eyes testing asks if she's your daughter! – and she doesn't let you forget it. With my wife to encourage her, boychik, I have to warn you that Anna could end up getting a face-lift. Like Myrna did before I met her. If you tell this to Anna, I'll fire you. Myrna thinks she has me fooled.'

'How did you find out?'

'A friend of Myrna's told me.'

'Some friend.'

'If you'd met some of those divorcées Myrna thinks are her friends, whose second-favourite pastime is stabbing each other in the back, you'd consider me fortunate that Myrna was the one I got hooked by.'

Irving smiled reminiscently. 'I was in LA for a convention, and I still don't know what got into me. There's something about those smart hotels where sales shindigs get held that can make a guy feel like a tomcat on the prowl. I've seen the staidest of married men succumb to the one-night-stand atmosphere. It had never got to *me* before, but I suddenly found myself thinking, what the hell!'

'Was that the night you met Myrna?'

'It sure was. In the singles bar a bunch of us guys went to, making like we were single. Myrna was there husband-hunting with her buddies. And the rest is history.'

'How do you know Myrna was husband-hunting?'

'What else? At heart my wife is a conventional woman. But she doesn't know it,' Irving added as his telephone rang. He lifted the receiver and issued a final instruction to James, 'Be sure to flush the toilet thoroughly, when you've done what you have to do.'

Did James have the guts to dispose of Anna's tranquillisers?

'It's Frankenstein,' Irving mouthed to him. 'He heard what I just said and thinks he's been put through to the men's room!'

'Thanks for the advice. I'll think about it,' James said.

'Action would be better,' said Irving, his hand now clamped over the telephone mouthpiece. If James believed the advice was just on Anna's account, he was wrong. Myrna had let slip, last night, that James had taken a tranquilliser. Was there nothing that women didn't tell each other? Irving thought, while he tried to exchange pleasantries with the none-too-pleasant Swiss. What had Myrna confided to Anna about him, that he didn't know she knew about? But that went both ways, didn't it? – like his own smart move in keeping to himself that he knew about Myrna's face-lift. Marriage could be a chequerboard – and a piece cunningly withheld could enter the game at a later stage and be used against you. The hell with chess! Irving didn't want his number-two guy at the agency getting his mind fogged by tranks, which was why he'd made up the story of the screenwriter heading for the skids.

James had left Irving's office with a mental picture of Anna on her knees beside the loo, trying to retrieve some capsules that had remained afloat. If he could bring himself to do what he should. He was also quaking with anxiety about Frankenstein having called the managing director instead of him. By the time he reached his own office his imagination had supplied him with a list of dire possibilities, and a vice had replaced his invisible too-small hat, which it did at least once a day.

'I just had a call for you from Geneva transferred to the

boss's office,' his pert new secretary said, as he strode through her cubicle.

'It'll have to be transferred back here, but thanks anyway, Tracy.' Did his relief show on his face? He'd worked himself up into a lather for nothing, like he did about every little thing, nowadays. But Irving and Neil were in the throes of middle age too – why weren't they losing their grip? Irving seemed no less forceful than when James first met him. And Neil was as assured as ever.

It did not occur to him that Irving and Neil, like many of his contemporaries, were better actors than he was, even when there was nobody there to play to but themselves. The only man James knew who admitted to feeling his age was Maggie's husband Mike. Mike appeared to have given up the struggle when he became a grandparent, James reflected while he waited for Frankenstein's call to be put through to him. Why was Irving taking all this time? Was Frankenstein telling him that he'd rather have someone young and go-ahead to handle his account? And there I go again. That's enough of that, James!

'Good morning, Doctor. How are you?' he said when the call finally came, and with an insincerity that not long ago wouldn't have been necessary. He used to enjoy his work.

'I am not pleased, Mr Ridgeway.'

Oh, God.

'First I am connected by error to your office urinal, and next to the person to whom I do not wish to speak.'

Why had Irving left it to James to sort out the mix-up? 'I won't tell my managing director you don't wish to speak to him,' James said, trying to be jocular – with a chap who had no sense of humour.

'I have already informed him myself.'

If you tickled Frankenstein in the ribs with a feather, you couldn't get him to laugh.

'But tell me, if you please, Mr Ridgeway, your office urinal has in it a telephone for increased productivity?'

James had to control his own laughter.

'I have engaged, last year, experts to advise on my clinic administration. They did not suggest it.'

'We don't have a phone in ours, either, Doctor — '

'Am I to believe that my ears deceived me?' said Frankenstein, sharply.

'Since I don't know what you heard,' James lied, 'I can't answer that. But right now, you're wasting money, aren't you?'

'How so?' came the reply James had anticipated – like a shot from a gun.

Making and saving money was what Frankenstein lived for, as James had quickly learned.

'The advertisements, they are not getting good results? I telephoned to inquire about them.'

'Exactly, Doctor. And we were wasting good telephone time discussing telephones in the — '

'Never mind the telephones. I wish to know about my campaign.'

James put him in the picture, and added a coat of rose-coloured varnish. 'We have high hopes, Doctor.'

'Kindly keep me informed.'

When the stressful conversation ended, James asked his secretary to go and find out how the first stage of the campaign was going. Discreetly worded copywriting, which nevertheless offered the tantalising prospect of rejuvenation, had featured in the ads placed in quality newspapers and up-market magazines. Attached to the ad was a coupon requesting the brochure James had not let Anna see. The agency was handling the inquiries, via a box number, on the client's behalf. So far, they had not exactly been snowed under, thought James, trying to stem his anxiety.

Tracy returned with the morning's crop of coupons in a wire tray. 'I've brought them for you to see.'

James would rather not have seen with his own eyes how few there were. 'I advised the client to let us use Freepost for this!' he vented his feelings.

'Why didn't he?'

'The reason he gave was that anyone not prepared to pay the price of a postage stamp isn't a serious inquirer. Needless to say, Tracy, I tried to convince him that non-serious inquirers can become serious ones after seeing the brochure. That our number-one job, with a tricky campaign like this, is to *get* them to see it – which includes making it easy for them.'

'He's a bit of a mingy devil, isn't he?'

But James had dealt with mingy devils before, and managed to handle them without *them* getting the better of *him*. 'Anyway, he wouldn't listen, Tracy. I even had trouble with him about the ads – he'd have liked them to be half the size they are. What he's after is quick results with the minimum outlay.'

Tracy was sorting out the coupons.

'Why are you doing that?'

'I have to do something while you let off steam to me, don't I?'

'Don't be cheeky.'

'I'm not being, Mr Ridgeway. Letting her boss sound off to her when he's having an off-day is part of a secretary's job.'

'I am not having an off-day.'

'If you say not, Mr Ridgeway.'

Marj, though she might sometimes have felt he needed humouring – what busy exec didn't? – wouldn't have put her tongue in her cheek like this kid. She would have produced a boiled sweet from the jar in her desk and given it to him like a soother. Oh, plump and motherly Marj, where are you now? Why did you have to desert me when I need you most? James eyed her saucy young replacement. Out to grass, though there was still life in her, was where Marj was. But who could blame her for thinking it was time she retired? Bit by bit, the agency had become a lonely place for her. Modern youngsters had taken over and nudged Marj's lot out.

The girls who had applied to be James's secretary had all been like the one he had engaged, with an independence about them that the old brigade hadn't had. That must be why he had felt so comfortable with Marj – he was the agency 'square', as well as a legend. Oh well, he thought drily.

'It's nice to see you smiling, Mr Ridgeway.'

'Believe it or not, there was a time when smiling wasn't foreign to me.'

He could hear Tracy thinking, 'You could've fooled *me*.'

'Do stop going through those coupons!'

'There's no need to shout. I just thought I'd count them — '

'Please don't bother.'

'And I'm curious about what kind of woman would reply.'

'Since the next stage – if they're hooked by the brochure – is an appointment with the clinic, not the agency, you're never going to know that.'

'But the addresses tell me something. If the house has a name, instead of a number, that tells me it's from someone with a posh home. But if it has a name as well as a number – well, that's just pretending you're posh, isn't it?'

'*My* house has a name as well as a number,' James informed her.

'Sorry, Mr Ridgeway. But I bet it isn't Bella Vista.'

'It is, as a matter of fact.'

'So are the names on two of these coupons. But sorry again!'

'As it happens, mine had the name on it when I bought it.' If there was one thing James had never been guilty of, it was pretending he was posh. But even the house you lived in was part of your bloody image – and not just the *size* of the house. He'd a good mind to take the nameplate off the gate!

'Do you always put people in pigeon-holes?' he snapped to Tracy.

'Only since the market-research stint I did, while I was making up my mind if I wanted to be a secretary or a hairdresser.'

She'd have made a good policewoman, the way she ferreted things out!

'I plumped for hairdressing, but the bleach they use got on my chest, and anyway, you don't get paid much while you're an apprentice. I'd done a secretarial course at school, so here I am.' She gave James an impish smile. 'Not before a few bosses before you had knocked the corners off me, though.'

This was the first personal conversation James had had

with her, and it wasn't like him. He had to start seeing her as a human being, as he had Marj, if they were to work well together.

'Why didn't you stick with market research?' he asked. It was almost lunch time and neither of them was going to settle down at their desk now.

'The bottom end of it's just knocking on people's doors, isn't it? And they don't ask you in. Before then, I didn't know a Fairy Liquid type from a Squeezy user,' Tracy added cynically.

'But that's what market research is about, isn't it?' James countered. 'Finding out which products will sell to which consumer category.'

Tracy smoothed her sleek fair hair and said coolly, 'Now who's putting people in pigeon-holes, Mr Ridgeway? And it's all a great big con. What the research is for, I mean, and what gets done with it. Everyone's being brainwashed, but they don't realise it.'

James took in the gaudy tights and the baggy tweed jacket that were the current uniform for girls of her generation. Image again! But he was in the bloody image business, wasn't he? – as Tracy had just reminded him, though she was a sucker for it herself. Weren't they all? And had she just been giving him lip again? Probably not, nor had it been lip before, when he'd ticked her off for it. Youngsters today gave as good as they got; if they had a point to make they made it, and didn't think of it as disrespect to their elders. All but his own darling daughter.

'If you feel that strongly, Tracy, what are you doing working in an ad agency?'

'I can't afford to be noble about it, my dad's been made redundant. Ad agencies pay their staff well. Or I should probably've stayed with my last office job, earning a bit less, but happy at my work.'

'I hope you'll settle down happily here.' She was a nice kid.

'That depends on how you treat me, doesn't it?' she said perkily, and harked back, 'But me being your girl-Friday doesn't mean that I have to approve of brainwashing. I'd be very upset if my mum let herself be lured into having cosmetic surgery – if she could afford it, which she can't.'

Tracy gave James a wry smile. 'But the way things are looking, Mr Ridgeway, face-lifts'll soon be available on the never-never, like everything else, and all hell will break loose all over Britain, while couples fight it out over which they're going to get into debt with, a new car for him, or a new face for her. But if a woman fell behind on her payments, I wish the clinic luck to repossess her face!'

She picked up the tray of coupons and headed for the door. 'Meanwhile, I'll go on giving my mum Oil of Ulay for Christmas, and hope for the best.'

James had to laugh. 'What an over-active imagination you have, Tracy.' But no more so than his own, nowadays.

CHAPTER EIGHT

CHRISTMAS CAME and went without James having summoned the strength to have it out with Anna about the tranquillisers. It was not just what being deprived of them might do to her, but the effect of this on their homelife, that kept him silent. Each evening as he drove home from the office, he would resolve to confront her immediately after dinner. When that time came, and he saw her seated opposite him with her knitting, he could not bring himself to shatter her serenity, false though it was, nor to disrupt his own peace beside the hearth.

Irving's advice to simply dispose of the capsules was the thinking of a high-handed man, which James knew him to be when necessary. James was not that kind in any of his dealings, least of all in his marriage, and it went against the grain to even contemplate doing what Irving would do.

If only his level-headed daughter were here to talk to. And to talk sense to her mother, though Kim would be amazed that it was necessary. What was she going to make of Anna when she got back? It wouldn't take Kim two minutes to see how the life had gone out of her mum. This had been her first Christmas away from them, and when she phoned to wish them all the best, James couldn't keep the tears from his eyes, but the capsules had not let Anna down.

So what? James had said to himself — but he couldn't keep on saying it. The longer she relied on them, the harder it would be for her without them. They weren't supposed to be addictive, but people could get addicted in their minds, think they couldn't get by without something, when they could if they tried.

Oh, for the time when home was a place I couldn't get back to quick enough, he thought, after a dayful of meetings with clients. Instead of another problem — and one I don't know how to deal with. If Anna were really herself, as she believed she was, she'd have said something about what wasn't going on in their bed any more, though James was glad that she hadn't. How the heck had the two of them got into the state where Anna needed tranks and James couldn't get it up? Could the menopause and that damn joke of Anna's really have caused all this? His loss of libido had to be part of it. But would he get it back, if and when everything else got back to normal? And that included having their daughter around again.

Anna had missed Kim dreadfully after she got married, but they'd talked on the phone every day, and Kim had dropped in often. It wasn't until she'd been in Australia for a few weeks that Anna got mad and threw the shoe at him.

He sat tapping his fingers on the steering wheel, held up at Henley's Corner, as always. Was Julie right? According to Neil, Julie thought Anna had suddenly had time to turn in on herself and realise a big chunk of her life was over and she didn't know what to do with the rest of it. But what had that to do with vanity – and in a woman who'd never displayed an ounce of it?

It was beyond James. Nor would solving the puzzle help him break her of the habit that afforded her relief, he thought, when home drew nearer and he was negotiating the car along the ice-crusted suburban avenues.

This was the worst January James could remember. The weathermen said there had been one just like it in 1947, but knobbly-kneed schoolboys, which James then was, neither feel the cold, nor suffer the ignominy of requiring thermal long-johns. Anna had gone to Marks & Spencer to buy some for him – and seeing himself in them did nothing for his diminished virility. Though Anna said women had been queuing at the cash desk, to pay for the ones they'd got for their husbands, that was no comfort to James. The first time he put them on was like bowing to middle age, saying, 'Okay. You win. I give up.' Nor had the dark days of winter helped his jaded spirits.

When he had garaged the car, and entered the house, he was still debating his nightly dilemma. It would be playing the heavy-handed husband even if he used only words, and cruel to try to deprive Anna of her solace. But if he let her go on taking the tranks —

In the event, he acted instinctively, and without hesitation.

'I've had some bad news,' Anna said when he joined her in the kitchen.

James's innards flipped over. Had something happened to Kim?

She went on stirring the soup. 'My mother's dead, James. She never really got over the flu she had before Christmas. It left her chesty.'

'But we didn't expect her to die.'

'This dreadful winter must have made an end of a lot of old people. Mam's house was nice and warm, with the gas fires we had put in for her. But she went out to get her groceries whatever the weather, though that nice young woman next door offered to shop for her. You know how independent Mam was.'

And how quickly and philosophically you've put her in the past tense, thought James. He couldn't believe that this was his wife talking about her own mother. It was as if the pain and shock hadn't touched her. When her dad died, James could remember her walking around red-eyed for weeks. But there she was, calmly adding salt and pepper to a pan of soup. Tranks might not have this effect on everyone, but Irving wasn't wrong. Zombie was the word for her.

'Where are you going in such a hurry?' she asked when he turned and strode from the room.

'To get rid of those bloody capsules! I want you to weep at your mother's funeral.'

CHAPTER NINE

ANNA DID not weep for her mother, or for herself, until the capsules she had craftily secreted in her handbag were all gone. She had learned from Myrna and Julie, who heard it from their husbands, what James was thinking of doing, and could not have contemplated managing without her tranks if he did his worst when the health centre was closed for the weekend.

James attributed her continued composure to lingering effects of the drug in her bloodstream, and steeled himself for the opposite of composure when it came. In the meantime, he made a dismaying discovery about his parents.

Anna's mother was buried on a Friday, and the Ridgeways had remained in Manchester for the weekend. James and his brother were having a Sunday morning drink together in the local pub, while Anna – who had said she preferred to do it alone – was sorting through the bric-à-brac of her late parents' married life and her own childhood. And if that doesn't move her to tears, nothing will, James thought while he sipped his beer. If her eyes were red when he got back to the house – well, he wouldn't know whether to be thankful, or sorry for himself.

'I must say Mam and Dad seem a lot less grouchy than they were when I was last up north,' he remarked to his brother.

'The doc put them on the same as Uncle Ted and Aunt Edith are on.'

'Come again, John?' James put down his tankard. 'I didn't know Uncle Ted and Aunt Edith were on anything.'

'How would you? It's ages since you've seen them. But take it from me, they'd reached the stage when they were ready for a Home.'

'What stage is that?'

'To put it in a nutshell, they couldn't cope with getting

old. Nor could Mam and Dad, before they were on what they're on now.'

'We're talking about tranks, aren't we?'

'They don't get called that up here. You've turned into a real Londoner, haven't you, lad?'

James drank some of his beer. 'Never mind what I've turned into. I don't like the idea of Mam and Dad taking those things.'

'Why not, if it makes life easier for them?'

'Our grandparents got by without them.'

'They didn't have to be frightened they'd get mugged, and all that. Nobody bothered locking their doors, it wasn't necessary, was it? Nor did they have to queue for a bus, in all weathers, to buy a bit of bacon at a supermarket; they had the corner shop. Where they could get things on tick, if they were a bit hard up. How would you like to have to manage on a pension, James, the way prices are, nowadays — '

'You and I've made sure our parents don't have that particular worry,' James cut in.

'But Uncle Ted and Aunt Edith have it, don't they? And it isn't just that, James. It's everything. We're living in very different times from how it used to be.'

'There's no need to tell me that.'

'Then what are you on about?'

'Our parents taking tranquillisers.'

'Since you weren't here to see what was going on, you'll just have to take it from me that they needed them. Old age affects different people in different ways, but from what I've seen, what a lot of them get afflicted by is hypochondria.'

'I don't remember noticing that in our grandparents.'

John downed his beer. 'Those were the days when the family doctor used to drop in for a chat, every so often. Remember how Gran always kept a few ginger biscuits in a little tin, because she knew he liked them? I used to pinch one whenever I visited her.'

James laughed reminiscently. 'Me, too, and she once caught me at it, and slapped my hand.'

'Where was I?' John returned to the present. 'Oh yes. Mam and Dad. After he retired, and she had him under her feet all day, squabbles wasn't in it.'

'After our next-door-neighbour retired, his wife said to Anna that she'd married him for better or worse, but not for lunch.'

'And that about describes it with Mam and Dad, James. Not to mention how every little ache and pain they got, they'd run to the health centre to make sure it wasn't the beginning of the end – that's why I mentioned hypochondria. Pathetic, isn't it? But I'm thankful to say none of this is going on now. They're happy as larks, like Darby and Joan.'

Darby and Joan in cloud-cuckoo-land, with a lot of other Darbies and Joans, thought James. And pathetic in a different way. His father had lost his bite, and the vagueness he'd noted in his mother wasn't the onset of senility. Was that what being a senior citizen had come to? Walking around zonked to the nines?

But there was nothing James could do about his parents – he could imagine what John would have to say if he tried. John was on their doorstep, and James wasn't.

He glanced at his brother's ruddy countenance, and the double chin that wasn't there in his thirties – but *he* still had all his hair.

'How's middle age treating you, John?'

'I don't have time to notice. Lucky for me my shop's wine and spirits, or I might've been in Queer Street now, along with a lot of other folk – especially up north.' John eyed the jostling throng beside the bar. 'My takings aren't what they were, of course. People've had to cut down. But it'd take more than unemployment for them to turn teetotal. How're things with you, James? You seem fine.'

Well, he'd learned to, hadn't he? And his too-small hat was invisible. James was tempted to unburden himself to his brother – even about how something was still making him deliberately leave the loo seat up at home. But the two lads who'd shared a bed and told each other everything were now men who'd gone their separate ways. Time and distance had come between them, fond though they still were of each other.

'I mustn't grumble,' James replied.

John got up to get them a refill. 'One for the road, and back to our wives!'

*　　*　　*

85

Anna took her last remaining capsule the day the Ridgeways returned to London, and the next morning called the health centre for an appointment immediately James had left for work.

'Dr Binns is doing evening surgeries this week, Mrs Ridgeway.'

'Then it'll have to be then.'

'I'm not sure if I can fit you in. Half a mo – I'll have a look.'

'All I want is a prescription.'

'So do a lot of other people. But you're in luck; I can squeeze you in at ten past seven, since the person before you's a prescription, too.'

Anna had come to think of this receptionist as the 'squeezer-in' – even if she hadn't recognised the girl's voice, she would have known it was her – and, with amusement, of herself in relation to the girl as a prescription.

She was still smiling when she replaced the receiver. After stacking the dishwasher, she poured herself the third cup of tea she always had after James had rushed off, and sat sipping it. What was she expecting? A fit of the shakes, because she hadn't had a trank? She could get by for one day without them, and had plenty to keep her occupied.

By early afternoon, she knew what the woman she had met in the waiting room had meant when she said *she* couldn't. The shakes were not part of it, but depression had Anna in its grip, and she could not sit down for five minutes without wanting to get up and busy herself. Panic and tears followed. Anger, too. What right had James to put her in this position, he wasn't the one who had to suffer it!

The telephone rang.

'Hi, Anna. I heard from Irv about your mother and I sure feel for you. There wasn't time to call you, before you went to Manchester.'

The mention of her mother was anguishing for Anna.

'Want me to come hold your hand? There's a tea at the synagogue, but I don't have to go to it.'

'No. I'm all right, Myrna.'

'It doesn't sound like it.'

Anna was sobbing into the telephone.

'It's just that I haven't got any tranks. James did what he said he would — '

'Julie is going to be pleased. She's never approved of you taking them. But with that stiff upper lip, why should she care?'

'Exactly.' Anna glanced at herself in the hall mirror. 'Half a day without a trank and I can't bear to look at myself again,' she sniffed, averting her eyes.

'That should only happen to Julie, it might get her to diet. Sure you don't want me to come over? Irv and I have a dinner date tonight – the way the weather still is, I might wear my mink boots – or we'd drop by and spend the evening with you, like we used to before the tranks put you right.'

'By tonight I'll be on them again, Myrna. And from now on, they'll be kept where James can't find them.'

James returned from the office to an empty house. Where the heck was Anna? She was never out when he arrived home. He called Myrna and Julie, without getting a reply from either number, and finally Maggie.

Mike answered the phone, and made light of James's anxiety. 'You're not going to ring up all Anna's friends because she wasn't in when you got home, are you, James?'

'But I would like a word with Maggie.'

'I'm afraid you can't have one. She's bathing the little monster – Shirley's gone out straight from work tonight.'

'Would you mind asking her if she's any idea where Anna is?'

'I'm not going to encourage you to behave like a mother hen with your wife, mate. Anna'd have a fit if she knew.'

'I'm sorry to've troubled you,' James said stiffly.

'I was only making myself a sandwich. When Shirley and her brother were little, my wife had my evening meal ready and waiting. Twenty years on, with just one kid suddenly here for her to look after, she seems to have forgotten how she did it.'

'It's that twenty years on,' said James, though he was in no mood to be conversational.

'And now I'm a granddad, and you're an old fusspot, James. If I came home and Maggie was missing I'd assume she'd gone to the West End, shopping, by tube, and got caught in the rush hour. Now why didn't you think of that, mate?'

Because dire possibilities are more my mark nowadays, thought James.

He was left to contemplate them for another half-hour.

'Where the heck've you been? You've worried me sick!' he tongue-lashed Anna when she came home.

'That's nothing to what you've done to me!' she retorted, slinging her coat onto the hall chair and stalking into the kitchen. 'How dare you forbid the doctor to give me what I need? And I've had the most terrible day. Because of you!'

'Shall I make you a cup of tea, love?'

'If you did, I'd throw it at you.'

'I don't remember using the word "forbid", when I rang him — '

'The way you put it doesn't matter,' Anna raged. 'That's what your call amounted to. You put the wind up him.'

'I intended to.'

'So he wouldn't let me have any more. But you weren't above taking a trank yourself, when you needed one.'

James didn't bother asking how she knew.

'And that makes what you've done to me all the more callous and despicable.'

'If putting someone back in touch with their own feelings is callous and despicable, okay, I stand guilty, Anna.'

'But you can manage without tranks, and I can't,' she said, dissolving into tears. 'What am I supposed to do now?'

James went to comfort her. She pushed him away. He gave her his handkerchief. She threw it on the floor.

'I'm glad to see you behaving like a human being again,' he said warmly, and received a freezing glance.

'You might not be when I tell you I can't look in the mirror, again. And I haven't cooked you any dinner.'

They were back with the face-phobia – and another spell of baked beans and the like. But that was better than living with a zombie, James thought.

'I love you,' he told his wife.

'I hate you,' she replied.

CHAPTER TEN

SOMEHOW ANNA found the strength to hold herself together; her household routine, too, though what had once been to her a pleasure was now a duty. Neither James, nor her home, was neglected. But her mind, which had formerly centred upon wifely pursuits, remained riveted upon her own uncertainties.

Women were said to 'turn funny' sometimes during the menopause, but Anna had thought it an old wives' tale until it happened to her. And if she had to get fixated about something – Julie's word, not hers – she would have expected it to be about something domestic, like cleaning the floor over and over again. The big mystery, she said to herself, is not that I've turned funny, but what about.

Little by little, as her grey days slipped by, she had stopped resenting what James had done. In that respect, her commonsense returned. She need not have let James win that battle; prescriptions for tranquillisers were available from doctors who practised privately, and she could have kept from James who her new doctor was and paid the bills from her savings account.

She had almost taken that step, then stopped short. What sort of marriage would theirs be from now on, if she thought nothing of deceiving James? He didn't know about the savings account, but that was her own little nest-egg, and what she intended it for would one day be a lovely surprise for James. As for the other deception, not telling him where she got tranks from, was she really that desperate? Like the junkies you saw on TV who'd do anything for money because they had to have their fix? Come on, Anna! Hold tight.

James had done what he thought best for her, and there was no denying he was right. She was ashamed of having told him she hated him, but couldn't bring herself to apologise. Why not? She just didn't want to. It was as if she somehow held him responsible for her plight, though he'd done nothing to deserve it.

What did she use to think about while she did her morning chores? This and that. But nothing that really mattered.

'I feel like a mole, suddenly burrowing its way into the daylight,' she said when a call from Julie interrupted her dusting. Why had she said that?

Since she had stopped taking the capsules, Julie and Myrna had resumed supportively calling her each day – and pulling her their two ways.

'It's as if I've been buried alive for a long time,' Anna crystallised her thought.

Julie's reply was: 'Marriage has that effect on a lot of women.'

'And wouldn't *you* be the one to say that.'

'They stop being who they are the day they become someone's wife,' Julie went on. 'How are you doing without your crutch, Anna?'

'This is the first time you've asked me.'

'I didn't think it was safe to.'

'I'm getting by, Julie. But I still can't be bothered with people who don't know how daft I'm being about my face.'

'Your local friends will think you've dropped them again.'

'No they won't. Maggie will explain that I'm not too good and want to be left alone for a bit. That's what I told her. How's Neil?'

'Getting more and more browned off as I get fatter and fatter. Hard lines! But I'm pleased you're making progress, Anna. Last time you fell apart, you didn't spare a thought for how your behaviour might upset Maggie and the others.'

'My mind wasn't really functioning.'

'Exactly. But nor has it been, the way it ought to, for many a long day. Now, you seem to be hobbling in the right direction.'

'How can you say that, Julie? When I still can't look at myself and that's what's wrong with me?'

'If you think so, Anna, you've a lot more hobbling to do yet. In my opinion, your obsession with how you look is only a manifestation of what's wrong with you.'

'And, since you're the clever one, try to solve this one,' Anna replied. 'I seem to be still bearing James some sort of grudge, though I'm not mad at him any more for doing me out of my tranks.'

Julie snorted. 'There's nothing to solve. If a married woman feels buried alive, who's the most likely candidate to've wielded the spade? But you didn't have to let it happen to you, Anna. I didn't,' Julie added unnecessarily, before someone demanded her attention, and she had to ring off.

Since Julie invariably called from her chambers, and more often than not the conversation was cut short as it was today, Anna was becoming increasingly aware of the narrowness of her own horizon compared with Julie's. With Myrna's, too. Though the two women led vastly different lives, the Sangers' West End apartment was as a window on the world compared with Anna's suburban scene. But why was she suddenly comparing her life with theirs?

She picked up the duster, sprayed some polish on it, and set to work on the dining-room table. It was all fine for Julie to accuse her of letting herself be buried alive, she thought, envisaging herself in her apron, standing trial, and Julie in her barrister's wig and gown, doing the prosecuting: 'This woman is guilty of making marriage her career.' But even with the benefit of hindsight, Anna would not have done otherwise. Nor were they lost years. There was her happy, uncomplicated daughter to show for it, and what greater reward could a woman have?

So what are you bitching about? Myrna would have asked her. If I knew the answer to that, maybe I'd stop hobbling, Anna mentally replied. And another good question was, why had the life she had built with James suddenly come tumbling down around her, like a house of cards?

Stop trying to fool yourself that it hasn't, Anna. They were back to pretending all was well between them, but what was the point of Anna's pretending to herself? They couldn't be natural with each other any more, and had nothing to fall back on, now the habit of being easy together had gone. Maybe a house of cards was all their marriage had ever been. Carefully erected by both of them, to serve the purpose. What purpose? Enabling them to live together, day in, day out. Under the same roof. Sharing the same bed long after their young passion had waned.

Julie would say she could hear Anna's brain creaking — and it certainly felt strange to be having thoughts like this. Like stepping back and seeing more of the picture, not just the bit that was driving you daft.

Anna would not have called herself a thinker, but she was not short of commonsense and it was this that carried her forward now. Every marriage was something the couple had constructed together. She had always thought her own soundly based. People said that when sex took a back seat, contentment went missing — or something of the kind — but it hadn't been like that with Anna and James. When they reached the age and stage where making love became less important than getting a good night's rest, they had laughed about it. But maybe James's laughter was just a cover-up for how he really felt. What a smug daftie she'd been, believing she shared his every thought and feeling. Had she let him share all of hers? Of course she damn-well hadn't. It was no wonder the house of cards had come tumbling down. And James wasn't laughing about their sex-life now, since they hadn't one any more. Nor was he talking about it.

Anna went on polishing the table, as if doing so was helping her push her thoughts along an unaccustomed track. The objectivity she had mustered was unaccustomed, too, but this was not to say she was not an intelligent woman. Like James, she had won a scholarship place at a grammar school, though it was one less renowned than the élite establishment he had attended. Had he set his sights on university — he had confounded his teachers by not doing so — Anna might have followed suit. In their teens, she had already begun moulding her life to his.

James's habit of clockwatching was a hangover from the impatience to get ahead which had gripped him in his youth. It was as if every minute had counted for him, and his refusal to spend time acquiring further education had not surprised Anna. Instead, he had answered an advertisement in the *Manchester Evening News* for a trainee account-executive. Though he had not, then, known the meaning of that term, it had sounded as if there was a future attached to it. Since the agency he had joined was small, and James astute and personable – two essential qualifications for the job – he had risen fast, and moved on to a larger firm.

Later, in London, he had found the big-league a harder climb, but had succeeded nevertheless. James was the kind whose natural diligence and pertinacity enable them to climb despite the lack of a single, driving ambition. He had entered, by chance, a field whose ethos was foreign to his nature, but had felt no discomfort until the insecurities of middle age brought home to him that the older one gets, the more difficult it becomes to hide behind a required veneer.

But Anna knew nothing of her husband's private traumas, and was at present too immersed in her own to dwell upon the possibility that he had any. She was dusting the living-room ornaments, her mind still clicking from thought to thought, when Julie called her again.

'Haven't you any work to do this morning, Julie?'

'Stacks. But I just got a brilliant idea about you, and I can only spare a few minutes to put it to you. You once told me maths was your best subject at school. I think it was when you mentioned you'd got a nest-egg in – wherever you had it, and I said you'd got no business sense — '

'That was years ago,' Anna interrupted. 'And I did what you told me to.'

'But now you've started thinking for yourself, why not ask Irving to find you a part-time job at the agency?'

'Is that your brilliant idea! Doing what?'

'Something to do with figures. Every firm has an accounts department. And you'd be helping to disinter yourself and paying James back at one fell swoop. He doesn't approve of married women working if their husbands can keep them.'

This reminded Anna of Myrna's saying that having cosmetic surgery would also be punishing James in his pocket. What were the two of them trying to do to her marriage! 'James has never said that,' she replied.

'Are you trying to tell me he isn't the woman's-place-is-in-the-home type? Come off it.'

'We've never discussed it, Julie.'

'What you and James have never discussed is part of your problem, Anna. And it would be one up for you, working at the agency right under his nose.'

'I don't want a job!' Anna exclaimed.

'Because you've let yourself grow lazy.'

'How can you say that, when I do all my own housework, though I could afford help?'

'More fool you. And I was referring to your mind.'

'What makes you think,' said Anna crossly, 'that in the age of computers Irving would give a job to a woman on the wrong side of forty who once got ten out of ten for her sums? When highly qualified young people are on the dole?'

'Myrna could make him do it. If you ask her, she'll oblige by turning him on specially for the purpose.'

'Are you being funny?'

'Like hell I am. How do you suppose she got that red fox jacket, when she already had a mink? Irving told Neil she was after one she'd seen at Harrods, but he had no intention of buying it for her. Contemptuous though I am of Myrna's methods, I have to hand it to her,' Julie declared. 'Are you going to do it, or aren't you, Anna?'

'Do what?'

'Enlist the aid of our chum the vamp.'

'I don't think I've seen Myrna wearing a fox jacket.'

'She had it on – it was the night I arranged a jolly sixsome dinner to cheer you up and you cried off – over a Forties cocktail frock, like you see in those old movies. When I saw the frock – her hairdo went with it – I thought she could pass for the Andrews sisters if there were three of her. Neil, needless to say, leapt right into his flatter-Myrna routine.'

'Why are you always so catty about her?'

Julie let the question pass. 'You could call and ask her your little favour now. You, no doubt, have already cleaned your entire house, and I've had a laborious consultation this morning, but Myrna will still be languishing in a frothy negligée, recovering from her and Irving's nocturnal delights.'

'Well, that's Myrna, isn't it?'

As always after one of Julie's quick calls, Anna was left hanging in the air and increasedly confused. Irritated, too. Her brilliant friend's feminist attitudes, which had once amused her, now affected her as steel wool on a Teflon-coated saucepan. Julie was scratching away at Anna's surface, as though beneath it was a female of her own kind. Julie would have said that surface was just conditioning, and would have been correct in some respects – but not in all. She had steered Anna's thought processes along lines they might not otherwise have followed, but that did not guarantee that the end product would be what Julie supposed. One vital element had escaped her: That some women choose to make marriage and motherhood their career, and Anna was one of them. As her self-searching had already determined, Anna had no regrets in that respect. Nevertheless, it was as though she had arrived at a crossroads.

While she drank her mid-morning coffee, she found herself thinking of Julie's sourness about the Sangers' sexual activeness. She and Julie had never compared notes in that department, but Anna would bet that the Newtons were once-a-weekers, like she and James were before she made the joke and threw the shoe at him. She hadn't worn those shoes since, as if she blamed them, as well as James, for whatever was wrong with her. And he was still leaving the loo seat up – that night was the first time he'd done it. What a pair of dafties they were. Getting back to sex and the Sangers, their marriage was still young even though they weren't – and Myrna knew all the tricks.

Talk of the devil, Anna almost said, when the doorbell rang and there Myrna was. But she couldn't tell Myrna she'd been talking to herself, back and forth inside her head, like she had since she came off the tranks. Saying things she couldn't say to James and coming up with her own answers.

What you and James have never discussed is part of your trouble, Julie's voice echoed in her mind.

'I thought I'd give you my daily pep-talk in person, for a change,' Myrna said.

'If it's going to be as long as all the others, we may as well make ourselves comfortable in the kitchen.' Anna led the way.

'You're a kitchen person, aren't you, Anna?' Myrna declared, glancing around the cosy room. 'Just like I used to be.'

'Whenever you come out with something like that, Myrna, I feel as if you're having me on.'

'So would Irv. If he found me sitting in our kitchen, he'd think there had to be a snake in the living-room. And I sometimes wish I could tell him.'

'Tell him what?'

'That the room I was happiest in, in the house I lived in with my ex in Beverly Hills, was the one where the cooking got done. Also how much I hate that penthouse. If I had a homey place like yours, I'd stay home a lot more than I do.'

'Why on earth can't you tell Irving what you've just told me?'

'It doesn't go with the picture he has of me.'

'There's nothing to stop you from changing the picture, Myrna.'

'After all the trouble I went to painting it? And what I painted it for? Also, it's the one Irving left his ex for, isn't it? To change back now would be short-changing *him*.'

Myrna's idea of honesty was somewhat confusing to Anna. 'Five minutes with you,' she said, 'and my head's in a whirl.'

'Okay, so I'm a dizzy blonde. But I wasn't always. Not even the blonde bit. Finding youself alone after having a guy by your side for fifteen years isn't easy, Anna. I was never going to get used to it. Maybe Julie could, but I guess you would feel like I did.'

'Probably.' There were times when Myrna came over like a character in a comic strip, but this wasn't one of them. And if she was really the homebird-at-heart she'd just made out, what a ridiculous set-up she'd created for herself.

'Shedding some pounds and getting a new face helped me find a replacement,' Myrna went on.

Anna was shocked. 'Is that all Irving is to you?'

'Not any more. But he was when I married him. Since you've never been in that position, and I hope you'll never be, Anna, you'll just have to take my word that a lot of second-time-arounders start out like that. I never used dating agencies, but some divorcées I knew did, and a few found husbands that way. What do you think, that they and others like them fell madly in love with the guy a computer picked out for them, there and then?'

Myrna got up to look out of the window at the frost-rimed trees in the back garden, but Anna sensed that she wasn't really seeing them, but re-living a time in her life she would probably rather forget.

'If you're lucky, and the guy's good to you, you can get to love him,' Myrna said. 'Now, I wouldn't swop Irv for Robert Redford – don't tell him I said that, he'll get too sure of me. But I made up my mind before I even looked for a replacement that I wouldn't make the mistake with him I made with my ex.'

She came back to sit in the Windsor chair, crossed her fabulous legs, and gave Anna a wink. 'When sex flies out the window is the beginning of the end.'

'That sounds like *you* talking,' Anna said with a smile. But it had echoed Anna's thought about sex taking a back seat in her own marriage, and a pang of uneasiness assailed her. Why was she heeding the words of a sexpot, which Myrna was – self-created or not – and she herself never had been? Look how Myrna was showing her legs off, even though there were no men around. And that white cashmere sweater she had on left little to the imagination. Myrna had small, high breasts, or maybe she just wore a good bra – which had to be made of gauze, the way it let her nipples protrude.

'How did you use to dress before you made yourself over?' Anna asked her.

'Like Julie does. I didn't bother to hide my bulges.'

'I wouldn't say you did now.'

Myrna laughed. 'But they're only in the right places, aren't they? You can be quite witty when you want to be, Anna.'

'Nobody's ever said *that* to me before.'

'Maybe you never wanted to be before.'

'Let me alone, will you, Myrna! I'm mixed up enough as it is.'

'If you're referring to your face, there's only one answer, and I've told you what it is till I'm tired of saying it. Once you deal with that, things will hot up where it's dangerous for a wife to let them cool down.'

'I sometimes think your mind is situated in your nether regions, Myrna. What has my husband been saying to yours? That he can't get turned on with a woman who looks ready for carting?'

'If he did, Irv didn't mention it to me. What does "ready for carting" mean? We don't have that expression in the States —'

'Take a good look at me and you'll know. But I've told you myself now, haven't I, that all we ever do in bed is sleep,' Anna said with chagrin. One way or another, Myrna and Julie were always getting things out of her! Lucky she hadn't let Maggie in on the act, as well.

'You didn't have to tell me,' Myrna answered. 'When trouble comes in through the door, sex usually goes down the tubes.'

'Is that another of your pet theories?'

'Cut the crap, will you, Anna? We're not going to sit here discussing the price of fish, with your marriage in the mess it's in. I'm here to help you, aren't I?'

'Did I tell you Kim will be home in March?' Anna tried to change the subject.

'That doesn't leave you too long to put yourself together, since it's now coming up to February.'

'If you came to pep me up, Myrna, you're having the opposite effect!'

'What would really pep you up is a good screw. But how about offering me a cup of coffee?'

Anna went to put the kettle on. 'Will instant do?'

'In your country how would I dare say no?'

'You dare say a lot of things, don't you? What makes you think you can get away with what you just said to me?'

'Other people think things and I say them. Shoot me. But

what I just told you is probably true. My friend Boo-boo, back home, went to an encounter group when suddenly her husband couldn't make it with her any more — '

'She sounds as way-out as her name,' Anna cut in.

'Okay. She is. But what she learned about herself there, even *she* didn't know. She told me afterwards she didn't have a single inhibition left, and it helped her to show her husband a good time. If she hadn't, some other broad would have – and the same goes for James, Anna. Maybe you should find out if they have encounter groups here in London — '

'They do. I read about it in some magazine or other, a few years ago. But no, thanks, Myrna.'

'Okay, not an encounter group. An affair perhaps. Anything to get you going again – and James, too.'

'You seem to think what's happened to James is because he's bored with me. I think I'm just not attractive to him any more.'

'It could be both.'

'But I'm not getting my face lifted, and having everyone who knows me find out how vain I suddenly am. Nor shall I resort to tricks in bed,' Anna added vehemently.

'How can you, when you don't know any? An experienced lover, I mean one who's been around – which James hasn't – could teach you a few, is why I suggested an affair.'

'And if there was a college course – a practical one – where I could learn the necessary, you'd be telling me to enrol for it!'

'It would be a smart move.'

Anna set the kettle down. 'There's something I'd better tell you, Myrna. For me, sex is an expression of love. I could never have a casual affair, since I'm unable to detach one from the other.'

Myrna's reply was, 'A lot of women suffer from that complaint. Unfortunately, it isn't that way for their husbands. Have you met James's new secretary yet? Irv told me she's shaped like a pocket-Venus.'

'Then he must have got her to take off her baggy jacket and let him inspect her – James said she always wears one.'

'I'm going to believe that one day she didn't. But I'd drop by the office, if I were you, Anna —'

'What are you trying to stir up!'

'Some drastic action, which your situation sure calls for.'

You and Julie both — and you both mean well. But neither seemed to realise that her way of handling it was not necessarily right for Anna.

After Myrna had left, Anna found herself laughing hilariously. If she followed the advice her two friends had given her today, she could finish up a part-time bookkeeper-adultress!

The next morning, she arose determined to take herself in hand. Though the weather remained chilly, today sunlight was streaming in through the bedroom window. Was it a good omen?

She made up her face carefully, which, mindful of James's jibe about liquid camouflage the night their trouble began, she had not bothered to do for a long time. Before taking the tranquillisers, her looks had seemed to her past redemption. While she was on them, she could not have cared less how she looked. The past-redemption feeling again applied, but taking herself in hand meant shrugging it off and making the best of a bad job.

Here goes, Anna! She put on her scarlet trouser suit, and a black hat with a big brim that she had bought when shopping in the West End with Maggie, last winter. Maggie was hat mad! With the pants tucked trendily into her black suede boots, nobody would take her for a middle-aged matron, she told her reflection, and even managed to smile at herself. Nor were there many women of her age who could still wear the same size clothes they'd worn in their twenties. Julie, who was tall and had always been buxom, used to wear size fourteen, but probably required an eighteen by now. Anna chided herself for feeling pleased, but it was Julie's own fault.

The last time she wore this outfit, a kerb-crawler had halted his car, Anna recalled while striding along the main street. But so what? What am I trying to prove — and who to? Myself. That I can still be eye-catching? Maybe it *was* just a late-in-life attack of vanity, and she had better stop searching for other explanations, like Julie was needling her to do.

'You're looking very fetching today, Mrs Ridgeway,' said the man behind the delicatessen counter in the supermarket, while he weighed a piece of Brie for her.

If she'd gone for some ready-wrapped Cheddar from the refrigerated serve-yourself section, she'd have done herself out of a compliment – and how lovely it was to get one. 'It's nice of you to say so, Ken.'

'And I'm the sort who says what he means. That daughter of yours must have to watch it with her boyfriends, with a mum who looks like you about,' Ken continued his repartee.

'Kim's married now,' Anna told him.

'Really? You don't look old enough to be a ma-in-law.'

Anna gaily added some expensive duck pâté to her purchases. Had she been at the wine counter, she would probably have bought champagne, instead of the Ridgeways' weekly bottle of plonk. She was humming a tune and contemplating some imported strawberries – the heck with the price! – when a young chap in workman's overalls accidentally bumped his grocery trolley into her and said, 'Sorry, Ma!'

The smile died on Anna's face. James wouldn't be getting strawberries for dessert tonight – his wife was back with her feet on the ground. She was so anxious not to be thought past-it, she'd taken an older man's flattery without a sensible pinch of salt, then a young man had returned her to earth. And how she felt now was what she deserved.

What exactly she meant by past-it, she did not let herself conjecture, and on the way home she briefly blamed everything on the menopause, a comfort she had not employed for some time. One morning she would awaken with all this behind her. But that could be a long time from now, and she couldn't go on this way. Only two choices were open to her: to grow old gracefully, or be the kind of woman who got described behind her back as mutton dressed as lamb. The incident in the supermarket was enough to show her the folly of the latter. But the former was easier said than done.

Her trim figure in the bright red suit attracted the attention of one or two male motorists driving past her, and she silently told them not to be fooled by a passing glimpse. An hour ago, it would have made her day. Now it was like grit on an open wound. But she had still put a false spring in her step, hadn't she? – as if she were really the young woman they supposed.

'You bloody disgust me!' she told her reflection in the hall mirror when she arrived home, and it wasn't just her face she was saying it to. It was her whole damn self!

She rushed upstairs and scrubbed the make-up off her face, as though doing so was a penance. And punished herself for her folly in the supermarket by calling Myrna and relating what had happened, chapter and verse.

Myrna reminded her that she had a third choice. 'What're you waiting for, Anna? The day when a dishy young guy bumps into you and says, "Sorry, Grandma,"? Think of all the wolf-whistles you could be getting between now and then —'

'It isn't wolf-whistles I want,' said Anna – though, in a way, it was.

'With you, I'm prepared to believe that. But they're a bonus that comes with a new face.'

'Stop trying to talk me into cosmetic surgery!'

'Would you prefer a psychiatrist's couch? I hate like hell to have to agree with the guys, but that's where you're headed, Anna. James told Irv and Neil, when they last lunched together, that he wouldn't care what it cost him to put you right. A shrink is their current thinking.'

Anna was outraged. 'They're holding meetings about me, are they!' If James were here now, she'd throw a boot at him, not a shoe! 'It's a wonder he didn't invite my friend Maggie's husband to attend it — '

'Cool it,' Myrna cut in. 'Since what James once called your momentary madness has proved anything but momentary, all of us who love you are trying to decide what's best for you, all the time. I don't recall, since we got back from the States – it was the same before we went on vacation – when Irv and I last spent an evening alone together without mentioning you and James. And Neil told Irv it's like that with him and Julie.'

Anna suppressed the urge to laugh. There they all were, night after night, discussing what she and James, though it was their crisis, carefully avoided talking about. And everything got bandied about, this way and that, between the lot of them. The only good thing about it was that Myrna and Julie, between them, had passed on bits and pieces that had kept Anna one step ahead of James.

The last time he'd seemed her enemy was when she learned he was planning to dispose of her tranks. He'd done it for her sake, but she couldn't help resenting how, afterwards, he'd just sat back and left her to tussle with herself. She was still bloody tussling! – and had never felt as lonely in her life. She hadn't thought a married woman living with her husband could feel lonely, but she knew differently now. Two people could sit together beside the fire chatting away and still be withdrawn from each other in the ways that mattered. 'Talk to me, love, let me help you,' James had once said to her. But how could she, when she knew he'd only see things from a man's point of view?

It did not occur to Anna that James felt as she did, in reverse. After twenty-odd years of harmony, their inability to share their deepest thoughts had come as a shock to them. It had already dawned on Anna that maybe they never had, and James, too, was coming to think that the togetherness with which they had thought themselves blessed was a sham. Yet they went on pretending, lest airing their new-found differences destroy the little they had left.

This was not to say that Anna was prepared to buy peace at any price. A picture of her husband and his sympathetic cronies deciding what should be done with her, over their pub lunch, now rose before her, and with it came a blast of fury.

'So James is plotting to put me away, is he!' she put her feelings into words. 'Now I know what the bugger's thinking about, when he hides behind his evening paper.'

'Cool it again, will you? Nobody has mentioned putting you away.'

'I'd like to see them try!'

Anna Ridgeway, the cause for concern. What a humiliating position to be in – and all because she'd made a daft joke and blackened James's eye. If the shoe had hit him where his clothes hid the bruise, their tiff would've stayed hidden, too. And how she felt about her face. Without Myrna and Julie egging her on, she'd perhaps have learned to live with it, and not gone delving into the whys and wherefores of things she'd always taken for granted. Gone to her grave wrapped in beautiful illusions, along with her shroud – instead of the Sangers and Newtons helping her to strip herself of them –

'I wouldn't be your buddy, if I didn't tell you what James has in mind,' Myrna broke the silence.

Anna didn't know whether to curse her or thank her. But Myrna and Julie were true friends. 'It's James I'm mad at, not you, Myrna. I shan't forget how you've stood by me.'

'What I've been trying to do is wise you up, like I said the day I dropped by with the wine.'

'And you've finally succeeded,' Anna replied. She was done with letting James lead her by the nose. 'Daddy knows best, love', was how he used to handle Kim. Never 'Do as you're told'. And it was how he'd handled Anna, without her knowing it. Well, she knew now! And just because she'd never had to make a decision didn't mean she wasn't capable of making one. It was time she began being a person, not just James's wife. Julie was dead right.

'I've a lot to thank you and Julie for,' she said warmly to Myrna. 'Not that I've enjoyed the tug-o'-war you've been having over me, but I'm sure you'll be pleased to hear that you've won. James is in for a shock.'

'All of a sudden you're opting for a face-lift? How come?'

'It's better than getting my brains tested, and I can't go on the way I am. Once I can look at myself without cringing, nobody will have to hold meetings about me any more — '

'But I wouldn't let the agency's client do it, Anna. After what James has done to upset you, he isn't entitled to get discount. Also, a cut-price face-lift could be taking a risk — '

'Let the person responsible for me cracking that joke make a profit out of it? Not likely, Myrna! I wouldn't dream of putting myself in Frankenstein's hands.'

'Are you sure you've got the name right?'

'His name didn't register with me. All I could think, when

104

James and I had dinner with him, was that he must be itching to take his knife and fork to my face. But I once overheard James call him Frankenstein and laugh, when he was talking to Irving on the phone. It stuck in my mind.'

'I advise you to prise it out. If you're going to think of yourself as a resurrected cadaver, you're not going to enjoy being reborn. And I'll come see you every day while you're in the clinic, like my girlfriend back home did me. Not that you'll need my company, those places are like smart hotels, except for the bandages.'

'I shan't want anyone to visit me *except* you, Myrna. That includes my husband.'

'Naturally. It isn't for a hair-do you're going – and I wouldn't let Irv see me under the dryer. But Julie will expect to come.'

'I doubt it.'

'Because I won, you mean?'

'Sort of.' But it was more than that. Anna and Julie had always had a lot of respect for each other, and it was going to be one-sided from now on. Her friendship with Julie would never be quite the same. But what she was about to do had already drawn her closer to Myrna. 'How long shall I be in there?'

'With just a face-lift, there's no black-and-blue; you'll come out looking like a million dollars, and before you know it. When you leave the clinic, we'll celebrate, Anna. Then you and I can concentrate on getting Julie to shed the weight, to save *her* marriage — '

'That isn't why I'm having my face lifted, and Julie's marriage doesn't need saving.' Nor did mine, before you lot got in on the act.

Myrna ignored the interruption. 'The way those two have begun getting at each other, and Julie always comes off best, anything could happen. I once saw a movie where all the guys had their wives' minds made over to suit themselves. If that could be done in real life, Neil would have Julie in the making-over clinic plenty fast.'

'*The Stepford Wives.* Julie lent me the book.' Had she been trying to tell Anna something? Probably.

Myrna's conversation dived in her favourite direction. 'Remember what I told you you needed, Anna? With your new face to turn James on, I guess there'll be no shortage in your bedroom.'

Did Myrna think Anna had given a thought to *that*, when she made her decision? Nor was she hitting back at James. For the first time in her married life she was going to do something solely for herself.

PART TWO: . . . and After

CHAPTER ONE

MYRNA COLLECTED Anna from the clinic in a white Rolls she had recklessly hired for the occasion.

'It's no wonder Julie sometimes calls you Mrs Over-the-top,' Anna said when they were settled in the back of the car.

'Two minutes out of the clinic and she's quoting Julie! And you don't have to lower your voice, Anna. The window between us and the chauffeur is soundproof.'

'Excuse me for not knowing that! I've never sat in a Rolls before, and I doubt if I shall again.'

'What sort of talk is that?' Myrna demanded. 'I'm launching the new you. And over-the-top is better than bored stiff. It'll be your own fault if you're ever bored again.'

'Thanks for telling me.'

'If the voice of experience doesn't, who will? My best girlfriend in LA picked me up from the clinic in a silver Cadillac,' Myrna reminisced, 'which sure wouldn't have matched my "before" image. "Here you go with your second chance, Myrna," she said to me, "and how you begin is how it'll be from here on." I guess that's what I'm saying to you, Anna.'

'But you seem to have forgotten that extravagance has never been my way.'

'I can see I'm going to have trouble with you. You need a whole new wardrobe to go with the face – or why did you bother getting it lifted? Meanwhile your husband is hopping mad with me; he thinks *I* advised you not to have him come visit you. And Julie has been so vinegary, she probably won't show up for the luncheon.'

'What luncheon?'

'The one I'm giving for interested parties. That's why I wanted you to leave the clinic on a Sunday, so the guys and

Julie would be free to come. I'm not taking you home, Anna. We're going to my place.'

'What did you say to them?' Anna said drily. 'Myrna Sanger invites you to come and inspect the goods?'

'I told you we'd celebrate when you came out.'

'But I thought you meant you and me. And not on the *day* I came out.'

'James will have you to himself tonight – and oh boy!'

There she went again. Anna had not let herself think as far ahead as tonight.

'I was up at the crack of dawn,' Myrna said, stifling a yawn, 'putting out all the deli I bought yesterday. We're having a cold buffet – with extra potato salad for Julie!'

'Neil won't thank you.'

'Julie, neither, if I didn't provide enough nosh – and her idea of enough! We really have to do something about her, Anna.'

'She rang me up at the clinic and said I'd let the side down,' Anna said with a smile. 'As though my face-lift has weakened the struggle for women's rights.'

'Maybe she thinks her over-eating will strengthen it.'

'You could be right.'

'Since when did you take my wisecracks seriously?'

Anna thought many of Myrna's wisecracks to Irving were *meant* seriously, and vice versa. 'Whenever I see Julie stuffing herself with food, I get the feeling she's blowing a raspberry at men.' Hadn't Julie once said she didn't care if she turned into a fat pig, she'd still be a hard-to-get QC? It was on an evening Anna was unlikely to forget! She could recall the grey misery that had caused her to put the Newtons off. The terrible desperation that sent her rushing out to buy the most expensive face-mask they had in the shop. And the promises it made on the packet, that raised her hopes. Julie and Neil turning up to disturb her privacy and finding her with the damn mask on. And later, James thinking it was plaster-of-Paris. It had crumbled on her lap, like the hope she'd never really had. But she was fine now.

Myrna was powdering her nose. 'If an apple fell off a tree she was walking under, and hit her, Julie would think a guy was up there shaking the branches. Adam getting his revenge on Eve, and the other way round, is how she sees everything. When I first met her, she was shaped like Raquel Welch, and Neil reminded me of one of those classy British actors. He still does, but any resemblance between Julie's shape and Raquel's is long gone.'

'Why must you keep going on about it?' Myrna was as catty about Julie as Julie was about her.

'I guess because she's never valued what she has, and it upsets me.'

'That's a bit of a sweeping statement about someone you haven't known all that long.'

'Long enough to have heard her ask what she's done to deserve the sons she's got.'

'I don't know what you're on about, Myrna.'

'Come off it. We're talking attitudes, and you know it. Julie's boys must have imbibed with their mother's milk that they were never going to come first with her. And if Neil didn't know that also applied to him, he's finding out now. That proving whatever she's proving is more important than keeping herself attractive for him.'

'As it happens, she didn't breastfeed the twins.'

'That doesn't surprise me.'

Anna smiled reminiscently. 'During the day, I'd give one his bottle, and Julie the other. And I always had to pop into their house to fetch up the babies' wind, before they were put down for the night. Neil never had any luck with it, and Julie hadn't the patience. Once, when I had a bad cold and didn't go, James and I could hear Paul and Mark screaming their little heads off, through the wall.'

'And how I read it,' said Myrna, 'is they haven't stopped screaming for attention, and it's their mother's attention they want.'

'You really have got a down on Julie, haven't you?' Anna had never before heard Myrna speak with such feeling.

Myrna gazed through the car window, as they glided along Park Lane. 'Would you believe how those two guys are jogging in their shorts and undervests in the middle of winter?' She added, too casually. 'I never told you I had a stillborn child with my ex, did I?'

Myrna was full of surprises, and they weren't all frivolous. She was also capable of seeing things in their true perspective, which Julie, for all her intellect, wasn't, Anna thought.

'Irv doesn't know, so that's another of my little secrets you now share,' Myrna said. 'Why would the madeover me bother telling him?'

'Didn't you and your ex try again?'

'The doctor said another pregnancy would be too risky for me. I was born with only one kidney – and don't tell that to Irv, either. I wouldn't want him to think he's making it every night with a freak.'

'You're a real nutcase, Myrna, the things you come out with!'

'But what I'm never going to be again is a *shlemiel*. My ex made me get sterilised. Irv probably thinks I'm on the pill.'

'Haven't you ever discussed contraception with him?'

'What's to discuss? He's not going to think I'd want kids this late in life, so he leaves it to me. If *he*'d wanted them, he'd have had them when he was younger, with *his* ex. Getting back to mine, he told me with tears in his eyes that he would rather have a live wife than a motherless child. But he ended up killing me in another way. The woman I was when he walked out on me died the day he did it,' Myrna said with a brittle laugh, as the Rolls halted outside her apartment block.

Anna could have wept for her.

But when they stepped out of the car, Myrna's brief poignancy was gone; she was again the dizzy blonde her friends knew, handing the chauffeur an over-the-top tip and dazzling him with her smile. 'Thanks for keeping me company on the way to the clinic. I wish I was going to that new disco with you tonight.'

'Me, too, madam.'

Anything in trousers! Julie would have said. And what was she going to say when she saw Anna looking thirty-five again? When Anna first saw herself, it had been like being thrown backwards in time – and what a shock Kim would get when she came home.

As they crossed the elegant foyer, Myrna harked back to

the effect her ex's desertion had had upon her, but it was the madeover Myrna who was speaking now. 'So if anyone tells you that you can only live once, don't you believe them, Anna. And here you go with your second chance, like I said.'

Anna's mind returned to the evening that had led to it all; when James, too, had said what Myrna had now told her twice: That his new client was selling a second chance for women. But Anna wouldn't know what to do with a second chance. Having a face-lift wasn't going to make her flighty, like Myrna was. She was still the same woman who'd gone into the clinic, though there was no denying that even before she went in she'd changed from the docile daftie she used to be. If she hadn't, she would never have done it – and that included making the decision without consulting her husband. What had he said when she told him? 'You must do what you think is best for you, love,' – and that was a new one! As if she'd driven him to desperation, which she most likely had.

'Irv said I picked this apartment block because the elevator is lined with mirrors,' Myrna said as they stepped into it.

'And the last time I visited you, I wished I was wearing a blindfold.' Confronted by her reflection, Anna still couldn't believe it.

Myrna smiled at her expression. 'I know just how you feel. Nobody values their youth while they still have it.'

'I don't look *that* young, Myrna.'

'All the same, younger is younger. It's what gives rejuvenation the edge over the first time around. Like Irv said after his haemorrhoids surgery, he had to suffer the pain to appreciate the relief. Don't look so nervous, Anna. Nobody's going to eat you, though the guys are going to want to.'

'Do I really look that good?'

'Like Liza Minnelli in *Cabaret*, without the nose.'

'What you mean is tarty! Why did I let you get at me with a comb?'

'What's wrong with tarty for a woman whose husband can't make it? And all I did was sweep a little of your hair forward, to hide the scars.'

'Since I didn't have brain surgery, there was no need to give me a fringe!'

'Cool it, Anna. Everyone is going to love how you look – though it'll choke Julie to have to say so.'

Anna resisted the urge to press the stop button. 'When I had my hair chopped off – I used to wear it down to my shoulders – I did it with James's approval, but I was still nervous about what he'd say when he saw me.' And thanks to well-meaning Myrna, this wasn't going to be a private viewing.

'Did you ever do anything *without* James's approval?'

'Now you sound like Julie.'

'But the difference between me and her is I don't use her thumbing-the-nose tactics. By the time I get finished with him, Irv *thinks* he approves. And you've forgotten the other thing I told you, Anna. How you start out with your second chance is how it'll be from here on.'

When they entered the living-room, Julie paused with a cocktail canapé halfway to her mouth. But Anna's appearance had arrested the attention of everyone.

'Who's the youngster you've got with you, Myrna?' said Neil.

'Is that an insult to me, or a compliment to Anna?' Myrna cracked back.

Neil gave her his winning smile. 'It's Anna's turn for the compliments today.'

Irving was the next to pronounce judgement. 'For a minute, I thought my wife had brought me what I've always wanted – a French au-pair girl.'

James was thinking that he would definitely have to get himself a toupée now.

'Well?' Anna said to him.

'You've rendered me speechless, love. Will anything come unstuck if I give you a kiss?'

Julie burst out laughing and helped herself to another canapé.

James isn't going to let me forget I've had a face-lift, Anna thought. She'd let herself hope this might be a new beginning for both of them. But it could still be one for her. 'Only my hair-do,' she replied. 'Myrna sprayed it with lacquer, after she'd combed it for me.'

'But James has my permission to disarrange it,' Myrna said helpfully.

'If the Ridgeways wouldn't mind postponing the rest of their ecstatic reunion until they get home, I'm ready to eat now,' Julie intervened.

Some ecstatic reunion, thought James.

Neil watched Julie waddle to the buffet – there was no other word for it – and said acidly, 'You're always ready to eat.'

'And I always was.'

'But before the menopause got to you, it didn't show.'

'Kindly don't mention that word in front of those two young ladies,' Julie jibed, with a glance at Myrna and Anna. 'You'll embarrass them.'

'Gee, thanks for saying I look as young as Anna,' Myrna replied. 'I wish it was true.'

'Who I have to say looks absolutely stunning,' Neil declared.

'I can't argue with that,' Julie said through a mouthful of Greek salad. 'But it isn't the real her, is it?'

'Don't be daft, Julie,' Anna answered. 'Only how I looked has been changed.'

'That's what makes what you've done so bloody ridiculous, Anna. It's what's inside your shell that counts.'

And you're getting fatter and fatter, proving it, thought Anna.

'That, I'll go along with,' said Irving, stealing a morsel of potato salad while Myrna's back was turned.

'But would you if your wife didn't look as delectable as she does?' Neil inquired.

'If that's a dig at me, darling, dig away merrily,' Julie said sweetly.

But everyone present knew that Julie was at her sweetest when she bared her fangs. If this is how she is in court, heaven help someone she's prosecuting, Irving was thinking. That lady could lacerate you with words before the smile was off your face from her show of sympathy.

'It obviously makes you feel entitled to your self-pity,' was her follow-up to Neil, 'which extends far beyond your having a wife who looks her age, I might add.'

'And I'm lucky you're against cosmetic surgery, aren't I, dear? It would cost me double to have your face lifted if the number of chins involved affects the price.'

Irving silently applauded Neil's answer – though he wasn't up to Julie's standard, he too was no slouch with the words. But their verbal rapiers had developed a lethal edge of late.

'I used to think you two enjoyed your little slanging matches,' Myrna said to them. 'But I don't any more.'

'You just took the words out of my mouth, babe,' said Irving.

'I'm not going to like it if they spoil Anna's new-face party.'

'Her fake-face party you mean,' said Julie. 'If we're here to celebrate something, let's be accurate about what we're celebrating.'

'In that caftan you have on, Julie, you look bigger than you are,' Myrna diverted her.

'You forgot to include the word "even", Myrna. And I prefer the image I project to yours and Anna's. What you actually remind me of is a pair of clones.'

Myrna stopped eating smoked salmon and telegraphed an eye-message to Anna: Did you tell the bitch I had cosmetic surgery? Anna signalled: No.

But Julie had always suspected it, and her suspicion was confirmed by the same silkily-tight patina around Anna's cheeks and jawline that she had noted in Myrna's.

In the split second of silence that followed Julie's remark, Neil, the only one of the men not in on Myrna's secret, looked puzzled. Irving and James avoided each other's eyes. Irving was also holding his breath. How was his foxy wife going to get herself out of this one?

Neil saved her the trouble. 'Even eminent QCs can be occasionally guilty of inaccuracy,' he enjoyed saying to Julie. 'What my dear wife obviously meant,' he told Anna and Myrna, 'is you're an example of the kind of women she holds up to ridicule because they care how they look.'

For once, Julie let him get the better of her. The sacrifice was for Neil's sake. Given Myrna's influence over Irving – she was wearing the red fox jacket when she walked in – if

Julie forced her to pick up the gauntlet, the end result might be Neil's losing the occasional work he did for the agency. Julie wouldn't want that on her conscience.

'But that doesn't mean Julie doesn't love us, Neil.' Myrna's laugh hid her relief.

Irving was relieved, too. Myrna having her shop-front torn down in public was not something he cared to contemplate, though it could make a difference to his life. James and Neil wouldn't believe it if he told them he had never seen his wife with her hair in rollers, or doing any of the things women did to beautify themselves. Myrna wouldn't let him in the bathroom if she was only painting her toe nails, though it was open house when she was taking a bubble bath without a hair on her head out of place. If he saw her minus mascara and eyeliner he probably wouldn't recognise her. And the same went for if she ever got into bed in the dark and didn't smell like a perfume store. It would be great to feel like a husband, instead of a resident boyfriend.

But Neil was a lot worse off. The poor *schmuck* didn't know he'd won the last round only because his wife saw fit to let him — and why she did was a mystery.

'Julie must have had a last-minute attack of pity for Myrna,' Irving said quietly to James. 'If you don't mind me interrupting the way you're sitting gazing at Anna.'

'She's really something, isn't she?'

'I guess you forgot what she once looked like, eh, boychik?'

'I must have done.'

'And if you'd like my opinion, Julie is now dead jealous of her, like she's always been of Myrna. Or why was she so goddamn bitchy? I don't think Neil knows what a complicated woman he's married to. She comes over as straight black and white, but that lady is far from it when it comes to herself.'

'She's a good deal more observant and perceptive than Neil is,' James said wryly.

'That could be why she's made it to the top and he hasn't, charming though he is. And these days she isn't, unless it suits her to be. Let me go refill everyone's glasses, James. I'll be back.'

Since the living-room was vast, it was possible for them to converse privately. Neil had joined Julie at the buffet and was trying to stop her from piling more potato salad on her plate, and James wondered what Anna and Myrna were talking about with their heads together, over by the bar. This wasn't the reunion with his wife that James had looked forward to. Good old Myrna had put her oar in again. The way she'd taken Anna under her wing was getting to be like the Myrna Sanger show.

'I don't want to appear ungrateful for your hospitality, but I wish your wife hadn't done this,' he said, when Irving returned with the cocktail shaker.

'There was as much chance of me stopping her as of putting my foot down about this damn-awful decor.' Irving glanced around with distaste. 'Myrna's gone Forties-mad!'

'This sofa we're on is very comfortable,' James tried to placate him.

'I'm talking about what it looks like, and there are four of them, aren't there? All shiny red leather – not to mention that pink-mirrored item that passes for a bar. Only the thought of what it cost me stops me from taking an axe to the lot of it.'

He was diverted by Neil's snatching a dish of creamy dessert from Julie and Julie's voluble response.

'Stop being so bloody macho, or I'll tell everyone you're not!'

She snatched back the dish, they fought over it, and it dropped from their frenzied fingers onto the carpet.

'Myrna is going to kill them both. When we had the pale carpet, she never served red wine at parties,' Irving said resignedly.

But all Myrna said was, 'I'd rather it went where it has, than put yet another inch on my friend's shape.'

Julie's response was to get herself another dish of dessert, while Neil cleared up the mess with a paper napkin.

'I'm beginning to think that this has nothing to do with food,' James said to Irving.

'When did the penny drop?'

'But what Julie's doing to herself still makes sense.'

'Except to a woman who stands or falls by her brains.

And how someone so clever can also be so foolish beats me, boychik. Why would Neil go on living with a female Mohammed who now looks like she's the mountain?'

Had Neil and Irving discussed James's marriage like this? Probably. When your friends are doling out sympathy and advice you tend to overlook that talking about you between themselves goes with it.

'When you asked Anna if anything would come unstuck if you kissed her, I nearly gagged on my drink,' Irving said.

'But Neil used the right word when he called her stunning,' James replied, turning to look at her. 'She was a nice-looking girl, but I wouldn't have called her stunning when she was genuinely young.'

'Since we're talking semantics, I'd avoid the word genuinely in that respect, if I were you,' Irving counselled him. 'Also other such verbal pitfalls. And I guess you didn't find her so fascinating when "genuinely" still applied because now she has a youthful appearance and maturity both. A combination that only money can buy! Did you get the surgeon's bill yet?'

'It landed on the mat yesterday, with another epistle from the person you're trying to make me have nightmares about.'

Irving clapped a hand to his cheek. 'What were you, born yesterday? If you haven't sought professional advice yet, when they come to get you don't ask me to bail you out.'

'Since I'm hiding nothing from the taxman, I'm not going to let you scare me into running up accountants' and lawyers' bills.' James fortified himself with a sip of his drink. 'In this country, you're innocent until proven guilty.'

'But the whole world over you can be made to feel over tax matters that it's the other way around.'

There was no need for Irving to tell James that! Nor was it only the taxman who loomed large in his ongoing nightmares – Ronnie had just been assigned an important new client, one whom James, though he would have felt over-burdened by it, had expected to get.

'I heard you and Myrna were invited to Ronnie's for

dinner last week,' he said to Irving casually. Casually nothing! but he hoped it didn't show.

'That boy sure knows how to keep in with me.'

And was doing fine.

'You should try smiling once in a while,' Irving said, topping up James's glass. 'If this doesn't help, nothing will.'

'I don't know what you mean.'

'Why do you suppose I gave the new client, with such big potential, to Ronnie?'

'You like his smile,' said James facetiously.

'What I don't like is what you let stress do to you, and you've been under a lot of strain from your marriage crisis.'

James had better get himself together, or it might soon be: Goodbye, boychik. I love you, but business is business.

'I don't let personal worries affect my work.'

One good lie deserves another, thought Irving. 'Of course you don't, James. But you should try not to make mountains of molehills, in your mind.'

James wanted to laugh, but it would have stuck in his throat. Where other people's problems were concerned, Irving was the prize exaggerator. If you went into his office and mentioned you'd just had a bout of cramp in your leg, you'd come out convinced that it needed amputating. James wouldn't have called his row with Anna a marriage crisis — and who'd told him it was one? After which his marriage had slid rapidly downhill. Nor would he have got worked up about a little tax misunderstanding, before he got told one of Irving's gloom-and-doom stories.

Irving was thinking that sending Myrna on that peace mission had got Anna a new face, but failed to forestall what he'd feared.

Since neither knew what the other was thinking, they exchanged a smile and clinked glasses, like they often did when having a drink together.

The trouble with my friendship with Irving is I can never be sure which cap he's wearing, the boss's or the buddy's. But he couldn't blame Irving for his fiascos in bed, James thought, when Anna briefly met his gaze across the room. Why didn't she come to sit with him? Or he go to join her? Once, they'd have done it naturally, one or the other of them, but they'd stopped being natural with each other. The glance they had shared had affected James as might a come-hither look from an attractive woman he didn't know – if his thinning hair and thickening middle hadn't put paid to him getting them – and led him to hope for a resurgence of activity where he was now tingling. If that went right for him, now she was satisfied with her looks perhaps everything else would?

'I'm looking forward to Anna and me settling back the way we were,' he said to Irving.

'Then take off your rose-coloured glasses, boychik. Marriage is one situation that never moves backward. Especially when it's veered in an unexpected direction after years of standing still.'

Irving was at it again! 'I'll let you know if you're right or wrong about mine.'

'You won't have to. My wife will keep me informed.'

And what Anna didn't tell them, Myrna and Julie would conjecture and surmise and give advice about. Hadn't James been treated to the same from their husbands? It was like being on a roundabout that was never going to stop – and the Sangers and Newtons were propelling it. James wanted to take Anna by the hand and leap off with her, back to the privacy that had been safe ground, but according to Irving it couldn't be done. He hadn't seen Anna so relaxed since she came off the tranks. But *he* still had that bloody tightness around his head – was it going to be there forever?

'You didn't tell me yet how your lunch with Frankenstein went,' Irving said.

There was no mistaking which cap he was wearing now. 'I had to take an indigestion tablet after it – and it wasn't from what I ate.'

'How come?'

'You know him! And all I need now is for him to find out my wife had her face lifted by someone else.'

'He can't complain that the campaign isn't off the ground, or he wouldn't have been in London to consult with prospective patients. That slow starter has turned into a runaway horse.'

'But does he give you a word of appreciation?' James said testily.

'If you're going to start expecting appreciation from clients — '

James rubbed his forehead. 'Leave it out, will you, Irving?'

'What's the matter? You're always doing that nowadays.'

'Nothing's the bloody matter! I'd just like to go home with my wife.'

Irving glanced to where Anna stood chatting to Myrna and Julie. 'I guess you're going to have to wait a little longer. She's enjoying chewing the fat with her girlfriends.'

Anna caught James's eye. 'I'm telling them about that funny letter from Kim, that you sent on to me while I was in the clinic.'

'After I'd sent it, I thought maybe I shouldn't have, in case laughing made you burst your stitches.'

Irving gave James a scathing look. 'Stitches are only mentionable when she drops one while she's knitting. *Shmuck!* You've done it again.' His gaze roved to Neil, who sat nursing a glass beside the buffet. 'Come join your buddies, Neil.'

'Would you mind if I didn't?'

'What're you doing? Guarding the nosh, so your wife can't get at it?'

James winced. Irving's wisecracks could be too near the bone.

'How's my babe doing?' Irving called to Myrna.

In a room this size, if you weren't sitting next to someone, you *had* to call to get their attention, thought James – and how daft it was, the Sangers paying the earth to live in a place like this, when there were just the two of them. There was a small room that Irving had made his study, with a TV in it, and Myrna had told Anna that that was where they spent their evenings when they were alone. Since the study was much less spacious than the Ridgeways' living-room, James had had to laugh. But a status symbol is a status symbol. Irving might hanker after a Bella Vista, but James couldn't see him shedding this bit of his image even if Myrna were to let him.

Myrna brought James some dessert and saw that he had only picked at the food she had heaped on his plate. 'Why aren't you hungry, James?'

It would take too long to tell her, and he had had a bellyful of his friends' concern and counsel. But how could you say that when you knew the concern was genuine – and the chief offender was your boss?

Myrna gave him a naughty wink and supplied her own answer. 'I guess any guy would be too excited to eat, getting his wife back after a separation – and how sexy Anna looks now.'

James couldn't argue with that. The new Anna made a man conjure up seeing her in black lace undies – stop it, James! Anna doesn't have any undies like that. But I've got a tingle again, and long may it last.

'Me, I'm getting the only dessert my wife ever gives me,' Irving said, when Myrna sat on his lap for a kiss and a cuddle.

'Hold everything!' said Julie. 'Our host and hostess are about to present us with one of their exhibitions.'

'And you're the one who always spoils their fun,' Anna remarked.

A moment of surprised silence followed. Anna was not the kind to stir things up.

'That wasn't very nice,' Julie said.

'Nor was what you just said.'

'Are you having a go at me?'

'Don't be daft. I was just speaking my mind, and why shouldn't I?'

It was an exchange which James would recall later, though he attached no significance to it at the time. He watched Neil again try to stop Julie from eating something.

'My sole consolation' – Neil tried to make light of it – 'is that if my wife cared about preserving her looks it would be costing me a fortune in health-farm bills.'

'Have you never met a big fat judge?' Julie said with her usual barbed sweetness. 'And no prizes for guessing who isn't going to end up a tall, handsome, slim one.'

'Why doesn't she just cut off his balls?' Irving muttered. 'It wouldn't take her as long.'

123

'If I were Neil, I'd bloody throttle her.'

'It's what she deserves. But not his style.'

Neil hid the wound he had just received, and said with a smile, 'Now we all know what my wife's ambition is.'

Irving came to his aid. 'And my wife is welcome to go out in the world and turn herself into the president of a big conglomerate, while I stay home with my feet up.'

'I wouldn't want to,' said Myrna, unnecessarily. 'How about you, Anna?'

'Not likely.'

Julie gave them both a scornful glance. 'Because you've let yourselves be duped into thinking you wouldn't and couldn't. Even women with careers have to keep reminding themselves that having one isn't a favour bestowed on them by the male community. It isn't easy to stop seeing yourself as nothing but a cook and a sex object.'

'You seem to have managed very well on both counts,' said Neil.

'And that's enough of that!'

'All the same he isn't wrong,' Myrna put in.

'If you don't like my cooking, I won't invite you for dinner again,' Julie flashed back.

'It was the other I was thinking about.'

'Well, sex *is* all you think about, isn't it, Myrna?'

'What I like about when us six get together,' Myrna said with a smile, 'is the nice friendly arguments all of us have.'

My God, she means it, thought James. Myrna never seemed to know when she was being got at. And a less friendly argument James had never heard than the one that continued to rage around him.

Was Anna thinking what he was? That if friendship was the umbrella folk sheltered under while they had a go at each other, he'd rather be alone in the rain. Where had he been all his life, that this was just getting through to him? It didn't use to be like this in the old days before Anna threw the shoe at him – and nor was it now with Maggie and Mike and that crowd. But once you'd let other people into your private life there was no getting them out, and somehow you got snarled up in theirs.

*　　*　　*

124

'Cosmetic surgery isn't going to solve Anna's real problem,' Julie said to Neil while they prepared for bed that night. 'She's too intelligent for that to be the answer.'

'May we talk about ourselves for a change?'

'What is there to talk about?' Julie sat down at the dressing-table to unpin her untidy bun and give her hair its nightly brush. 'If you say my girth, I'm going to behave like a woman and scream.'

'We've been so involved in the Ridgeways' crisis, you may not have noticed that we now have our own. And I *married* a woman.'

'Oh, I thought you married me because I wasn't just a pretty face.'

'It's got lost in the avoirdupois.'

'And you don't like what there's left to see.'

'What there's left to see includes the avoirdupois.'

'You just won't let up about it, will you, darling?' Julie began brushing her once-chestnut mane.

'I was about to add, since you're deliberately helping your hormones do their worst to your shape.'

'Thank you for not saying menopausal hormones.'

'You're not denying it, then?'

'You haven't got me in the witness box. Let me get on with my one concession to the beauty stakes, will you, Neil?'

'Why bother, when you now wear what was still your crowning glory when it turned silver, in that bloody awful style.'

'You're beginning to sound like James.'

'And to know what he went through with Anna, only the opposite way round. You're a one-woman crusade in everything you do, Julie. In a way I admire you for it, or I might if I didn't have to live with it. It struck me today, at the Sangers', that you're the only one of the lot of us who isn't fighting middle age.'

'What's the point, when you know you can't win?'

Neil hung his brocade waistcoat in the wardrobe and paused before closing the door. 'Most people would rather not accept that they have fewer years to look forward to than they have to look back on.'

'Since I don't have time to think about it, that aspect doesn't bother me. But I'd advise those it does bother to do something useful with the time they have left. I tried telling that to Anna, though less bluntly, but she opted for what she's done.'

'I don't want to discuss Anna. If the Ridgeways had gone on being lovebirds, you and I might not have come to this.'

For the first time since Neil began getting at her about overeating, Julie experienced a qualm. 'There has been a bit of a chain reaction, I suppose,' she said, brushing aside her uneasiness.

'Some of which I'm looking at right now. Your rump is spilling over the edge of the chair.'

'Didn't I say insulting me wouldn't get you anywhere?'

'What I'm actually doing is stating facts.'

'You'd do better to put on some weight yourself, darling. A plump countenance does fill in the lines.'

'Plump is one thing, dear. Obese is quite another,' Neil hit back. 'I'd rather *your* countenance were a mass of wrinkles than have you the way you now look.'

Julie met his gaze in the mirror. 'But you're not having me, are you, Neil?'

'When was I last allowed to?'

'From my point of view, that aspect of our relationship – what there was of it – could have been curtailed before it was. I continued it as a concession to you — '

'It's lucky for me you *dis*continued it,' Neil cut in, 'or given your unappetising flab, *I'd* be making the concession, not you.'

'There's no way I'd let myself be laid by a man who's more interested in my body than he is in how I tick,' Julie informed him.

'And the man who doesn't see women that way doesn't exist.'

A fraught pause followed.

'Is the eminent lady-QC lost for words?' Neil inquired.

'She thought she'd found the exception to the rule.'

'But she was only a student then.'

'And for twenty-six years he kept her fooled. I thought it

was me-the-person you made love to, Neil, but you were doing what all men do in the hay. Using me, in the one situation where brains don't count and, biologically, the male is the dominant partner.'

Neil thought back to the passionate nights of their youth. 'Are you telling me you didn't enjoy it?'

'I wouldn't have, if I'd known what I know now.'

'You have the makings of a lesbian, my dear.'

'But only in my mind – or I wouldn't be here with you.'

Another of Neil's resentments sprang to life. 'And I wouldn't have the kind of sons no father could be proud of.'

Julie put down her hairbrush and bit into a chocolate biscuit she had brought upstairs with her. 'Are you blaming me for how the boys have turned out?'

'Who else?'

'How about their weak-as-water father?'

'I'll let that pass. Since you removed them from my influence at the age of eight, and except for holidays they never lived under my roof again, it's irrelevant.'

'You didn't have to agree to their going to boarding school, did you?' Julie challenged.

Neil laughed. 'There's another kind of man who doesn't exist, Julie: one who's stronger than you. I knew before we married that I'd met my match. But that was what I wanted. An Anna, or a Myrna, wouldn't do for me.'

'But you find Myrna attractive, don't you?'

'If I thought you were jealous, it would kindle hope in my heart – but that's another female attribute you lack.'

Like hell it was! 'Do go on.'

'I intend to. And the things I'm saying should have been said a long time ago. I thought our marriage would be an equal partnership, Julie, which is more than many men offer their wives, but it didn't turn out that way. I made all the sacrifices, while you forged ahead.'

'What the hell did you sacrifice on my account?'

'Are you so blinded by your own importance that you can't see for yourself? I'd have swopped my life for James's dull, domestic scene without thinking twice.'

'It would have had to include a wife like Anna.'

'Don't bother telling me that I can't have it both ways. I know. And despite everything, I still love you, Julie.'

'I still love you. But where will it get me?'

'To a health farm, I hope.'

'You cunning devil! Was this what Myrna whispered in your ear before we left? You'd subject me to colonic irrigation, not to mention starvation, because you don't like to be seen with a woman who looks like me!'

She pulled off her nightdress and flaunted her flab, beside herself with anger. 'I don't go with your image of yourself any more, do I? Too bad!'

'Let's leave my image out of it, and just say that suet pudding was never one of my favourites.'

She threw the nightdress at him. 'If you really loved me, it wouldn't matter to you how I looked! And if Myrna thinks she can make me over, as she has Anna, she had better think again.'

'A face-lift and dieting are not comparable, Julie.'

'But at my time of life and Anna's, the motivation for either is the same.'

'And you'd rather be a bulky female who would really prefer not to be one,' Neil said with a sardonic smile. 'Why else would a born-beautiful woman – given that she's also a rabid feminist – perversely do what you've done to yourself? There'll soon be no room for me on the sofa. We shall have to change it for a four-seater.'

'Go to hell!'

'Some might think me already there. I'm certainly not in heaven – which isn't to say I'm not attached by marriage to a barrage-balloon. Would you mind putting your nightie back on, dear? Your wobbling thighs are giving me vertigo.'

'Save your wit for your courtroom appearances,' Julie retaliated. 'I understand they could use some. My not being physically attractive any more is your opportunity to belittle me on a personal level, because my success has done that to you professionally.'

'Since I'm trying to persuade you to make yourself attractive, that argument doesn't hold water.'

'But you're guilty of mixed motives, whether you know it or not.'

'Nonsense!'

Julie put on her nightdress and declaimed, with it flapping around her like a barrister's robe, 'The real nonsense is this whole matter of what makes a woman attractive. Venus de Milo wasn't exactly a sylph. And the females Rubens painted were the stereotype beauties of that era, who today would be outsize, like me. What more proof is required that fashion, through the ages, has dictated the current interpretation of feminine beauty? And what is it all about, but women being stupid enough to fall over backwards to please men?'

Neil heard her bed creak as she got into it. 'If *you* fell over backwards – *or* forwards – we'd have to get the builders in to repair the hole in the floor, and a crane to heave you up. But there's no danger of your doing either to please me.'

He switched off his reading lamp and settled himself for sleep.

Julie found it less easy to switch her mind to the documents on the bedtable, awaiting her attention, but forced herself to do so. Mind over matter had got her where she was – and she had not come this far to be sidetracked by her female instincts.

The lunch party had been a strain for Irving, as it had for everyone but Myrna, and he had not taken kindly to having to help her clear up. She hadn't asked him to share the chores, and seemed surprised when he'd offered to – but why wouldn't she? That wasn't the picture she had of him. What did she know of his homey lifestyle with his ex? – who would not have thought of hiring help when she entertained friends, like Myrna did.

Nor would Myrna, before she set out on her second chance, though her husband could easily have afforded it. But Irving could not have known that.

How could she be so energetic whatever the hour? he asked himself as he crawled into bed. The answer was that sex revitalised a woman and drained a man! He felt like an empty vessel – but that wouldn't stop Myrna from wanting some action, he thought while she did the nightly striptease that was her way of undressing. He could barely keep his eyes open, but if he closed them she'd think he'd lost interest in her.

'When the dishwasher let me down, as well as the maid, I remembered that trouble usually comes in threes,' she chatted, 'so I'm waiting for something else to happen. Do you like my cami-knickers, Irv?'

'To me they look like all your others, babe.'

'You never saw me in camis before. I got just one set to try out on you.'

She was letting them slip to the tigerskin rug when Irving lost the struggle with sleep and a loud snore reverberated through the room.

Myrna came to nibble his ear. 'You know something, doll? I think you and I are the only truly happy-together couple I know – and this is for why.'

Was this happiness? Irving had his doubts. And when she called him 'doll' she really meant business! 'Tonight your lover is bushed,' he had to tell her.

'But his babe will revive him.'

'He's unrevivable.'

'Who is that an insult to? You, or me?' Myrna pouted, and went to straddle a chair – her personal imitation of a centrefold model. But all he wanted was sleep.

'I did good with Anna, didn't I?' she briefly digressed.

'The surgeon did good,' Irving replied, 'and that hairdo you fixed for her is all wrong for her personality,' he added while registering that the show his wife was putting on for him was a waste of her time tonight. Once, her breasts – carefully supported on the chairback – the curve of her hips, and that promisingly pouting mouth would have sent him crazy. But a guy could have too much of a good thing. Well, one who was going on forty-nine. That when you were younger you thought you could never have enough of it, was the big laugh.

'I'm not going to let Anna keep her old personality,' Myrna announced.

'What are you? Svengali?'

'Some drastic action is called for, Irv, like I've told her. Or James might never be able to make it with her again.'

Your kind of action, thought Irving, is liable to make certain of it. 'If James is having that kind of trouble,' he said, putting off the moment when he would again have to prove his own stamina, 'I'm not surprised the poor guy feels he's over the hill.' The things you found out about your buddies through their wives could be like pieces in a jigsaw puzzle. But what the hell were they finding out about you on the same network? A question he'd asked himself before.

'Did James tell you that, Irv?'

'He doesn't have to. I work with him, don't I? And I'm doing my best to reassure him he still has what it takes, or I'd have had to fire him, wouldn't I? Friend or not. Short of saying this to him outright, there isn't too much I can do.'

'You could pay for the black lace suspender-belt I'm thinking of getting for Anna.'

'How did a suspender-belt get into this!'

'If Anna wearing it has the same effect on James as me wearing mine has on you, the end result could be you wouldn't have to pep-talk him any more. Maybe I should go put mine on now.'

'Just get into bed, will you!'

Myrna obeyed the order and wound herself around him.

'Would you mind if we take a raincheck, babe? Unless you want to wheel me to the office in a bathchair.'

'That's no way for a loving husband to talk to his wife.'

'It doesn't mean I don't love you.'

'Then why don't you prove it?'

What am I doing having this inane conversation, when the rest of the middle-aged fraternity is sound asleep? Irving asked himself. There was such a thing as moderation, but his wife didn't know from it. OTT was how she lived her life, sex included. He felt like telling her to be her age, but that was something she'd made up her mind not to be when she had her face lifted. Now she was trying to stop Irving from being his, but with a guy it couldn't be done.

'You're going to have to manage with less proof,' he told

131

her. If she didn't like it, she would have to do the other, though he feared what it might be.

Myrna left him in no doubt. Trouble sure did come in threes and this was *big* trouble. 'I'll find out who the woman is if it costs me every nickel you've got!'

James, who for Irving personified the middle-aged fraternity, was winding his alarm clock at a much later hour than usual. Anna had taken one look at the dust and clutter he had let accumulate during her absence, and had set to there and then to put her home in order.

So much for the cosy evening by the fire he'd hoped for, he thought as he got into bed. It was the sort of thing she usually did when they got back from a holiday, but he hadn't expected her to tonight. More fool him! – and his tingle had bloody gone.

'I'd like you to keep your hair that way,' he said when Anna emerged from the bathroom.

'Maybe I will, and maybe I won't.'

Was she telling him that the days when she'd do anything to please him were gone for ever? 'That sounds like Myrna or Julie talking, not you,' he said.

Anna smiled. 'Myrna and Julie could never be said to speak with one mind.'

'But the way you put it could be seen as either coyness or bloody-mindedness.'

'Take your pick, love. But I wasn't being either. And as for being coy, well, I don't think I'd know how to be. I have got a mind of my own, you know, though I was daft enough to let myself forget it. I never shall again.'

She returned to the bathroom to brush her teeth, leaving James to digest what she had said. Was it some kind of threat?

'Were you saying I've done all your thinking for you?' he asked when she joined him in bed. 'Like Julie once said?'

'We had that kind of marriage, didn't we?'

'I could bloody shoot Julie! What do you mean, "had"?'

'The way we used to be. After I came off the tranks, I

132

began asking myself questions about why I'd got into the state I had, and I didn't like some of the answers I came up with. I'm as much to blame for it as you are, James — '

'Thank you for that. Would you mind telling me what I'm sharing the blame for?'

'Burying me alive, if you want the truth.'

'When are you joining Women's Lib?'

'I don't think they call it that any more. You don't like it when I speak my mind, do you?'

'That's the second time you've used that phrase today.'

'But you don't, do you?'

'Not when I know it isn't your own mind you're speaking. Nor was it when you told me you'd decided to have the face-op, though I can't say I object to being married to such a smasher.'

'I'm pleased you think so. But we shall get nowhere, love, if you keep harping on about Myrna and Julie. All they did – between them – was prod me out of my rut.' And make me reel with confusion, she privately added, but I'm confused no longer. She'd stepped out of the clinic with something added, and it wasn't just her new face. More like reaching the other side of the road safely, when the traffic lights had changed from red to yellow, but not to green until you'd got there.

James had switched out his bedside lamp, so Anna would not see his hurt expression. 'Is a rut what you think being happily married to me was, Anna?'

'We were in it together, James. But you've got another life, at the agency, haven't you?'

'And it isn't all beer and skittles.'

'I've never thought it was.'

'If you've thought of it at all.'

'It's lovely being home again, James. Please don't spoil it for me.'

And what about her spoiling it for him?

'Did you miss me?' he said.

'Yes.'

'Same here.'

'Then why don't you try making love to me?'

Why did she have to say 'try'? 'It used to be me who

made the advances – but you've been seeing a lot of Myrna, haven't you?' he said crisply.

'Why don't we just invite Myrna and Julie to come and sleep with us?' Anna retorted. 'Then you could say things directly to them! And wish you could do with all three of us what you've stopped being able to do with me.'

James would not have thought fury an aphrodisiac, but a brute force he had not known was in him took him in its grip.

'Give me time to unbutton my nightie, James — '

But he wanted *sub*mission, not *per*mission, and behaved accordingly. Was this really the agency-square, tearing his wife's nightie off her? The pipsqueak should see me now! was his last coherent thought.

'If that was making love, you've never made love to me before,' Anna said when he lay spent.

'Would it help if I said I'm sorry?'

'It was a bit of a shock, but I'll get over it.'

James was not so sure that *he* would. How could he have behaved that way with a woman he loved and respected? His final and comforting reflection before sleep claimed him was that their daughter was due back from Australia next week. He might not have slept so soundly had he known how Kim would react to her rejuvenated mother.

CHAPTER TWO

ON THE way from the airport, Kim told Anna and James they were going to be grandparents.

'How about me?' Harry said with a grin, after Anna had hugged and kissed her daughter.

'If you were in the back with Kim and me, you'd get the same,' Anna told him warmly.

'I'm not letting you near Harry, Mum. Not now you look like you do!'

Harry turned round to look at his transformed mother-in-law. 'If I were you, James, I'd consider it worth the price.'

'But don't expect me to have my face lifted when I'm my mother's age,' said Kim. 'I wouldn't dream of it, and I wouldn't have dreamt she would. What on earth got into you, Mum?'

'I shall have to leave you to find out when you *are* my age, love.'

Harry was still looking at Anna. 'She must've been a real beaut, when she was *really* young, pumpkin,' he said to Kim.

Ouch! It was the kind of dig Anna kept getting from James − except that Harry's remark wasn't a dig. And she was learning to laugh at James's. When he stopped doing it, they could settle down to their life together. If the sex came right again. There hadn't been any since the night she'd rather not remember. Nor had he stopped leaving the loo seat up. They had a long way to go yet.

'I see Harry still has that daft pet-name for you,' she said with a smile, to Kim.

'When he first met me, he probably thought me a vegetable, Mum!'

'If I did, pumpkin, I made a mistake.'

'What would a vegetable be doing working at the BBC?'

said Anna. She was proud of her bright daughter. 'And you're a production assistant now, aren't you, love?'

'But, thankfully, she doesn't emit the kind of vibes that put me off career women,' said Harry. 'She's a nice sensible girl, who managed to catch me.'

Kim leaned over and tugged his beard.

'This was how she did it,' Harry said with a grin.

'What he means,' said Kim, 'is I didn't use the methods all the others did.'

'Well, you're your mother's daughter, aren't you?' Anna put in.

'I used to think I was, but now I'm not so sure. And as for Harry calling me "pumpkin", I'm going to be shaped like one soon. Just so long as he never calls me a sheila – his spell down under has got to his vocabulary. Did you notice, Mum, how he said you must've been a real beaut, when you were really young?'

Kim wasn't getting a dig in, either. But Anna sensed her daughter's disapproval. 'It doesn't go with his Oxford accent,' she joked. 'But the two of you have given Dad and me a lovely surprise. We're thrilled to bits.'

'James hasn't managed to get a word in yet,' said Harry.

'It couldn't have been a happier surprise.' And a shot in the arm for a chap badly in need of one.

Kim borrowed Harry's comb, to tidy her shoulder-length hair.

'Haven't you got one of your own, love?' asked Anna.

'No, we share everything,' Harry answered for her.

Anna hoped that Kim would always agree that they did. That she wouldn't find out in her forties how she had let life hoodwink her. Though Kim's generation of young women were more clearsighted than Anna's lot, she was not another Julie. Anna hadn't needed Harry's remark about career-woman vibes to know that her daughter was a homebird at heart.

'Mum's looking very thoughtful,' Kim said to Harry, with a wink.

'She's turned into a thinker, didn't you know?' said James.

Another dig – but less easy to laugh at. And Anna hadn't

failed to see Kim's wink. If there was one thing she wasn't supposed to be it was a thinker.

'I'm getting the feeling there's a lot that's gone on in my absence that I *couldn't* have known,' Kim said, glancing from her mother's face to the back of her father's head – she would have liked to have seen his expression when he made his light comment. 'Would one of you care to tell me about it?'

Harry became aware that the kind of atmosphere he associated with his boyhood was crackling in the car. His father was the strong, silent sort, and his mother a chatterbox until she suddenly stopped chattering, as if she were nursing a grudge. Maybe her chattering was her way of trying to get through to Father, and she had finally realised it couldn't be done? Whatever, it had finally led them to split up. But Anna and James? Never. If he made documentaries, and were making one on the ideal marriage, he would want to make it on location in their home. He'd thought there was no such thing until he met them.

'All right, you wouldn't like to tell me about it,' Kim said to the silence. 'But getting back to the surprise we gave you, what you gave *me*, Mum, was a real shock. I mean, fancy being waved off to Australia by a nice, comfy mother-figure, and being met on your return by competition! It's enough to make a girl spit.'

'And you are spitting, aren't you, pumpkin?'

Kim laughed. 'Who wouldn't? Here's me, in my crushed boiler-suit, resigned to stepping out of the beauty stakes until I give birth – and I suddenly get landed with a mother who looks like Joan Collins – apart from the size of her bust.'

'Why do I have to be compared with this film star or the other?' Anna asked. She'd combed back the Minnelli fringe Myrna had given her. The way James responded to her looks that first night . . . No thanks!

Kim gave her a straight answer. 'You've done what they do, and you're not one. How do you expect everyone to react?'

'Maggie didn't take it like that. All she said was she wished she had the nerve.'

137

'What did the rest of that crowd say?'

'The ones I've run into since I had it done said they wouldn't have thought *I'd* have the nerve.'

'And why wouldn't they? I thought I knew you, Mum.'

Me, too, James echoed silently.

Kim went on with her quizzing. 'What's all this about you turning into a thinker?'

'Not just a thinker, a letter-writer as well,' James added.

'Why can't I write to a newspaper if I've got something to say?'

'Come off it, Mum! You never even read a newspaper. All I've ever seen you do is cook, clean and knit.'

'You forgot the gardening, pumpkin.'

Anna couldn't blame them for their attitude. 'When I was in the clinic, Kim, all the papers and magazines were laid on a big table in the lounge every day.'

'That must've been one of the extras I paid for,' James cracked.

'But it did me as much good as the surgery.' Anna smiled at Kim. 'What you said about me not being the face-lift sort is right, love. If I hadn't known that before I decided to have one, I'd have discovered it when I went into the clinic. A fish out of water about describes how I felt in that lounge. There we all were, with our dressings on, like a uniform – but that was the only resemblance between me and the others.'

'And I shouldn't think there was *any* between my bank balance and their husbands',' said James.

'People who have cosmetic surgery for reasons that aren't considered vanity can have it under the National Health,' Anna countered sharply.

'I wouldn't have let you do that.'

'Then what are you on about?' Anna resumed relating her experience in the clinic. 'I noticed that all the other women had their favourite daily papers, and they were never what Julie calls the quality kind. The *Guardian* and *Times* and *Telegraph* never got touched. As for the magazines – well, there weren't enough copies of *Vogue* and *House and Garden* to go round. There weren't any copies of *Woman's Weekly*, of course! And it set me thinking how everyone gets put in a bracket by their income and how they live.'

'One affects the other, doesn't it?' said Harry. 'But the *Woman's Weekly* bracket, encouraged by James and his lot, have pipe-dreams about emulating the *Vogue* lifestyle.'

Anna set about him. 'Don't you go knocking how your father-in-law earns his living! You'd do better to consider the ethics of how you earn yours.'

'Is this really your mother I'm having this conversation with?' Harry said to Kim, tongue-in-cheek.

'I warned you, didn't I?' said James. 'And it was TV series like yours, Harry, that she wrote to the papers about.'

'It's been done before.'

'Maybe. But the more who do it the better. And I haven't yet got to the point of what I was trying to tell you all.'

James said, 'I'm included, am I? Thanks.'

'Since you seem to think I just woke up one morning and thought, "Right, Anna, it's time to improve your mind and become a thinker, we'll start by reading newspapers," you're damn right you're included. It wasn't like that at all. It began to dawn on me, bit by bit, in that swanky place, that me being there made me just like all the rest who'd come to be made young and beautiful. And what a shallow lot they seemed to me.'

'Like Myrna, you mean,' James butted in again.

'I've found out she isn't, as it happens. And I could be being unfair to some of the women I met there. I can only tell you how being among them made me feel. That they were all bracketed together, and not just by their backgrounds. Some had Cockney accents and big diamond rings. Another was the Honourable something-or-other. Two of them were in show business, which won't surprise you. There was one from Berkshire, who always wore twinsets and pearls, and kept away from the Cockneys — '

'What? No Sloane Rangers?' Harry cut in with a grin.

'I wouldn't know one of those if I tripped over one, Harry. But there *was* one who said her son is a punk and she's disowned him. What I'm trying to explain — '

'It's taking you long enough, Mum!'

' — is I began to feel as though I were on a little island, where nobody was interested in anything but how they look. But what was I doing there, if I was any different? If I wasn't, I damn-well ought to be! If I'd been thinking aloud, they'd have heard me ticking myself off. Then it struck me that there were only one each of the newspapers nobody touched, because the clinic knew exactly what kind of lady-patients they were bound to get. That was when I got bolshie, to prove I wasn't like the rest, and asked them to go out and get me a copy of the *New Statesman*.'

Harry roared with laughter. 'Did you actually read it?'

'I'm afraid I didn't – but I'm keeping it as a souvenir. I did start reading the *Guardian* every day though, and I still do.'

'Good for you.'

'But I don't think James thinks it's good for *him*, Harry.'

'Not when you nearly let the Sunday roast burn, like you did today while you had your head in the *Observer*.'

'That kind of thing is my lot, too, isn't it, Kim?'

'But it was never my dad's lot,' said Kim.

'I'd keep out of it, Kim, if I were you.' Much as Harry liked his parents-in-law, he wouldn't want a situation where his wife was pig-in-the-middle, as his married sister had been with their parents, and she ended up with Mother living with her. Kim was a dutiful daughter – and who wanted a resident mother-in-law?

'That's easy for you to say, Harry. But this isn't the homecoming I'd looked forward to – in more ways than one. My parents haven't stopped snapping at each other since we left Heathrow – that's shock number two – and for another thing, I keep wondering where my lovely mum's gone.' She eyed Anna reproachfully.

'I'm still here, Kim.'

'But that motherly face you had isn't. And I suspect that what you're after, Mum, is to have your time again.'

Anna kissed Kim's cheek. 'Without the benefit of hindsight, what use would that be, love?'

'If I had my time again, I'd probably do no differently than I did,' said James. 'And wouldn't you know it, I'm held up again at Henley's bloody Corner!' – a place he was coming to associate with some of his most painful thoughts.

'You didn't use to swear at minor irritations, Dad,' said Kim.

'Nor,' Harry observed, 'did he have the habit he seems to have now of fingering his brow.'

And so much for James's hope that Kim's return would help to loosen his invisible hat. On the contrary. 'What was I saying?'

'That you'd do no differently,' Anna reminded him. 'Which was more or less what *I* meant.'

James stopped tapping his fingers on the steering wheel, lest Harry notice him doing that, too. 'In their youth, a person has neither the experience, nor the wisdom to make the right choices,' he said wryly. 'By the time age equips them to, it's too late.'

Harry smiled. 'My father used to tell me that youth was too good for the young.'

'He had a point. Not that I made a choice about what to do with my life,' said James. 'I just slipped into it.'

'Does that include marrying Mum?'

'She couldn't have been more than three when she began tagging on my shirt tails, so I'd have been six. We lived next door to each other, didn't we? Does that answer your question, Kim? When we were in our teens, our parents clubbed together and got us a tandem bike for Christmas. I've no regrets that we stayed on it.'

'Me, neither,' said Anna.

Their daughter said, 'I'm relieved to hear it.'

Harry would have liked to add, 'Me, too.' 'What you said, though, James, confirms a feeling of my own.'

'And what might that be?'

'That advertising isn't your scene.'

'I haven't done too badly in it, have I?'

'Look at the big wedding he gave us,' said Kim with a laugh. 'And Dad's never struck me as being unhappy in his job.'

'He's the kind who makes the best of things, pumpkin.'

And he was still trying to. 'Would you two mind not discussing me as if I'm not here?'

'What I was getting around to saying, James, is that sooner or later I hope to have my own production company. Since I'm liable to run away with myself on the creative side, I shall be looking for someone to keep my feet on the ground.'

'Are you offering me a partnership, Harry? I'm fine where I am, thanks.' Better the devil you know!

Anna interrupted. 'I wouldn't want James to join up with you, Harry. Not unless you change your ways. While I was in the clinic I watched telly every night, and I had to work hard to find a programme with no blood and guts in it.'

'That has to be an exaggeration.'

'But only just. And it struck me, not for the first time, that the streets not being safe any more can't be just a coincidence.'

'The research says otherwise.'

'I'd trust my commonsense against a computer any time. Where do folk, and youngsters in particular, get their ideas from, if it isn't from films, books, and TV? There used to be a commercial – though it's not them I'm talking about – that showed someone spreading butter on a hot muffin and eating it. And what did Kim use to do, whenever she saw it? Go and make herself a hot buttered muffin, or a slab of toast, if there were none in the bread bin.'

'You were a compulsive hot-buttered-muffin eater, were you, pumpkin?'

Anna let Harry have it. 'If you really think this is a laughing matter, you're not the lad I think you! People like you have the power to influence the kind of life we all have – and look what you're doing with it.'

Harry looked like a whipped schoolboy, Kim thought before he turned round to stare through the windscreen. She wanted to tell her mother she'd got too big for her boots in that clinic – but that'd be behaving as she was.

'Everyone's always thought you a kind and pleasant person, Mum,' she said, 'but if you go on thrusting your opinions down people's throats – well, there're nicer ways of saying what you think. There's such a thing as being diplomatic with it.'

'Beating about the bush you mean? – and in the end you *haven't* said what you think. I've done that for most of my life, Kim. And finished up getting my face lifted.'

'I don't get the connection.'

'How would you? Shall we drop it, love?'

'What I really meant, Mum, is there's a happy medium to everything. Like – well I plan to go on working when I'm a mother, which you didn't; you became a full-time house-wife when you got married. But I shan't take Julie Newton's approach, either. How is Julie?'

'Still carrying a banner – and getting fat on it,' James said cryptically.

'Talking of carrying banners,' said Harry, 'neither of you is going to believe what your daughter wants to do.'

'And I'm going to.'

'If you weren't pregnant, I'd let you.'

'Don't you start using the word "let" to me, Harry.'

'What with your sandy hair, like your dad's was, and Harry's red beard, the baby will probably be ginger,' said Anna to distract them.

'Is that a comment on Dad's turning grey, Mum, or a joke about his thinning top?' Kim leaned forward to stroke her father's head. 'There's even less of it than when I went away.'

Small wonder!

'It was just a remark,' said Anna.

'What's all this about you and carrying a banner, Kim?' asked James.

'I'm going to Greenham Common, Dad, to join the peace-camp women. Harry will have to find himself a new PA.'

'That isn't the aspect that bothers me.'

James's reaction was, 'Have you gone daft, Kim? Lying down in the mud inviting Yankee vehicles to ride over you?'

'If she weren't pregnant, I wouldn't try to stop her,' said Harry. 'Since she is, I've said that kind of thing till I'm blue in the face.'

'And you can both have a blue fit if necessary. As for the way Dad put it, well, that's more useful than letting things *wash* over you, like most people're doing.'

'I'm against what's going on as much as you are,' said James.

'But you're not standing up to be counted, are you?'

'I've never been an activist of any kind, Kim.'

'Nor have I. But there's never been anything that got me going. There hasn't been a word from you yet, Mum. Have you lost the tongue you've suddenly found?'

Hearing her speak to her mother that way compounded

James's feeling that he hadn't known either of the women in his life, he had only thought he did. And after the harmonious example her parents had set her, James wouldn't have expected Kim to stick to her guns against her husband. Anna had never had to. Or was the real picture that she'd had no reason to? She was making up for it now.

'I'll drive you to the peace camp, Kim. When are you going?' he heard her say.

'Are you out of your mind!'

'Keep your eye on the road, James.'

He'd let the car swerve. And this would be one journey he was unlikely to forget.

Kim recovered from her surprise. 'Are you serious, Mum? I thought you'd side with them.'

'They're men. And we're women, aren't we?'

Julie bloody Newton again!

'I shall worry about you being there, of course, love. But I'm proud of you for it. If I had the guts I'd join the peace camp myself.'

'This is positively Kafka-esque!' Harry exclaimed to James.

'I could think of another word for it.'

Harry turned to look at Kim. 'Your mother hasn't just undergone a transformation, pumpkin, it's more of a metamorphosis.'

Kim linked her arm through Anna's and shared a smile with her. 'And I'm getting to like it.'

Even mothers and daughters could be sisters under the skin. 'I've made Harry his favourite supper, seeing as you're eating at our house before you go home. There's Lancashire hotpot sitting ready in the oven.'

'If you weren't too immersed in the colour supplement to remember to switch on the timer before we left for the airport.'

'Stop getting at Mum, Dad.'

And it hadn't taken Kim long to change sides, thought James as the conversation changed to less stressful topics.

'For my money, the Aussies are turning out better films than anywhere else in the world,' Harry was declaring when James halted the car outside his garage. 'When I saw *Picnic*

At Hanging Rock – I was still at college – I thought it was just a one-off phenomenon. It wasn't.'

'I hope your enthusiasm isn't going to lose me my daughter to Australia.'

'What? Me leave you and Mum to fend for yourselves in your old age, Dad? Not likely.'

Harry laughed. 'That's why it won't, James.'

Although Anna hadn't wanted to leave Manchester for London – they weren't short of ad agencies up there – it hadn't entered her head to try to talk James out of it. But her daughter's marriage was a real partnership from the off.

During supper, Harry had kept them laughing with some tall stories he had heard from an Aussie cameraman.

'But when did Kim decide to join the peace women?' Anna harked back, while she was making some tea.

And wouldn't you know! thought James. She couldn't leave well alone.

'It was getting pregnant that did it, Mum. I mean, if mothers don't try to protect their children – born and unborn – from the missiles that politicians are letting be dumped in our midst, who will? There aren't enough fathers, *or* prospective ones, taking it as seriously as they should.'

James retorted, 'That could be because they're too busy being the breadwinners.'

'Being a good provider has been your life's work, hasn't it, Dad?'

'And if that's a crime, I'm prepared to hang for it.'

'I didn't say it was. But where did you yourself come into it? And more so if what Harry thinks about you not really enjoying your work is true.'

'Enjoying what they do to earn a living is a luxury few people are blessed with, Kim. And in my day, a lad from my background wouldn't even have given that a thought.'

'You still haven't answered my question.'

'If you're asking what my reward was, love, the answer is I achieved what I set out to do, no more and no less: to give you and your mother a good family life.'

'And that's enough for you, is it, Dad?'

James smiled ruefully. 'It was. But I'm getting the feeling it's all being flung back in my face.'

'Then you're guilty of harbouring expectations,' his son-in-law informed him. 'Anyone who does that with human relationships is asking for disappointment.'

'I've got what I deserve then, haven't I?'

'And you're making me feel I've let you down, Dad.'

'Because his attitude instils obligation, pumpkin. How could it not?'

This was one of the times when James wished he had a less intellectual son-in-law. When Kim brought Harry home for the first time, James's heart had not exactly sunk, but nor had it soared. But lately enlightenments of one kind and another had been coming at him from all sides. What was one more among the many?

'My father's attitude had the same effect on me,' Harry told Kim. 'I still get these pangs of conscience, because I opted for what I'm doing, instead of for a steady, nine-to-five life in the City, like his.' Harry stirred his tea reflectively. 'One thing you and I are never going to do, pumpkin, is see our kids as little extensions of ourselves.'

'I'm with you there.'

'Does that include not wanting the best for them, since everyone wants it for themselves?' James inquired.

Harry and Kim shared a glance. He let her answer for them both.

'You just don't understand what we've been talking about, do you, Dad?'

'But I do,' Anna chipped in.

'Well, you're the new clever-breeches around here, aren't you!'

'And you don't seem to like it. Go on with what you were saying, Harry. I'm finding it interesting.'

'My mother put a different sort of pressure on me.' Harry smiled at Kim. 'But one of her hopes will materialise in time for next Christmas.'

'Harry's sister and her husband have decided not to have children,' Kim revealed.

'Why would any couple make a decision like that?' Anna asked.

'You'd be surprised how many do, nowadays, Mum. Even those who decide to have a family might think twice about bringing a child into the kind of world where there may be no tomorrow.'

'Decisions, bloody decisions!' James got up to refill the teapot – how would he not feel parched from all this? 'In my day, people went by their instincts and everyone was a lot better off for it. If your mother and I had sat worrying about hydrogen bombs, we might have decided not to have the child who turned out to be you, Kim. That was in the sixties and the world is still spinning round.'

He brought the teapot back to the table, plonked it down, and glared at Kim and Harry. 'The trouble with your lot – among other things – is you're letting yourselves lose hope.'

'Not entirely, Dad, or I wouldn't bother going to Greenham Common.'

'Maybe you and Harry *should* emigrate, if I'm to have nothing but aggravation from you! You could take your newly-emancipated mother with you.'

'You don't mean that, Dad?'

'Of course I don't.'

'But getting back to my father,' said Harry.

'Must we?'

'Since I started the story, I'd like to finish it and make my point. Father probably saw me as a budding stockbroker from the day he announced my birth in *The Times*, though he did no more than raise his eyebrows when I told him, after Oxford, that I'd applied for a Beeb trainee-director course. Expectations don't have to be put into words, do they, pumpkin?'

'And your dad isn't one for speech-making.'

'But it's those raised eyebrows I can still see. Get what I mean now, James?'

'How could I fail to?'

But James hadn't known he *had* an attitude. He'd just got on with his life, playing it by ear – before others began teaching him to read the music. That included not pausing to dissect his relationship with his parents, and theirs with him. They were just Mam and Dad to him, and when their lives ended, James and John would have those two

147

meaningful words carved on their headstones. But for Kim's generation, something had gone from that meaning, and the freedoms they'd claimed – and their parents had allowed them – had to account for it.

'When you lived under this roof, you weren't like you've become!' he let fly at his daughter.

'There was something about this house, and you and Mum, that didn't let me be.'

'We stifled you, did we?'

'Those're your words, not mine. But I was a different person when I wasn't with you. Ask Harry.'

'Why didn't you leave home, then?'

Harry grinned. 'It wasn't for the want of asking.'

'I bet it wasn't. But I'd like an answer from Kim, if you don't mind.'

'Weren't you listening to what Harry told you about expectations, Dad? I didn't want to upset the applecart, did I? Remember when Shirley left home, and there was all that kerfuffle about it?'

'If I'd been Maggie, I'd have been glad to see the back of her,' said Anna.

'And where but home has she gone back to with a kid, so her parents can look after it while she runs around,' James said with asperity. 'But Shirley never cared if she upset her parents, and you did.'

'That's what I'm trying to tell you, isn't it? When Mum wrote me about what's going on with Shirley, I thought back to when she decided to move out and asked me to share a flat with her. I said, "How can I do that to my parents?" And she said, "I know what you mean."'

'And what *did* you mean?'

'Another kerfuffle was neither here nor there, in her family, was it? I used to go to Shirley's a lot when we were at school together. I'm sure her parents are fond of each other, but they were never the happy apples you and Mum used to be.'

Kim sipped her tea and glanced from James to Anna and back again. 'While I was away, somehow the applecart got tipped over. In a way it upsets me – but it's a relief not to have to play tiptoe-through-the-tulips with you any more.'

She got up to give both her parents a kiss, winked at Harry, and said to them teasingly, 'Tiffs, then kiss-and-make-up, can be fun when you get used to it. But when I went to the loo right after Dad did, and saw that he hadn't put the seat down, I thought, "Is it my imagination, or is there a mutiny going on in this house?".'

'Your dad's been hit by middle-aged forgetfulness, love.' On this topic, Anna was keeping her opinion to herself.

James had to let the crack pass. The only forgetfulness he was suffering from was when he sometimes did from habit what she'd trained him to do, and then had to slam the seat back up again! – and she damn-well knew it. He'd once caught her loitering in the hall when he emerged from the cloakroom – as if she'd been listening for the sound of two consecutive thuds and having a private laugh.

Harry became aware that the atmosphere he had felt in the car was now crackling in the kitchen. Kim felt it too – and her parents were carefully not looking at each other. Had the loo seat got something to do with that? And why her sensible mother had had a face-lift remained a mystery. Despite the inhibiting effect upon her, the secure and peaceful childhood and youth they'd given her was comforting to look back on, and rare among the people she mixed with. Why had they had to spoil it for her now? She felt like banging their heads together!

CHAPTER THREE

MYRNA CALLED Anna one morning to confide that she was having Irving 'tailed'.

Anna's reaction was scathing. 'Only you would leap to the conclusion you have!'

'If I'd leapt to it about my ex when I should have, I'd have got myself made over and saved the marriage. This time I don't need the beautifying, but I still have to do something. It will probably be cut the broad's throat.'

Anna had to laugh. Though James's sexual problem – and she must now accept that it really was one – was far from funny to her, if she'd read into it what Myrna had into Irving's inevitable slowing down, she'd be having James followed, too.

'While Irv is under surveillance would be a good time to make him miss me. How would you like to join me for a little break, Anna?'

'I couldn't just now, Myrna. I'm seeing as much of Kim as I can.'

'It's natural that you'd want to after that long separation. *My* baby would've been about Kim's age now.'

Anna wanted to ask if it had been a girl or a boy, but, for Myrna's sake, could never bring herself to prolong the occasional glimpses she was allowed of her friend's true self. Since a makeover could never be more than superficial, it *had* to be her true self – and raising the shutter, however briefly, must be painful for someone whom hurt had caused to lower it.

Myrna answered the un-asked question. 'She had silky, dark hair – but I never got to touch it.'

Nor to watch your daughter grow up, and share in her ups and downs. 'Look, Myrna,' Anna said impulsively, 'I mentioned I'd be driving Kim to Greenham Common,

150

didn't I? Why don't you join us? She's going on Friday, and you and I could stay there with her for the weekend —'

'My idea of us taking a break,' Myrna cut in, 'was along the lines of two married broads on the loose in Paris – not chaining themselves to a barbed-wire fence.'

'Probably. But if my pregnant daughter is prepared to stay at the peace camp indefinitely, you and me giving moral support for a couple of days isn't a lot to ask, is it?'

'In theory, no. But I don't see myself in that ambience.'

'Me, neither – but that probably applies to a lot of women who put in a salutatory appearance, and Kim says they do. Are you coming or not?'

'Wouldn't you rather take Julie?'

'We could ask her, too.'

'Then count me out definitely. With all the nosh she'd bring along, there'd be no room in the car for my clothes.'

'Anyway, she couldn't take the chance of going there, could she, given who and what she is.'

'There has to be some reason why she isn't already there making with the barbed-wire cutters. And you and me too could end up on the wrong side of the law.'

'Since neither of us is aiming to be a judge, we oughtn't to let that matter.'

'I used to think I had more guts than you. You're turning into one big surprise, Anna.'

To herself, too. She'd found the courage to take a step that set her apart from most women of her kind – and not out of vanity. Desperation had driven her to it. The need to shove herself forward. Standing still couldn't be done. It was forward or under. Now, her face was incidental, though she wasn't going to kid herself that knowing she looked good hadn't made her feel good. And somehow, what I've done has given me a confidence I've lacked all my life, she was thinking when Myrna stopped chatting on about this and that and said:

'What're you wearing for the peace camp?'

'Good for you, you *are* coming.'

'You've shamed me into it. If spring weren't also winter here, I could wear my Bermuda shorts.'

And if it was announced that the world would be blown

to smithereens tomorrow, Myrna would spend today planning what to wear when she entered the next one! 'I shall wear something warm and sensible, and I advise you to do the same.'

Myrna's interpretation of that turned out to be her mink coat and hat.

'All we need now is the white Rolls!' Anna exclaimed.

'I don't have the kind of *schmattas* you're wearing,' Myrna replied.

'Thanks for the compliment to my sheepskin jacket.'

'I'm sure it was lovely when it was new. Do you mind if we take my car?'

'Would you rather not be seen in my second-hand Renault? It certainly doesn't go with your outfit,' Anna snapped.

'Since when was I a snob?'

'All right, I'm sorry. But I should have known when you insisted on coming over here to save me getting snarled up in the West End, that something like this was up your sleeve.'

'Something like what?'

'What's that big basket I can see under Lord knows what else, on the back seat of your car?'

'I had Fortnums pack us a picnic. We have to eat, don't we?'

'And you knew, if I came for you, I'd say there wasn't room for it in my car!'

'Well, there wouldn't have been, would there? With all Kim's stuff, when we go to get her. Nor for the folding table and chairs I have in the trunk.'

'You don't intend being deprived of your creature comforts, do you, Myrna?'

'If it would make any difference to whether the button gets pressed or not, I'd gladly dispense with them.'

'Which button?'

'Now who's forgotten where we're setting off for? And you've already made us late to pick up Kim.'

Anna took her small holdall from her own car and sat with it on her lap in Myrna's Mercedes. 'Kim's lending me Harry's sleeping-bag. Did you remember to borrow or buy one?'

'It's in that Harrods bag that's hiding the hamper.'

A Fortnums picnic at Greenham Common! And nobody could have the last word with Myrna. The same went for Julie. Though they operated very differently, and wanted different things from life, in one way you could lump them together. They had to win, even when it was just a to-ing and fro-ing of words. With Julie, it was as if she was powered by some kind of dynamo that wouldn't let her give up on anything. As for Myrna – well, hadn't she said she was never going to be a loser again? She'd used the Jewish word for fool when she said it, but a loser was what she'd meant. They were Anna's dear friends but they suffered from tunnel vision. And how wrong James was to think that she was modelling herself on either of them. Was he ever going to accept that she really did have a mind of her own? He was still blaming Anna's support for their pregnant daughter's actions on Julie, as though Anna had caught an infectious disease she was too weak to resist. And every time he looked at Anna's face he probably thought: damn Myrna and what she'd done to his pocket, though it was Anna who had actually done it. Oh well.

When they reached the Victorian villa that housed Harry's garden-flat, Kim was pacing the drive impatiently, with all her gear heaped around her. She let out a shriek when Myrna got out of the car.

'You can't go to Greenham dressed like that!'

Anna would have been surprised if Kim hadn't reacted as she had.

'Does that mean ladies in mink aren't allowed to stand and be counted?'

'There's such a thing as suitability, Myrna.'

'But there shouldn't be,' Anna heard herself say.

'Come off it, Mum! The peace-camp women aren't going to appreciate Myrna treating Greenham as a fashion show – and she'd probably get torn limb from limb by those who think fur should be left to keep the animals warm.'

'Would you prefer me not to come?'

'Kim can prefer what she likes,' said Anna. 'You're

coming and the car's yours. If what you're wearing matters that much to her, Kim will have to find another way of getting there.'

'And so speaks my new mum!'

'She's sure changed her tune,' said Myrna. 'When she first saw me, she said the same as you.'

'It was that word "suitability" that got to me – and your remark, Myrna, that made Kim use it.'

'Irv would call it projecting the right image, I guess.'

'And when they see yours,' Kim answered, 'the women who've deprived themselves of all but the bare necessities, for what they believe in, are going to think Nancy Reagan has sent a proxy to thumb her nose at them.'

Anna flared with anger. 'Are you saying, Kim, that what they'll think of her should stop Myrna from doing what she feels she should? How does my sheepskin qualify me to make my gesture of support, and Myrna's mink disqualify her? They're only the trappings, aren't they?'

'Too true! And what I'm really saying is I'd like to lend Myrna my tweed coat, the one with the warm lining.'

Anna stood her ground – there was a principle at stake for which she must fight not just Kim, but herself, though her face would be as red with embarrassment as her daughter's when they got to the camp with Myrna. 'Never mind the lining, Kim, we're talking about what shows – and compared with what Greenham's all about, we're wasting time on what Julie would call social hypocrisy. To add an opinion of my own, dressing down to make the right impression is no different from dressing up. Shall we go? I'll help you put your stuff in the car.'

Kim shrugged resignedly. Mum was right, of course. 'Maybe I should nip back into the flat and we'll tape that little speech you just made and play it to the peace women!'

When they were on their way, Myrna quipped, 'If I do get torn limb from limb, you can pick up the pieces, Anna – but be sure to put back my vital statistics where Irv expects to find them.'

Where they were headed for hadn't dislodged Myrna's mind from its customary groove. 'Did Irving try to talk you out of coming?' Anna asked.

'Especially since the missiles we don't want in our country were put there by yours,' Kim put in provocatively.

'As it happens, he didn't,' Myrna answered. 'Which makes me sure I'm doing the right thing,' she said in an aside to Anna.

'Good for Irving,' said Kim.

But Anna knew Myrna was referring to having him watched. 'While the cat's away, the mice will play' was typical Myrna-reasoning – and she'd deliberately provided him with the chance to prove it. Most women, if they suspected what she did, would make sure *not* to provide the chance. But Myrna was hell-bent on proving she was right, and there'd be trouble if she was wrong and Irving found himself being followed. That was where the tunnel vision came in.

Myrna overtook a line of cars held up by a monster European container-vehicle. 'Everyone has such patience over here. I don't know how they do it.'

'It could lengthen their lives.' Anna never felt safe with Myrna at the wheel.

'Getting back to my beloved, when he told me goodbye this morning, he said, "Go prove your loyalty to our British friends, babe."'

'American sentimentality,' Kim said with a snort, 'which unfortunately stops short at the Pentagon.'

'Your daughter's turning into a politico, Anna.'

'If that's what you call not wanting to be led blindly to destruction, you're right,' Kim declared.

'I'd apply that thinking to your marriage, if I were you,' Myrna replied. 'Or when you get back home you might not have one.'

'Have a fruit pastille, Myrna.' Anna popped one between Myrna's lips and handed the packet to Kim.

'Your mom is trying to shut me up, Kim,' Myrna said, sucking the sweet. 'But someone has to tell you that an indefinite separation, like the one you're setting up, can be a killer. What's the girl like who's replaced you with Harry's film crew?'

'Kindly stop trying to do to my daughter what you did to me!'

'What did Myrna do to you, Mum?'

Helped me blow up a squall into a tempest. But I finished up a new woman, if not a happier one. 'You know Myrna, love.'

Well enough to take what she just said from where it came, thought Kim. 'Before we get there, I'd better admit I'm ashamed of what went on before we set off,' she found the good grace to say. And added impishly, 'I'm proud of you two matrons for coming with me, even though it's just for a weekend.'

'Did you hear what your daughter called us, Anna?'

'Well, it's what we are, isn't it?'

'Speak for yourself.'

They were to find that the peace-camp population included many older women, from all walks of life, and even Myrna could not but be chastened by the experience. This was not to say that the pervading atmosphere was one of gloom. A spirit of determined cheerfulness prevailed, though the backdrop against which the campers had set themselves was the opposite of cheering.

'I didn't know it was actually a number of small camps,' Anna said when they had attached themselves to one of them.

'But they encircle the perimeter. That one beside the gate nearest to the cruise silos is where the militant feminists hang out.'

'That one would do for Julie,' Myrna said.

'But not for me,' said Kim. 'I heard they don't allow any men around — '

'It definitely isn't the place for *me*.'

' — and I'm hoping Harry will visit me whenever he can,' Kim finished her sentence.

'It could be jail he visits you in,' said Myrna, while Kim began pitching the tent.

Kim shrugged and smiled. 'I'm not here for the beer, am I? The last count I heard, over five hundred women had been arrested this year, and it's only the end of March. For making a nuisance of themselves! I believe the legal term is "incursions" into the base.'

Anna watched her tall, strapping daughter slamming a

tent peg with a mallet and wanted to remind her she was pregnant, but thought better of it. 'How did the camp get started, Kim?'

'When some women walked to the base from Wales. Hand me another peg, will you, Mum? That was nearly four years ago – look what it's grown into. It isn't just a British effort any more.'

'I already heard some American accents,' said Myrna, adding a Shetland shawl to her incongruous outfit. 'Boy, is this an Arctic breeze, or just the English spring?'

'Women come here from all over the world, to demonstrate how they feel about what this base signifies,' Kim said with feeling. 'And one way to stop shivering, Myrna, is to make yourself useful. I wouldn't mind something to eat.'

But wait till you see the catering! Anna thought.

'I wish I hadn't made that cheap crack about you and me chaining ourselves to a barbed-wire fence,' Myrna said quietly, while Kim's back was turned. 'To tell you the truth, if my girlfriends in California saw this place, they'd go right out and order themselves a satin-lined coffin.'

Kim overheard the last bit. 'Instead of just hoping the talks at Geneva won't be stymied by your president's pet project,' she added. 'By the time all the talking is over, my unborn baby could be a schoolkid – if they let it live that long. And by the way, your alligator shoes are splodged with mud, Myrna!'

'I read in a paper about the mud here, or I'd have worn my matching mink boots.'

But Myrna's appearance had evoked no more than some raised eyebrows and a few smiles – and just one cutting comment from a young fellow-countrywoman:

'Terrific! The dinner-at-Sardi's troops have landed.'

'So where's the food you said you'd brought?' Kim said to Myrna.

'I'll go lay the table.'

'What do you mean, you'll go lay the table? Just hand me a sandwich from that hamper I lugged from the car – not to mention all your other stuff! – and I'll eat it.'

'I don't have any sandwiches.'

Myrna went to prepare her spread.

'I don't believe this!' Kim exclaimed when she saw her carefully put a cloth on the folding table.

'Nor would I, of anyone but Myrna. And keep your voice down, Kim, or you'll attract more attention than she's doing.'

Kim watched the selection of delicacies being set out. 'You might have to put a gag on me!'

'I could use one myself. I'm as embarrassed as you are, love. But I'm not going to let it get the better of me.'

'I'm having the same fight with myself, Mum.'

Anna linked Kim's arm and smiled up at her, remembering when it was the other way round. It was hard to relate this young woman to the baby she had carried in her womb and nursed at her breast, but Anna's maternal protectiveness was no less strong now. Maggie had once said that her own headstrong daughter thought it could be turned off like a tap, once children were grown up. It couldn't be done. Nor was it easy to see life through the eyes of a generation whose values were so different from your own. Anna and James had thought Kim the exception. The Kim who'd returned from Australia was proving how they'd deluded themselves. To Anna, it was less of a disillusionment than a lesson. Her former relationship with her daughter had been no more than a silent and affectionate agreement not to differ, as with James, and she hadn't been aware of that, either. If she was now to have a real relationship with Kim, they were going to have to start seeing each other as people, not just as mother and daughter.

Thankfully, they had already begun to. 'That fight we were just talking about,' she said to Kim. 'The ones we have to have with ourselves are the hardest, aren't they, love?'

'When did you find that out, Mum?'

'Since I've been having some.'

Kim gave her a quizzical glance.

Were the other women here discussing things far removed from what they'd come to Greenham for? Anna briefly pondered. It was lunchtime, and she could see a large woman, wrapped in a gaudy blanket, frying something on a primus stove, with two little lads waiting beside her with tin

158

plates in their hands. It was so there'd be a future for kids like that, that women came here, but even with the base in full view, people got hungry and ate, smiled, and no doubt chatted about this and that.

'You've had some sort of cathartic experience, haven't you, Mum?' Kim said.

'I must look up that word in the dictionary, but it sounds right.'

Kim was still studying her. 'It was that that made you have the face-lift, wasn't it? It would've had to've been, for *my* mum to do a thing like that.'

'I don't suppose I shall ever know exactly what it was, Kim. And I'm over it now.'

'But Dad's still worried about you.'

'Are you sure it isn't himself he's worried about?'

'Why don't you ask him that?'

'The answer would be, "Don't be daft" – and it wouldn't be said nicely.'

'I can't argue that he hasn't turned into a bit of a grump. And why he's suddenly forgotten his house-training is a mystery,' Kim added.

'Not to me it isn't.'

'Come and get it!' Myrna called.

'There's a bottle of hock on the table, Mum!'

'And it's going to stay nice and chilled in this March wind. Those women over there are sharing a bottle of wine, Kim.'

'But they're not drinking it out of real glasses, with stems.'

'You're at it again.'

'I'm the one who'll get treated like a leper when you and Myrna have gone, though I know it makes sense about ladies in mink being allowed to stand up and be counted. But I can't help it, Mum. Nor is it just that I mind Myrna's get-up, and what she's doing, reflecting on me because I'm with her.'

What Myrna was doing when they joined her was squeezing lemon juice onto some smoked salmon.

When I said there's such a thing as suitability, I should have said, "of what's fitting", Kim thought. And that had nothing to do with top show. There'd be no Fortnums hampers in the hereafter. But most people were too preoccupied with the here-and-now to spare time for ensuring there would be a tomorrow. Myrna was making a token gesture and would then return to the Park Lane lifestyle she'd brought with her.

'I don't feel like any salmon, thank you,' Kim said. 'Some brown bread and a hardboiled egg will do me fine.' If Myrna knew why she'd refused something her tongue was hanging out for, she'd say, 'Is that going to stop the world from coming to an end?' But logic couldn't be applied to feelings, and Kim was making *her* gesture to a scenario stripped down to the basics of life itself and the threat hovering over it.

'I didn't expect it to be so quiet here,' Myrna said to her.

'Friends of mine who've done a stint tell me it's mostly just sitting tight and stifling your yawns. Things will hot up next weekend, no doubt, on Easter Sunday.'

'While they're having the Easter Parade in New York.'

'Do they have one in Washington, too?'

'Possibly.'

'Then why don't we send them one of their cruise missiles, and tell them to put an Easter bonnet on it!'

CHAPTER FOUR

IRVING DECIDED that their wives' absence was an excuse for him and James to have a night on the town.

'The British version of that is a pub crawl,' James told him.

'Then what are all those girlie-clubs for, that I never get the opportunity to enter?'

'Not for the likes of us.'

'Happily married men, you mean? And how you can still put yourself in that category, boychik — '

'I was having a peaceful Saturday morning, Irving – until *you* rang up.'

'You, me and Neil are three men in a boat! Have you heard from him recently?'

'No, as a matter of fact.'

'Me, neither. The poor guy must have his head in his hands, by now.'

And James's head was still wearing what it had been for going on a year. If he ever got rid of it, he was going to miss it.

'I wish there was something you and I could do for Neil, James.'

'And letting him sort things out for himself is what it'd be. If he wanted our advice he'd ask for it.'

'But we didn't let that stop us from coming to your aid, did we?'

Would that it had. And Irving especially. 'Did you get a call from Greenham?'

'Would I expect to? And I might just end up doing what my wife believes I am. Tonight could be the night,' Irving said with bravado.

'Where did Myrna get that idea?'

'From her own one-track mind, where else? I hate like hell

to have to admit this, boychik, but the time has arrived for me to slow down in the hay. And I'm not enjoying the consequences, or should I say the suspense. There is no way my darling babe is going to leave it go at that.'

'That could be all in *your* mind.'

'Have you ever sat in a room with a cat that's purring, but you know it's waiting to pounce? And Myrna has green eyes.'

James felt himself lucky that Anna didn't function like Myrna, since she had every excuse to think he no longer wanted her. There'd been no evidence that he did since the beast in him had made that brief appearance that shocked them both.

'Not only does she think I have to be putting it around, with my wife there is also the insult to her charms,' Irving went on. 'If there's one thing Myrna prides herself on, it's her ability to turn a guy on like clockwork.'

If you asked Irving to lend you some change for the parking meter, he'd delve into why you hadn't made sure you had some, thought James. 'You'd have made a good shrink, Irving.'

'And also a fortune, if I were one back home. Hang-ups are the late-twentieth-century disease, boychik. And Myrna's are all in her crotch.'

'Don't bother telling me where mine are.'

But who but Irving had led James to discover them? This time last year, he'd thought himself an uncomplicated person, able to accept philosophically – apart from losing his hair – that life did not begin at forty. Whoever coined that phrase must have had his tongue in his cheek. What began at forty was a gradual reducing of speed on the stretch to the next milestone. Three years hence James would have reached it – and if where he was at now was just an acute case of what happened to everyone, small wonder they called it 'over the hill'.

Equating men with vehicles, Irving's reluctant admission proved that the time came when even a racy engine had to bow to its length of service. But slackening off is not yet the scrap-heap, which was how James had begun to see himself in that respect.

'Much help it is to you to know how Myrna ticks,' he interrupted another outburst of marital spleen.

'But I don't have to take it lying down, do I? – which is the position she prefers me in. The other night, I slipped a sleeping pill into the hot chocolate she has while we're watching the ten-o'clock news. Needless to say, I'm not allowed any. She was snoring the minute she hit the sack – but the sun had not yet risen in the sky, when a tiny hand roused me from my slumbers, though not to action. If I could get hold of some, I'd put bromide in her hot drink like they used to do to stop prisoners from getting horny in jail. Drugging Myrna is the only way I'm going to get any peace.'

'But you didn't approve of Anna being on tranks, though it gave me a respite,' James replied testily.

'What you needed a respite from didn't make your legs buckle. Have you and Anna ever taken separate vacations?'

'We wouldn't have wanted to.'

'I note that you put that in the past tense. Sooner or later, boychik, what couples need a holiday from is each other. But who would admit it to anyone but their buddy? Tonight you can watch me put away a million calories, behind Myrna's back.'

They were tucking into some canelloni at Gennaro's when Irving noticed a tubby man seated at a nearby table. 'Haven't I seen that guy someplace before?'

'He looks familiar to me, too.'

'Then maybe he works in our office building.' Irving dabbed some rich sauce from his chin. 'If Myrna saw me now, she'd send for a stomach-pump. The food is good, but that's why I'm enjoying it even more. The pub crawl comes later.'

'What, no girlie-clubs?'

'In my satiated condition it'd be a waste of money.'

The man at the nearby table was reading a newspaper while he ate. James glanced at him again and a memory clicked into place. 'He was reading a paper the last time I saw him, though not the first time.'

'Who?'

'That chap. It *was* in our office building.'

Irving was more interested in adding another sprinkling of parmesan to his canelloni.

'You're really going off the rails tonight, aren't you?' James said with a grin.

'And when you reach the stage where you can only do it with food — '

'Myrna'll have her tape measure out the minute she gets back.'

'Why the hell d'you suppose I'm doing it?'

'I'd call a halt before you get to Julie's stage, if I were you. Since your motives are loosely what hers are.'

'Now who's the shrink? Which firm do you think that guy works for? He looks the computer type to me.'

'Let's not turn this into a market research exercise, Irving! I don't think he does work in our building, though. If he did, why would he sit reading a paper in the foyer at lunchtime? I was on my way out and he asked me for a match. I had a book of 'em in my pocket and I gave it to him.'

'The plot thickens!' said Irving. 'Why were you carrying matches when you don't smoke?'

'Some of my clients do.'

'That takes care of that. And the guy could've been waiting for someone to meet him there.'

'For an hour and a half? When I got back, he was still there, but he wasn't sitting reading. He was leaning on the wall, by the lifts.'

'I should be lucky enough to take such a long lunch break.'

'But not in the company I lunched with. It was Frankenstein, needless to say. Last Tuesday.'

'That was the day I was so busy, I had to send out for my lunch. And by now, Frankenstein's clinic must be turning out new faces like a sausage machine. He can't have any complaints about the campaign.'

'But leave it to him to find some.'

'How did we get into this, when we're having a night out? Pass me the pepper mill.'

'Does pepper have calories?'

'What are you? A watchdog for Myrna?'

Irving would have lost his appetite had he known then that the watchdog she had engaged was dining at his expense. The man was enjoying a cigar with his coffee when they left the restaurant. And still puffing it when, after they had moved on to a pub, James nudged Irving and said, 'There's that fellow.'

'Which feller?'

James pointed to where the man was chatting up a couple of girls.

'So he's having himself a drink, like we are – but unlike us, he's in the mood for female companionship.'

'But wouldn't you say it's an unlikely coincidence that he's picked the pub we're in – out of all the pubs there are around here? And happens to have been loitering in our office building recently?'

'You didn't use the word "loitering" before.'

'But that's how it strikes me now.'

'You think the cat's pounced, don't you?'

'If she has, your suspense is over.'

'But first we have to be sure. Finish your drink, James. We'll move on to the pub along the street.'

While they walked the short distance, the sights and sounds of night-time Soho all around them, James was assailed by a sense of unreality. Garish neon lights plying the voyeur-pleasures within. Girls in black net stockings and leather jackets, standing in doorways – was leather the in-thing for ladies of the night, this year? How the heck would a home-guy like me know that? He could hear the beat of disco music coming from somewhere, and raucous laughter from a gang of lads he'd just passed. Some of them were wearing football scarves, and had he seen the flash of knuckledusters? Never mind what the world was coming to, what was James Ridgeway doing out on a Saturday night in the midst of all this – and his wife miles away being a crusader – helping a high-powered American set a trap for a possible private detective his dizzy-blonde wife had also-possibly employed to tail him?

Let's stop playing games and go home, James felt like saying to Irving, whose expression was as grim as the night sky. But who'd put the 'tail' idea into Irving's head? James. You couldn't be involved with the Sangers without getting drawn into their games. If it weren't for the wind – that had to've come from Siberia – whipping around his legs, he wouldn't believe this was happening.

'Why don't you just wait till Myrna gets back and say to her, "Look here, mate, are you having me followed?" Take the bloody woman by surprise?'

'That's no way to refer to my wife, boychik.'

'And who was it called her a cat?' James retorted as they reached the pub, and made their way to the bar.

'Go grab that empty booth, James, before someone else decides to take the weight off their feet. Are you drinking the same as before? Lager with lime?'

'If you're buying, I'll make it a whisky. I need fortifying.'

They were on their second round and Irving was lecturing James on the dangers of an over-fertile imagination, when the man entered the pub. He had brought the two girls with him, and had an arm around each of them.

James saw him first. 'What were you saying about my imagination?'

Irving turned his head and exclaimed, 'That does it! If this was office-business, not monkey-business, you'd get a raise.'

'How's Ronnie doing with that big account you gave him?'

'The hell with Ronnie.'

James wished he meant it.

'You and I have a job to do here, boychik. And the drinks are on me for the rest of the night.'

'If you're thinking of a punch-up, Irving, I haven't brought my boxing gloves – and that chap's only doing his job.'

'Would I be so crass? You should know me better, James.' Irving knocked back his whisky. 'Don't look so tense. I'll be back.' He went to get them another round, and said when he returned, 'I'm going to need your co-operation — '

'D'you want me to go and ask him for a match, to jog his memory, and let him know we're on to him?'

'He's using a lighter tonight, isn't he? And, *schmuck,*

what would you light with the match? But we now have the answer to the lengthy loitering. He was hoping to tail me to a lunchtime matinée, but picked on a day when I ate at my desk.'

'Come again, Irving?'

'In New York, also LA, they're very popular. The motels and hotels do a big midday trade – and when else would Myrna think I'd get the opportunity?'

'For me, that's a new interpretation of the word "matinée"!'

'But you're catching up on your education, aren't you? Myrna's seen my secretary, so she can't think it's her I'm making it with, on the office sofa.'

'For all we know, he could've been tailing you for some time. How long is it since you slowed down?'

'What're you doing? Keeping a diary?'

'If you went and asked one of those girls he's with to spend the night with you, he could put it in his report and your troubles'd be over,' James cracked.

'What goes into that report should be something more than Myrna bargained for. I hate to do it to you — '

'Oh yes?'

' — But on the other hand, her having me tailed is going to cost me, and why shouldn't I get my money's worth out of it and cut short the tailing at one and the same time?'

James didn't like the diabolical gleam in his eye. 'Whatever it is, I'm not volunteering.'

'That's why I daren't tell you in advance. You're going to have to forgive me, boychik — '

He clasped James in his arms and kissed his bald patch.

'What the heck – !' But the protest was muffled against Irving's jacket. Was it the drink, or had Irving gone bonkers? James tried to struggle free, but Irving clamped a hand to the back of his neck. He couldn't breathe, and to crown everything, he felt Irving nibble the lobe of his left ear. Would it make any difference if it were his right ear? They were going to be taken for what they weren't. The penny dropped. That was what this daft Yank – who ran the agency with cool efficiency and didn't pull his punches, but played ducks and drakes in his marriage – was after. How cunning could you get!

The barman came to James's rescue. 'Er . . . if you gentlemen wouldn't mind, this isn't a gay pub. I can tell you one that is.'

Irving allowed James to disentangle himself. 'I guess that'd be useful info for when we're next around here.'

James straightened his tie. If his face was as red as it felt, it must look like a ripe tomato. 'We're not gay,' he said stiffly. 'My friend's had too much to drink, he was horsing around.'

'I do wish you'd stop trying to kid people, honey.'

James got up and left the pub.

Irving followed him, but not before announcing to the interested onlookers that it was just a lovers' tiff.

Irving had to run to catch up with James's angry stride. 'So you had a few minutes embarrassment to help me get back at my wife, and I'm grateful. The real gays don't get embarrassed.'

'I'm glad they don't have to any more. But you're probably going to regret what you did.'

'It's what Myrna deserves. And how she handles it, without knowing I set it up — '

'Will keep you running circles around yourselves and each other for the foreseeable future. Just count me out!' James quickened his pace.

'You're in a big hurry.'

'I'm going home, Irving.'

'Please don't. I need you to talk to.'

'All right. But if you lay a hand on me again, I'll slay you.'

'The guy has what he needs and it's juicy. I guess we've seen the last of him. If he did show up, I wouldn't have the nerve to do it again. And in the unlikely event of Anna finding out I was with you — '

'When the cabin crew on planes use that phrase, I always spend the first half of the flight waiting for the crash!'

'If there is one, it's going to be mine, not yours. And afterwards, maybe Myrna and I can settle down like I hoped we would. But I'd have to tell her first that I've known since our wedding day that her youthful face isn't a special favour from God to a woman her age.' Irving paused reflectively. 'And I don't see myself doing it.'

They walked along in silence for a moment or two, each with their private thoughts.

'How I'll put right what I did tonight, James, I still have to figure out. The idea came into my head, and I was so mad at her for putting a tail on me, I gave way to an impulse I already regret. Why in the hell can't she trust me?'

'One way and another, you might be better off without her.'

'What are you talking about, boychik? I love the dumb broad.'

James, who was coming to think on his own account, as well as Irving's, that love was a form of masochism, hid a smile. Who needs this? a man might ask himself over and again when his wife was putting him through the mill. But what was he to do if, despite everything, he went on loving her? It was the last bit that sometimes made the whole thing seem like self-inflicted pain.

CHAPTER FIVE

ANNA RETURNED from the peace camp with a sense of her own insignificance. Being shoulder to shoulder with women of all kinds who shared a common purpose had been a strengthening experience, but in another way she felt cut down to size. For close on a year, she'd been wrapped up in her own problems. Two days at Greenham Common had made her see how unimportant she and they were.

'That could be said about most people, I guess,' Myrna said, when Anna voiced her thoughts on the drive back to London. 'And all of the time, not just when they're up to the neck in some personal crisis.'

'More so when a woman is mentally housebound,' Anna reflected.

'Since Julie used that expression, you keep coming out with it. If it ever did apply to you, it sure doesn't now, Anna. But that doesn't mean you'll now have all the shit that's going on in the world on your mind night and day. The weekend had an effect on me, too. How could it not,' she added. 'But once I'm home, I won't have missiles on my mind while I'm cooking, or getting laid. And nor will you. Do you think the Ethiopian famine is in Julie's mind, when she's pleading a case?'

'All I'm saying is it's brought me up short.'

'But you seem to have forgotten that preserving the human race, so people can go on living their selfish everyday lives, is what the peace campaign is all about.'

'Why do you play the dizzy blonde, Myrna, when you're really nothing of the kind?'

'Is my hair showing dark at the roots?'

'That wasn't what I meant, and you know it.'

'Like I said to you once before, it was the DB whom Irv married – and what kind of wife did he leave for her? He never talks about his ex – but his mother does, like she's in permanent mourning after the divorce. I found a photograph of her in a box of old snapshots at my mother-in-law's apartment. And who she put me in mind of, I don't have to tell you. Me when I was Mrs Comfortable.'

'It isn't your looks I'm referring to, Myrna. It's the daft things you get up to, like putting a private detective on watch because you've got a wild idea in your head.' Among other things.

'The woman who isn't one step ahead of her husband is headed for disaster, I'm here to tell you. And let me tell you something else, a Mrs Comfortable should prepare to wave goodbye to a middle-aged husband. In case you didn't know it, Anna, now is the time when they itch for what could be their last fling. It's good you got your face lifted.'

'My husband's last fling has got no further than leaving the loo seat up, when he used to put it down.'

'You're lucky that's all he's doing.'

It was early evening when they reached Bella Vista.

'I was just going to scribble a note for you,' James said, before they had time to greet him. 'Now you're here, we can all go over to Fulham together. I arranged to meet Irving at the Newtons'.'

'If Julie's giving one of her last-minute dinner parties, I'll have to go home and change,' said Myrna.

'Far from it,' James answered tersely. 'She rang a few minutes ago to say that Neil has disappeared. It seems he's been gone for several days – but she's only just bothered to tell us!'

'I wonder who the broad is?'

'I'd be obliged if you didn't say that to Julie.'

'You'd rather I let her be an ostrich?'

James thought of the far-reaching effects of Myrna's influence upon his wife. 'I'd rather you didn't do anything! How's my daughter, by the way?'

'Fine. And she's Anna's daughter, too,' Myrna responded to his sharpness.

'But I wouldn't say that Anna's encouraging her to go to

Greenham in her condition is what many mothers would've done.'

Myrna replied, 'You know something, James, that's one of the few times I ever heard you tell Anna what's on your mind.'

And when you tell Irving, you do it with a wisecrack and he still doesn't know where he is with you, James silently answered. 'I'll get the car out and go. You two can follow in Myrna's.'

'At a time like this, we should all be together,' Myrna said.

Oh God! And damn Neil. They were full steam ahead for some more of those times. James sometimes thought the Sangers revelled in it. 'Then Irving will have to drive you back to collect your car.'

'But we won't come in for coffee. I can't wait to soak in a bubble bath. Did you see Irv while we were away?'

'What? No, I didn't!'

'Why is he snapping at me, Anna?'

'Don't ask me, ask him.'

'I've got a bit of a headache, from sitting watching TV the whole weekend.'

'Now he's giving you his alibi, Anna, when you didn't ask him for one,' Myrna said with a laugh.

This must be how criminals felt when they lied through their teeth, James thought.

On the way to Fulham, Anna tried to reassure James about Kim. She could have been talking to a brick wall. He made no reply.

She tried again. 'Before we left, some women we'd made friends with invited Kim to eat with them in their tent tonight. When Myrna and I looked back at her, she was unpacking some of her tinned food and one of them was with her — '

'I've said what I have to say,' James cut in.

'Then why don't we change the subject? A dime to a dollar what I said about Neil's taking off is right.'

'I'm getting the feeling you'd be disappointed if it wasn't,' said James.

'He's still getting at me, Anna.'

'Because I don't want you to add to Julie's anxiety by planting your kind of ideas in her head.'

'You always did believe in pussy-footing around, didn't you, James? And where has it got you?'

A good question! And James would rather not answer it. But he made no bones about replying to the first bit. 'If you call sparing the other person's feelings pussy-footing around, Myrna, what you said about me is correct.'

'I love you all the same. Did Irv mention what he did to amuse himself in my absence?'

'I'm not his keeper, Myrna.'

'There he goes again!'

James changed to a safer topic. 'I asked Julie if she'd informed the police that Neil's gone missing. She nearly had a fit at the mere idea.'

'Well, if they found him shacked up with whoever,' said Myrna, 'it could get into the papers and sully her professional reputation.'

Not to mention his. 'Are you saying that Julie would rather Neil were found in the river?'

'If Irv did this to me, I'd consider the river too good for him.'

'But we don't know what Neil's done,' Anna returned them to the facts. 'It could be amnesia — '

'That's a name for a broad?'

'Stop it, Myrna. What I'm trying to say is that our job is to help Julie give him the benefit of the doubt and do anything else we can for her.' Why was Myrna always at her dizziest when being practical was called for? Did she really believe that nonsense she talked?

Irving was parking his car outside the Newtons' home when they arrived.

'The kissing can wait,' he said when Myrna made a beeline for him. 'Julie's need is more urgent than yours, babe.'

But nobody would have thought Julie in need of comfort when she opened the door, munching a Mars bar, with a pencil stuck behind her ear, and her half-moon spectacles perched on her nose.

'Oh my! A posse!' she said as they trooped past her into the house. 'What are you lot doing here?'

Myrna gave her a sympathetic smile, and an unwelcome kiss on the cheek. 'What are friends for?'

If James heard that cliché one more time— Why the heck had he come? He knew how it felt to be on the receiving end of this, didn't he?

Since it was now Julie's turn, she replied in her own style. 'To help the bereaved dissect the corpse. I'm capable of doing that without assistance, thank you all very much.'

But hastening to the side of a friend in trouble was instinctive, James silently defended his uninvited presence.

'If the corpse you mentioned is your marriage, it's a bit soon to see it that way,' Irving said as they followed Julie into the living-room.

What you did when you'd hastened there was another matter. James hadn't come scalpel in hand – but Irving took one everywhere he went.

Julie sat down at the table where she had been working, picked up her pen, and said, 'That depends upon who's doing the looking, Irving.'

'And from where I'm at, I'd take some convincing that Neil's taken off because he doesn't love you.' What but love could have kept the poor guy chained to her for so long?

'I'm with you there, Irving,' said Anna.

Julie threw down the pen and glared at them over her glasses. 'Love has nothing to do with it! If Neil and I didn't feel deeply for each other, we'd have parted years ago, since our marriage has not exactly lacked its ups and downs. And it was holding together quite nicely before Anna and James's trouble began.'

Anna tried to exchange a glance with James, but he was staring down at the carpet. 'Are you saying that taking sides about us has caused this, Julie?'

'Not exactly. But Neil and I agreed – when we were still agreeing about anything – that there *had* been some sort of chain reaction. At the time, it was just a phrase I used, like I use a lot of others. It summed up my feeling about it, but I hadn't given it a lot of thought.'

'And now you have?' Anna prompted.

'Well, it stands to reason, doesn't it, that you being so concerned about your ageing face must've pointed up for

Neil that I didn't give a damn about the menopause blurring my shape.'

'But you didn't have to help it, did you?' Myrna rebuked her. 'And I'm supposed to be the dumb one.'

'If you were as dumb as it suits you to let everyone think,' Julie replied, 'your scheming would be a good deal less successful than it is. I find it remarkable that a man as intelligent as Irving hasn't tumbled to you yet.'

Irving wished he could tell Julie that he had.

'And in my opinion,' Myrna responded, 'a woman who lets herself go, like you have, doesn't deserve to have a good-looking guy like Neil love her.'

James wondered if his newly-outspoken wife was enjoying seeing her friends suffer the truths they had just fired at each other. But no doubt they'd be calling it a friendly argument in a minute!

Julie smiled, and said lightly, 'We're back to the reason Anna had her face lifted.'

'Not as far as I'm concerned we're not,' Anna declared. 'But it's your trouble, not mine, that's concerning us all at present.'

Why didn't she just shout from the rooftops: If anyone thinks I had myself beautified to please my husband, they're wrong! One day James might wake up and find he'd just had a bad dream. A woman who looked her age and didn't mind it would be lying beside him, and he'd gather her close and make love to her, never mind if it made him late for the office. And wouldn't all that be lovely? But it was never going to happen.

'Will someone please tell me why whenever I try to help my buddies, one way or another I land in the shit?' Myrna inquired. 'And the Newtons aren't the only ones who've had their ding-dongs since Anna threw the shoe at James.'

'But it doesn't have to happen to you lot over Neil and me,' Julie declared. 'You're welcome to keep out of it. Nobody asked you to come tonight.'

'Then why did you call James to tell him that Neil had split?' Irving asked. 'And don't give me any of that courtesy-call crap.'

'All right, I won't.' Julie hadn't asked James to tell Irving, and wished he hadn't. The sympathetic-sixsome was getting to be a habit. But one of them was missing. She took off her glasses and dropped her pretence. 'I'm bloody miserable. And livid, too! If Neil can't take living with me any more, why didn't he do the civilised thing?'

'Is there one, at the stage you two'd reached?' Irving asked.

'You don't miss a trick, do you? And the same probably goes for the lot of us about each other. If I'm ever reincarnated, I'd like it to be as a hermit, on a desert island where there aren't any natives to be friends with.'

'I think Julie's trying to tell us something, boychik.'

And James knew what it was.

'But since you're here,' she said, 'well, if I didn't talk to you, I'd be talking to the wall.'

'After you'd finished your work,' Irving cracked.

'If you're going to be your usual self — '

'My usual self is all I have to offer. Take it or leave it.'

'I'll take it.'

Julie had to be desperate, thought James. But he knew *that* feeling, too.

'Neil could've told me to my face, couldn't he?' she went on. 'Or at the very least, written "Fini" in red ink across the brief I'd left on the kitchen dresser.'

'That would have been very fitting,' said Irving.

'And don't think I don't know it.'

'But you don't know he's told you "Fini".'

'Perhaps he's trying to teach you a lesson,' said James.

'I'm the one who needs teaching all the lessons, am I? What loyal friends my husband has! I don't hear mine speaking up for me.'

'What is there to say?' was Myrna's response.

'That you haven't already said!' Julie looked at Anna.

'If you want the truth, I think you've been a fool, Julie.'

'Now I know what it feels like to stand alone in the dock. As for my errant husband, if he'd left me a note I'd know where I am, wouldn't I? And so would his current clients. It isn't just me Neil's walked out on, but apparently his career, too.'

Irving exchanged a glance with James. A man would have

to have reached the end of his tether to toss aside all he had striven to achieve.

'Are you sure he hasn't showed up at his chambers, Julie?' said Irving.

'A disappearance is a disappearance, chum. His clerk called my chambers the morning after my true love did a bunk. Needless to say, I hadn't yet got around to checking with him. "Is Mr Newton ill, Mrs Newton? It isn't like him not to call if he's going to be late," said Neil's clerk. "As a matter of fact, he is, Mac," say I, coolly. "I intended letting you know, but you know how it is, that my husband's in bed with a virus — "'

'You should have said a viper,' Myrna cut in, 'and I wonder if she's a blonde or a brunette.'

'You know that diamond frippery your mother-in-law gave her dog?' Julie said to Irving. 'Why not get one for Myrna, but make it a muzzle!'

'It wouldn't muzzle how her mind works.'

'And Julie's doing herself no favours by muzzling her real thoughts. If she doesn't face the facts, how is she going to deal with them?'

Anna interceded. 'As I said to you earlier, Myrna, the only fact is that Neil has gone.'

Then they heard the front door open, and all five of them rushed to the hall.

Paul Newton stopped short in the doorway and gave them a friendly smile. 'Who were you expecting? It can't've been me, I don't rate a reception committee. Are you having a party, Mother?'

'Am I dressed for one?'

Paul took in Julie's baggy, grey-jersey frock, 'All your clothes look more or less the same to me.'

'What he means is you're just his mom,' said Myrna helpfully.

'Let's go back in the living-room, shall we?' said Julie. 'What he means is what he said.'

'I can't stay long,' Paul said, following her.

'Do you ever?' Julie watched him fold his tall, lean figure into an armchair. The twins were not identical. Mark looked like her – well, he still did when she last saw him! –

and Paul was the image of Neil. Painfully so, she thought. 'Who's the lucky lady tonight?' she asked him cuttingly.

'Read William Hickey's column tomorrow, and you'll find out,' he said flippantly.

'That's certainly one way of keeping in touch with your doings.'

'Would you like a daily bulletin?'

'No thanks! And since you're a night-worker, it would have to be a nightly one.'

Paul glanced at the piles of documents on the table. 'You're a bit of a night-worker yourself,' he said lightly.

'If I didn't work night and day, who would supplement your income from that escort agency, darling?'

Her sweet tone and the smile that matched it prepared the Ridgeways and Sangers for the dart she now shot at her son.

'Somebody has to keep you in Gucci shoes, etcetera – or you wouldn't look the little-gigolo part, would you, Paul?' She eyed his black velvet suit, and the fancy silk shirt he was wearing with it. 'And I must say you look it tonight.'

Paul managed to put a smile on his own face, and said to the others, 'Nobody could compete with my mother in the word-stakes.'

'And I advise you not to try.'

'But the word you just applied to me has gone out of fashion.'

'What it means hasn't. Have you seen your brother lately?'

'What would the likes of him have in common with the likes of me?'

'You both smoke grass,' Julie said sarcastically.

'I've given it up.'

'For what? Older women?'

'If you must know, I decided it wasn't fair to you and Father – if I got caught, I mean. Son of two barristers found smoking cannabis – all that.'

'Thanks for the token gesture.'

But at least he had made one, James thought. From Irving's expression, he must be thinking the same. Julie's was deadpan, but she'd probably had her chips with both her sons. James wasn't surprised at her reference to grass.

Mark had been sent down from college on that account. And when James recalled that painful episode in the Newtons' lives, Julie's anger and Neil's resignation, it was as though Julie'd been unable to understand it, but Neil had been expecting something of the kind. They had still had high hopes for Paul, and like his brother he could've gone far. Both had the brains for it. Instead — ! But what was it that Harry had said about expectations leading to disappointment? Good old Harry. He certainly had a point.

'If it's a handout you've come for tonight, Paul — '

'There's no need to tell your friends how good my parents are to me, Mother,' he cut in with an embarrassed laugh. 'Though I don't mind them knowing. I had half an hour to spare and I just thought I'd drop in on you and Father. Where is he?'

'You may well ask!' The question released a spate of fury in Julie. 'Maybe he's had it with his sons, as well as with everything else. I certainly have, and I'm finished with cushioning you from reality, Paul. You and the glitterati you mix with make me want to throw up. The same goes for your brother and his lot. You've ended up a pair of leeches, and that is some admission for a mother to make. To me, there's no difference between feeding off people who think money can buy anything, and being the drag on society that Mark is.'

'Your boys haven't yet ended up,' Irving said when Julie paused for breath. 'Twenty-four is young enough to change.'

'That's what my father keeps telling me,' said Paul cynically. 'But why would I want to change? To work myself into the ground, like he does – and for what? No thanks. There are pleasanter ways of keeping body and soul together.'

'And you seem to have found them,' said Julie.

'Where's Father?'

'You'll probably be pleased to hear he's walked out on me.'

'Why would I be pleased? But I can't say I'm astounded.'

'Exactly.'

'Where's he gone to?'

'How would I know?'

Paul glanced at the Ridgeways and Sangers. 'I seem to've dropped in at the wrong time, don't I?'

'I wouldn't have expected a son to think so,' Irving said brusquely.

Paul looked at Julie, who was carefully not looking at him. 'But we're not your average family, are we, Mr Sanger?'

'You can say that again!' Julie flashed. 'Just get out of here, will you, Paul! Go where you're going!'

He managed to smile at her friends. 'I seem to've had my marching orders. And I mustn't keep my date waiting,' he added with bravado to Julie.

A silence broken only by Julie unwrapping another Mars bar followed Paul's departure.

'If you don't care about your shape, at least spare a thought for your teeth,' Myrna said.

'The hell with my teeth!' Julie bit savagely into the chocolate. 'I sometimes wonder why I bothered having kids.'

Anna saw the flicker in Myrna's expression. There must be times when she had trouble in keeping the shutter closed. What was that look on her face, if it wasn't another glimpse of how she really ticked? Of the woman who'd had the corners knocked off her by a man, and had polished them to an artificial gleam.

'Kids can tear you apart without even trying,' Julie went on, morosely. 'But it would've been nice to have the sort who'd rally round me now.'

Irving was moved to put a kind hand on her shoulder. Would she tell him to stick his American demonstrativeness? She didn't. This was like seeing an iron structure suddenly buckle. 'You can rely on us,' he assured her. 'We won't let you down.'

A kaleidoscope of recollections rose before James. Irving telling him he had a marriage crisis. Julie angrily frying onions, and giving him a dressing-down. Finding the wine bottle in the dustbin and Anna with an evening hangover. The grousing sessions he'd shared with Irving and Neil, over their wives, and his speechlessness when Anna decided to do what she had. Nor had he found his tongue, or she hers, until after the deed was done. Anna's second out-of-character decision — to spend this weekend at the peace camp. His learning that Myrna had used it as an excuse to set Irving up for the kill; and the way Irving had set her up, instead. Lord knows what ramifications of that were yet to come. And hovering over all was the remembrance of Anna's 'new-face' party, when James had likened the way he felt to being aboard a roundabout with the friends who'd got in on the act. But tonight he'd got in on Julie's, hadn't he? And she hadn't tried too hard to keep any of them out.

'I'll make some tea,' Anna said. 'It'll do us all good to have a cup.'

James noted the 'us'. *Your troubles are my troubles, pal.* And who'd want to be just a fair-weather friend? Nobody in this room. That's what had kept the roundabout whizzing. The tea and sympathy. But Neil had had the guts to leap off it before he was given the kind of advice he didn't want to listen to.

Chapter Six

When Myrna read the detective's report, she resisted the urge to pour herself a double brandy and rang Julie at her chambers.

'It's nice of you to call, Myrna. But I'm hellishly busy.'

'How're you doing?'

'That's the same stupid question Anna asked, when I had to get out of the bath to speak to her, this morning.' Julie had hoped it might be a call from Neil, and had snapped Anna's head off. She was now doing the same to Myrna. When you were trying not to let things get the better of you, probing phone calls, however well-intentioned, were no help. Had Anna thought that, at the height of her crisis, when Julie kept calling her? Probably, she was thinking, when Myrna said:

'Is homosexuality grounds for divorce?'

Julie did a mental double-take. 'I thought this was a comfort call. Is there something you know, that I don't, about Neil?'

Myrna stared down at the typewritten words that had shattered her – except she wasn't going to let that happen. The ex-Mrs Comfortable had learned to be a survivor.

'From where I'm at now, Julie, I have to say it's possible there are things none of us know about our husbands.'

'What are you trying to tell me?'

'I've just found out that mine swings both ways. And Irv is a lot more macho than Neil is.'

Julie brushed aside remembrance of her husband in one of his fancy waistcoats, talking intimately with a young male colleague at a party. 'That's one book that could never be judged by its cover, Myrna.'

'And haven't I just seen the proof?'

'May I ask how you came by it?' Julie sat tapping a pencil

on the desk, edgily, while Myrna told her. 'People who look for trouble usually find it,' she responded brusquely. But it could also come to those who shut their eyes to what was hovering over them.

'There's trouble and trouble, Julie. Some kinds are easier to deal with than other kinds. It seems that while Anna and I spent the weekend trying to save the world from destruction, our husbands were having themselves a gay time. The report says the guy Irving was with works in his office building. By the description it has to be James.'

It all seemed to Julie as bizarre as Myrna's preamble about spending the weekend trying to save the world. Ten days ago Julie wouldn't have thought it possible that anything could rock her own world. It had come as a shock to find that she too was prey to the doubts that weaker women experienced.

'There'll soon be only one intact couple left in the sympathetic-sixsome,' she said. 'And I can't say I'm too sure about them.'

'What gave you the idea I intend to leave Irving?'

'Wasn't the mention of divorce how this conversation began?'

'A card up my sleeve would be good insurance,' Myrna replied. 'Do I have the grounds, or don't I?'

'I'd have to check with a colleague who specialises in divorce. You think ahead, don't you, Myrna?'

'If you had, you might not be in the spot you're in now. I tried to warn you, didn't I?'

Was that what all Myrna's cracks about Julie's appearance were about?

'But you thought I was just being bitchy.'

'If you want an apology, you've got one!' Julie said ungraciously. 'Are you going to tell Anna what you've told me?'

'Why would I, when I know she couldn't handle it?'

'You're the only woman I know who could.'

'And wait till you see how. Would you like the name of my private eye? I guess I no longer require him.'

'If having Neil traced could unearth something I'd be

better off not knowing, I'd rather he came back of his own accord, or not at all.'

'Knowing what he's up to could be to your advantage either way — '

'Get off the line, will you, Myrna! Enough of your insidious comfort, I've got work to do.'

'Okay. Put your head back in the sand, that's what your work is for you.'

Julie was left to ponder on whether Myrna's parting shot was true. Preoccupation with work hadn't stopped her from being aware of Neil's discontent, but she'd attributed it solely to his professional envy. And hadn't tried to compensate by letting him have the edge over her in their personal relationship; why the hell should she? Since she knew she was cleverer than him, pretending she looked up to him would be using the kind of guile Myrna employed. But as things worsened between them, hadn't she blotted it out with work? One up to Myrna again! And where was Julie now? Trying to blot out thoughts of what life without Neil would be like. Where was the thoroughly self-sufficient woman she'd thought herself? If Neil came back to her, could she bring herself to take a leaf or two from Myrna's book? Since she loved him, she'd have to – and how ironic it was that Julie Newton QC had learned the error of her ways from a dizzy blonde.

CHAPTER SEVEN

ON THE Thursday after they learned Neil was missing, James and Irving lunched together in the wine bar. Since tomorrow would be Good Friday, they had pre-arranged their monthly meeting with Neil for today.

'Did you make a note of what you wanted to check with him?' James asked.

'What for? He isn't going to show up.'

'You're as pessimistic as your wife.'

'Realistic would be a better word.'

While Irving told him for the umpteenth time and at length that he wished he hadn't engineered the gay incident, and how the suspense was killing him, James's mind strayed to matters nearer home. Were things ever going to come right for him and Anna? They couldn't even brush their teeth side by side any more, without something one or the other of them said causing ructions. Like last Sunday, when they got back from Julie's. Ructions wasn't all that particular spat had caused.

On that occasion, it was James who began it. 'Much chance there is of women winning a peace campaign, when they can't even get on with their husbands,' he remarked while he was spitting out toothpaste.

'If that's a jab at me for doing my tiny bit this weekend, I might have expected it.'

'I was referring to Julie.'

'But I still get the message.'

James rinsed his mouth, and left her to absorb it.

'I shouldn't think Irving is spouting that kind of pillow talk, when Myrna's been away from his embrace for two nights,' she said when she got into bed.

And if that wasn't jabbing at James . . . 'Myrna's hot stuff, you're not,' he hit back.

'I never was, but you still made love to me, didn't you? If you're blaming your little problem on me, James, you'd better think again.'

James wanted to say that middle age affected different men in different ways, but it would seem a lame excuse. 'There used to be nothing we couldn't chat about,' he said instead.

'Chat was what it was. What did we ever talk about of any importance?'

'Like the economic situation, you mean? And what went on at the last Labour Conference?'

'If we did, there'd be things we disagreed about and you wouldn't like that. You want your yes-woman back, don't you, James? But you're never going to get her back.'

That was when the beast in James had taken over again. And he could remember wondering if wanting to tame her in the only way left to him was responsible for it, before the gust swept him away.

That time, he hadn't apologised afterwards, and Anna had said if that was the only way he could now make love to her, and she wouldn't call it that, she'd rather do without sex.

He was returned to the present by the waiter placing his meal before him, and asking where the other gentleman was.

James and Irving wished they knew.

Since an answer was called for, Irving said, 'Barristers are busy men.'

'Is he a barrister? He looks like an actor.'

Who isn't one? thought James.

'One of the old school,' the waiter added before leaving them to it.

'We'd better not tell Neil that last bit, Irving!'

'If we ever see him again.' Irving ate his salad as unenthusiastically as always. 'Meanwhile, I'm toeing the line about my diet again – and living in fear and trembling of that goddamn report arriving.'

'So you keep saying. But how can you be sure it hasn't already arrived?'

'I'm still alive to tell the tale.'

'Is Myrna really that vicious?'

'Did you ever encounter a cat that didn't have claws? So far she's only let me see the pads, boychik.'

This was James's chance to get his own back on Irving for the horror-stories he had had to endure. 'I once saw a cat biding its time with a mouse and enjoying it.'

'I'd rather not hear this, but tell me more.'

'The mouse didn't know the cat was watching it, getting a kick out of the anticipation — '

'Since when could cats get a kick out of something? You're putting me on, aren't you!'

'Not about Myrna, I'm not. If I know her, she'll pounce when she's ready to, and not a minute before. Meanwhile, you're left to stew.'

'She doesn't know I'm stewing.'

'A lot of good that's doing you.' James forked some chips into his mouth and said thoughtfully, 'It's time we turned our attention to trying to find Neil.'

'Supposing he doesn't want to be found?'

'Then it's up to him to tell us so; this needn't involve Julie. He may be able to exist without his wife, but he couldn't live without doing his *Times* crossword. Why don't we put an ad in the personal column, asking him to contact us in confidence, at the agency?'

Neil walked into the wine bar and saved them the trouble.

When Irving got his breath back, he said, 'The only thing Myrna didn't foresee was the viper being neither a brunette nor a blonde. Get an eyeful of that, boychik!'

Hanging on to Neil's arm was a young girl with flaming red hair, made more so by the sugar-pink streak on one side of it. She had on a brief yellow tunic, and her long legs, encased in royal-blue tights, caused every male head in the place to turn in her direction.

'And there was me feeling sorry for him!' James exclaimed, as the incongruous couple approached.

'But don't tell me what you're feeling now, isn't envious.'

'The feeling that's uppermost in me at the moment is that a pal of mine must have gone off his rocker.'

'It happens,' said Irving. 'I could tell you a story about a buddy of mine and a cute little hat-check girl. He was a lawyer, too — '

Fortunately for James there wasn't time.

'Sorry I'm late, chaps,' Neil said when he and his startling companion joined them, and as if he had been delayed at his chambers.

'Don't apologise. Take the weight off your feet, the both of you,' Irving said pleasantly, while thinking: The *chutzpah* of this guy! 'Hand Neil the menu, James.'

'I can pick it up myself, Irving, since I usually do.'

If anyone was feeling awkward it wasn't Neil, thought James. 'We didn't expect you to show up.'

Neil studied the menu – without putting his glasses on, his friends noted – and helped himself to a breadstick. 'I might have done something unpredictable, but there's no need to treat me with kid gloves. You'd like your usual burger, wouldn't you, pet?' he said to the girl.

'After you've introduced me. Or shall I just introduce myself?' she said with a laugh. 'I'm Mandy, and Neily's told me your names,' she said to James and Irving. 'Why don't I guess which is which?'

When she got it right, Neil kissed her cheek and patted her hand approvingly.

'It wasn't hard. People grow to look like their names.'

James and Irving were not sure how to take that.

'I wonder what Neil will grow to look like, now he's been renamed "Neily",' Irving said, tongue in cheek. 'And what you did wasn't exactly unpredictable, Neil. Only the way you did it.'

They were interrupted by the waiter coming to take the extra orders and view Mandy at close quarters.

'Is there a smut on my nose?' she said to him matily.

'Where're you from? Melbourne, or Sydney?'

'Wellington as a matter of fact. Can't you tell a New Zealander when you hear one?'

The lad gave her a wink. 'I wouldn't mind learning to.'

'If I had the time to spare, I wouldn't mind teaching you.'

Neil noticed that his friends were avoiding his eye, and said when the waiter had gone, 'Mandy's a nice friendly girl, aren't you, pet?'

She mouthed him a kiss, with lips that reminded Irving of the kind the agency used in lipstick ads, and said, with a dimpled smile, 'Neily says I've saved his sanity.'

Since this was the opposite of James's and Irving's judgement, they kept their expressions deadpan.

Mandy said, 'All New Zealanders're friendly. My great-great-gran was a Maori, that's where my bushy hair comes from. The red's from an Irish ancestor,' she added with another of her fetching smiles.

'Mandy's a real little melting pot, aren't you, pet?'

'I am if you throw my Scottish granddad in!'

And if Neil said 'aren't you, pet?' one more time . . . 'When are you going back to New Zealand?' James inquired. The pointed question meant nothing to the girl, but he saw Neil's lips tighten.

They loosened when Mandy looked at him. There was certainly something about that smile, thought James. Like being bathed with honey – and Neil was drowning in it.

'My dad staked me to a one-way ride,' Mandy replied. 'I've done a spot of waitressing, between seeing what he still calls the mother-country — ' She paused when the waiter brought her lunch and Neil's to the table, and transferred her attention to him. 'Good-oh! Thanks a million. I hope the burger's as good as the service! Did you hold the onions on the other one? Have a gander, Neily, before he takes off — '

Neil 'had a gander'. 'All's fine, he held the onions, pet.'

'You were telling us when you're going back to New Zealand,' James prompted Mandy.

'When I've earned my fare. Pass me the ketchup, Neily. And the pickle.'

They watched her drench and dress her burger until the meat was no longer visible. Oh, for the digestion of youth, thought James.

'You can have my chips if you like, pet. The burger is more than enough for me.'

James exchanged a glance with Irving. If Julie saw this, she'd have apoplexy. But Mandy's eating didn't show, and the time when it would was light-years away.

'I'll eat yours when I've finished mine, Neily. Good-oh! Time to feed the animals!' She sank her teeth into the burger. 'Great! What was I saying?'

'Why don't I say it for you, pet? Mandy's in no hurry to go home, chaps.'

She licked some ketchup off her fingers, as naturally as a child. But when a child did it, there was nothing sensual about it. Mandy had sex written all over her, though James had to admit there was nothing calculating or calculated about her. If there were, Neil would surely have seen through it. Mandy's combination of innocence and allure made her more dangerous!

'When exactly did you two meet?' he asked, trying to sound casual.

'I was hitching my way to see Land's End when Neily gave me a ride.'

Irving allowed himself a mental leer, and thought crudely, I guess, since whenever that was, you've given him plenty of rides. What else was there in it for Neil, with a teenage raver?

'I never got to see it, did I, Neily? If you don't want the rest of your burger, I'll have it. Thanks a million! Great.'

The guy's been shacked up in a motel with another food-addict! thought Irving. But this one Neil didn't mind – or hadn't he seen the irony? The way Mandy was gobbling up everything in sight, including the rest of the pickle in the dish, was like watching a fast-eating competition.

'Mandy has a healthy appetite, haven't you, pet?'

Something else that had to be seen to be believed was Neil's fatuous smile – and the irony had sure gone over his head.

'We spent the first evening getting to know each other, didn't we, Neily?'

Biblically, thought Irving.

'Telling you my troubles was very comforting, pet.'

Irving wanted to ask him if he'd handed her the 'my wife doesn't understand me' line.

Mandy confirmed Irving's cynical supposition. 'When I heard what he'd been through I wasn't surprised Neily took off.'

Neil displayed his first sign of embarrassment. 'I just gave you the potted version, pet.'

'Some potted version,' Mandy said with a giggle. 'I asked you why you looked so blue, when we stopped on the motorway for some supper. You were still telling me when we came off it and I saw that place we stayed at, and I said you looked too tired to drive on.'

After which the talking stopped, thought Irving.

James's thoughts were on a less earthy plane. Only a kid could think the story of how a marriage – and one that'd lasted for more years than she'd been on earth – had come to grief could be unreeled just like that. Oh the naïveté of youth, as well as the digestion! At Mandy's age – she looked no more than eighteen – what a man and woman put into a long-standing relationship couldn't even be envisaged. When you stood on the threshold of it, marriage seemed to you a flower-strewn path. And the youngsters who bothered with it, nowadays, didn't enter it with their parents' for-better-or-worse approach. It was more like 'if I've made a mistake, it's easily rectified'.

Meanwhile, this perky kid was an added complication in the Newtons' marriage, one Julie could do without. You'd have to be blind and deaf not to notice the alarming transformation in Neil, just because he'd met Mandy, and the fondness she seemed to have for him. In Neil's vulnerable state, anything was possible. Irving would say anything in a skirt would've been possible, but James wasn't so sure. 'Anything in a skirt' didn't include protectiveness towards its wearer.

He tried again to prise them apart. 'If you're looking for waitressing work, Mandy, and want to see some of England's finest scenery, why not hitch up to the Lake District? Now's the time to do it, while they're taking on temporary extra staff ready for the season. When you see Langdale Pikes, and Tarn Hows — '

'Why don't you just provide her with a travel brochure?' Neil cut in rudely. 'This would be as good a time as any for you to go and powder your pretty nose, pet.'

'Good-oh! I can take a hint. Order me a choc nut sundae, for when I get back, Neily. Make it a double. And tell 'em heavy on the nuts.'

The three of them were bathed in her smile, and fell silent when she left them to it.

'I told her to give me a minute for a private word with you two,' Neil said. 'But I'm getting the feeling I'm on the mat! She's some girl, isn't she? You can't deny that. When I saw her at the roadside, what with her hair, and her get-up, I thought I was seeing a rainbow,' he added with a laugh.

'And you're behaving as though you've been hit by one,' said James.

'The rain will come later,' Irving added.

'Allow me to correct you, Irving. A rainbow *follows* rain.'

'That doesn't mean the sun's going to shine on you from here on.'

James said, 'Why are we talking this daft imagery? Instead of saying what we bloody mean?'

Neil drank some of his lager, and put the glass down. 'I really am on the mat, aren't I? Well, well. The expressions on your faces remind me of our gloomy lunches of the old days.'

'They're already the old days to you, are they?' said James.

'In the way that matters, yes.'

Neil had leapt off the roundabout with a vengeance. 'And what way is that?'

'I haven't had a miserable moment since I met Mandy. When I told her she'd saved my sanity I wasn't kidding. We've all heard the expression "breaking point", but nobody knows what it is until they reach it.'

'But where does Julie fit into this situation?' Irving demanded.

'I'm afraid she doesn't.'

Irving clapped a hand to his cheek. 'A few nights with a cutie has done this to you? I'd credited you with more sense, Neil.'

Neil sipped his lager reflectively. 'I'd forgotten what it's like to feel light-hearted. It's as though a burden has gone from my shoulders.'

'That was your sense of responsibility,' Irving told him.

James said, 'I'm with you there.'

'What a couple of Dutch-uncles you've turned out to be.'

'Didn't someone once say the onlooker sees more of the game, boychik?'

'And we're sitting here seeing it.'

'What you're actually doing is being mouthpieces for my wife – or that's how it strikes me!'

'What *I'm* actually doing,' said Irving, 'is trying to wise up a guy who doesn't want to be wised up. And if you'd seen Julie the way we did, you'd shed a tear for her.'

Neil laughed. 'The day anyone needs to feel sorry for Julie, I'll eat my wig.'

'Does that mean you won't be requiring it any more? How will you keep your cutie in rainbow get-ups? And you don't deserve the way your wife is lying to your clerk to keep your options open for you.'

'It's the least she can do, and I knew she would. I'll be back in my chambers after Easter,' Neil replied airily. 'Not that I gave a damn if she did or not, when I made my getaway. Work was far from my mind.'

He laughed again. It was years since James had seen him so carefree. James had thought of Neil as the serious sort, but he hadn't always been, had he? It had happened gradually, as he grew older.

'And like you said, you knew you could rely on Julie, didn't you?' James harked back. 'That counts for a lot.'

'But not for everything. And without her constant competition fanning me in the face, I can stop striving for what I'm probably never going to achieve. And by the way, Irving, would you please stop calling Mandy a cutie? There's more to her than you two are at present prepared to see – as you'll discover when you get to know her.'

Irving's cheek received another clap. 'Are we going to have time to?'

'You are if it's up to me.'

'Why don't we just give up on this, James? Let him go get his fingers burned.'

'If I do, I'll blow on them myself,' Neil replied. 'I shan't expect you and James to kiss them better.'

'Whatever, we'll still be your buddies, Neil.'

'Then what the hell is this inquisition about? Julie's

193

capable of taking care of herself – a lot more so than I am. The least I'd expect from my friends is they wouldn't grudge me a little happiness.'

And there was nothing they could say to any of that, since all of it was true.

'If you hadn't met Mandy, what would your next step have been?' James wanted to know.

Neil paused before replying. 'It's hard to say, James. I just knew that if I didn't get away from Julie, there'd be nothing left of me. Let me put it this way, Julie is the irresistible force and the immovable object combined – and I'd suddenly had it. It was out or under.'

He paused again, as if sunk in recollection, and stared at what was left of his lager. 'When I got back from court that evening, Julie wasn't home yet. Have you ever felt silence? – that's how it was. A chilling emptiness, too. But I felt that inside me even when Julie was there. There's an old photo of me on my degree-day, on the living-room mantelpiece – you must have seen it. I stood gazing at it, and all the things I'd hoped for then, few of which have materialised, came flooding back to me. Given my age, if I didn't do something now, the number-one lack in my life was going to remain lacking unto the grave.'

'Everyone's looking for that elusive bluebird,' Irving said.

'Neil thinks he's found it.'

'Who doesn't, at some time or other? And I'm here to tell him that abiding happiness doesn't come in feminine form. Irrespective of age, shape, brain power, and whatever, a woman is trouble sooner or later.'

'Here comes your bluebird, Neil,' James said tongue-in-cheek, as Mandy emerged from the ladies' room. 'Long may it last!'

Mandy's first words when she rejoined them were, 'Where's my choc nut sundae, Neily?'

'I couldn't catch the waiter's eye, pet.'

Mandy had no difficulty in doing so, and said after ordering her mountainous dessert, 'Don't you think Neily should tell his wife about us, and get it over?'

James changed his mind about her not being calculating. 'That's up to him, isn't it?'

194

Irving said – for her benefit, 'After such a short acquaintance, what is there to tell?'

'Didn't Neily tell you he's asked me to move in with him? When we find a place, that is. For now, we've dumped our bags in a hotel.'

'I was just getting around to telling them, pet. Mandy wants to see all there is to see in London, chaps, so I thought that would be a nice idea.'

Irving did a mental face-clap, and James saw permanency looming ahead.

'I shall call Julie to let her know I haven't been run over by a bus,' Neil said with a grin.

'When she knows the full score, she's likely to push you under one,' said Irving. 'Myrna would.'

Mandy dug into her dessert, which had appeared with lightning rapidity and another wink from the waiter. 'Who's Myrna?'

'His wife, pet. And James's is called Anna.'

'If yours'd push you under a bus for leaving her, Irving, she must really love you a lot.'

Given his uncertainty about what Myrna was currently plotting, Irving thought it remarkable that he managed to smile. And what Mandy had just said meant she ticked the way Myrna did. Neil had probably gone from the frying-pan to the fire.

'We'll all get together for you to meet Myrna and Anna very soon, pet,' Neil said to the new female in his life.

If he hadn't been so distracted by her, he would have seen the glance of consternation that passed between his friends.

'What we should've done, pet, was ask James or Irving to lend us their guest room, till we get fixed up.'

'Do either of you live in the centre of town?' Mandy expertly negotiated some chocolate sauce from beneath her lips, with her tongue. 'I want to be where everything's at, Neily.' She mouthed him a chocolatey kiss. 'You promised.'

'Irving does.'

'Are you out of your mind?'

Neil laughed. 'I was just testing the water.'

'The one you'll have to test it with is my wife.'

195

'Myrna and Anna are friends of Julie's, pet.'

'Oh, I see what you mean.'

Mandy was cleaning the inside of her sundae-dish with her finger, and carefully licking the finger after each dab. If she asked for another one, James would be sick on her behalf.

'Isn't she delightful?' Neil drooled. 'There isn't an inhibition in her, bless her heart.'

Irving and James doubted that some of the top-drawer folk Neil mixed with would see it that way.

'But I wouldn't dare do this if my ma was around,' Mandy said with a giggle. 'She'd call it a waste of my upbringing, wouldn't she, Neily?'

'Since Neil hasn't met your mother, how would he know?' James asked.

'New Zealanders often end their sentences like a question, don't they, Neily?'

'And you're a girl-and-a-half, aren't you, pet?'

Nor had it taken Neil long to follow suit! But he was going to have to stay on his toes to keep up with a girl of his sons' generation, James thought. And he could find he'd swopped one kind of pressure for another.

Mandy gave James and Irving her dimpled smile and harked back to their wives. 'I'll just have to make Myrna and Anna like me, won't I?'

Since there was as much chance of her succeeding as of getting a stoat to like a snake – Irving could think of no better way to put how middle-aged wives, and Myrna in particular, responded to the potential husband-stealer they saw lurking in every attractive young girl – his silent reply to the one who'd proved them right was: Don't bet on it, sweetheart.

CHAPTER EIGHT

ANNA'S REACTION to the manner of Neil's reappearance surprised James.

'It isn't for us to pass judgement,' she said after a silence that lasted so long, James thought it the calm before the storm.

Since he had had to steel himself to tell her, her response was something of an anti-climax. And how could she take it this way, when he was so upset about it?

'Is that all you've got to say, Anna? You must have been thinking something, when it took you all that time to reply.'

'If you really want to know, I was thinking what it must've been like for you, when I was going through my bad patch. Soaping over the mirrors, not making you proper meals, and all that – which was only the half of what you had to put up with. Looking back on it, and considering what Neil's done, I can see how much stronger you are than he is.'

James gave her a rueful smile. 'If that's a compliment, thanks.'

'Call it what you like. But you didn't up and leave me, did you? And that says something for the kind of man you are.'

'In fairness to Neil, love, shocked by it though I am, he walked out of a marriage that hadn't been right for years. I had no bad times piled up to get bitter about.'

'But they're piling up now, aren't they?' Anna said. 'We're having a conversation about our private thoughts, by the way!'

'What have I ever kept from you that matters?'

'The same that I've kept from you.'

'And what's that?'

'The thoughts that if I'd spoken them could've led to us not seeing eye to eye about everything.'

They had just finished dinner, and Anna was pouring coffee. She spooned some sugar into James's cup, and said, 'I've always done the little things for you that a considerate wife does, and you've been that way with me. But you and I've never really talked, James — '

'I seem to have heard this record before.'

'Only because I still haven't got through to you what I mean. Whenever I try to, you cut me short. And it isn't just the talking that matters, James, it's listening to each other properly. Trying to see things from each other's point of view.'

'How could a man and a woman ever do that? And you sound like a marriage guidance counsellor! Tracy was saying the other day, in the office, that her brother and sister-in-law are seeing one — and what the sessions consist of are mostly listening to each other spout.'

'Then there's no need for us to see one, is there, love? I seem to've put my finger on what's wrong without help.' Anna sipped her coffee, and said carefully, 'Well, part of what's wrong. For the other problem you probably need to see a sex-therapist.'

James leapt from his chair as though blown from it. 'Lord spare me from know-alls! Why does everyone suddenly think they know better than I do what's best for me? If you go on like this, I could end up following in Neil's footsteps!'

'If you can find a girl who doesn't mind being brutalised,' Anna was stung to reply. 'I've heard there are some like that.'

A silence followed, then Anna carried her coffee into the living-room.

We're living separate lives under the same roof, she thought with distress. Whenever she said something James would rather not hear, it ended like this. He would now be sitting at the kitchen table wishing they could go back to how they once were. But all that was left of the house of cards was the trappings. On Sunday they'd give each other Easter eggs, and James would present Anna with the bunch of spring flowers he'd have hidden in the garden shed, as he always did. On Easter Monday they'd join the throng at the fair on Hampstead Heath, and feed their faces with

198

candy-floss — if they didn't, it wouldn't be like Easter Monday to them. But something had gone and now — well what did it all mean? They were creatures of habit, but it wasn't *that* Anna wanted to change. And the house of cards had been better than this — when she didn't know it was one. But illusions were like wallpaper; stripped off they lay in shreds around you. Anna was trying to replace them with something meaningful. How could she, without James's help?

It did not occur to Anna that she had gone from one extreme to another and was, unreasonably, expecting James to do the same. Or that he was unable to deal with the self-revelations their crisis had imposed upon him, as it had upon her. Anna's skin-deep rejuvenation had revitalised her in other respects, too. She felt like a new woman. But James was still walking around fearing that he was a has-been — and only had to glance at his wife for the feeling to be reaffirmed.

When he came into the living-room, Anna tried again to get him to open up with her. 'I noticed you got another letter from the income tax today, James — '

'And I can do without being reminded of it!'

'But what's it all about? Why do they keep writing to you?' she persisted.

'Your guess is as good as mine, and they're keeping me guessing,' he snapped. 'And even if I knew, it'd be nothing you'd understand.'

'Why're you fingering your forehead? You're always doing it, James.'

'And the first time you noticed me doing it, you said something like, "Oh, it's only a bit of tension, love." I haven't noticed you inquiring again.'

'It'd be more than my life's worth to keep questioning you.'

'But for your information, I've been trying to shift an invisible hat off my head for going on a year — '

'Isn't it time you saw a doctor?'

'And get given what you were? Tension and pressure is an executive's lot; if we all walked round tranquillised the business world would grind to a halt. Why d'you think the first thing most chaps do when they get home from the office is pour themselves a drop of something to relax them?'

'I hadn't thought about it, but thank you for telling me.'

'And since you want to widen your horizon, you might as well add this. When I leave here in the morning, I'm not swallowed up into thin air! I drive off to a world you know nothing about. Where people are often nice to you only because it suits them to be, and you have to be the same way with them. Where everyone, one way or another, is out to get everyone else, and everything they do is for their own ends. They call it earning a living, and it's getting to be a strain keeping up with it.'

'If that's a confession that you've no respect for how you earn yours, I'm surprised it's taken you so long to admit it to yourself.'

'I'm talking about sweat and tears, and she's talking ethics! What I just said applies to the whole business world, Anna, not just to my bit of it. All an ad agency does is put the gloss on the system.'

'And make people who can't afford it want to buy, buy, buy.'

'That's what the system's all about.'

'Are you thinking of opting out?'

'At my age?'

James was sitting in his favourite wing-chair, and Anna noted his weary posture. He meant everything to her and it was time she said something warm and encouraging. 'You're not too old to turn your talents to something more rewarding, love, even if it meant earning less than you do. If you made up your mind to, I'd support you in whatever you did.'

James's response was not the one she had hoped for.

'You've become a supporter of causes, haven't you? First the peace movement, which you got out of your chair to support for a weekend, and now me! Well, armchair support, with the occasional sacrificial gesture, is something I've always despised. It's Kim, not you, who's still knee-deep in mud at Greenham Common, like it'd be me, not you, who bore the day-to-day brunt of changing direction at my time of life. What I'm looking forward to now is my retirement.'

'And anyone not yet fifty who feels like that is already out to grass in their mind,' Anna answered. 'I shall have to take back what I said about you being stronger than Neil. At least he had the courage to do something about his lot before it got too late.'

'Is that an invitation to leave you?'

'If you've stopped loving me, you're welcome to go.'

'I haven't, as a matter of fact.'

'Nor I you.'

'Then what is all this bloody-well about?'

'I'm trying to help you sort yourself out.'

James paced the hearthrug like a man demented. 'How did I suddenly become a case for treatment!'

'That's the second admission you've made this evening. You're making progress, love,' Anna said with a smile.

'You may find it amusing, but it isn't to me. And when I look back at all that's gone on since you made that damned joke about your face, what's happened to me isn't sudden. What I'm suffering from is like the effects of water dripping onto a stone. Less than a year ago, I was sound in mind and body. A man who had his feet on the ground, who was without a worry in the world — '

'It would be truer to say who thought he hadn't,' Anna interrupted.

'And since happiness is a state of mind, what's wrong with that?'

'Why don't you just quote the one about ignorance being bliss?'

'If it weren't, it wouldn't be a cliché,' James countered. 'And if it were possible to wave a wand over you and me and return us magically to that blissful state, I'd foot the bill for the wand whatever it cost.'

'Like you were prepared to do to get me put right in a different sort of clinic from the one I put myself in.'

'Who told you that? Myrna, who got it from Irving? Or was it Julie, who'd heard it from Neil?' James smiled sardonically. 'What would we do without our loving friends?'

'They meant well.'

'I can't deny that. But has it never struck you, Anna, that what they've done between them is inject us with some of the poison that's done their own marriages no good?'

'We didn't have to let them.'

'And I wish, now, that I'd told the lot of them to go to hell. But once they'd got a foot in the door, it was too late to shoot the bolt. Before I knew it, I didn't know if I was coming or going. For a while, I couldn't be sure if I was thinking Irving's way, or my own.'

'Do you know now?'

'At present I'm trying not to let myself think. Too much introspection puts a chap off his stroke – and that's where I've been for some time. I was better off in the old days, playing everything off the cuff.'

'You mean plodding along. And right now, we're communicating, by the way.'

'Are you keeping a record of all the admissions I make – and our conversations that fulfil your new requirements? If Neil had to stand for this from Julie all his married life, I'm surprised he stayed with her for as long as he did.'

Anna let the sarcasm pass. 'Myrna's theory about why the Newtons' marriage went adrift is that sex flew out of their bedroom window.'

'If sex flew out of her bedroom window, it'd be wearing a hostess apron and no knickers!'

Anna had a vision of Myrna sailing over the penthouse balcony and along Park Lane, and had to laugh.

'When did Myrna ever have a theory about anything, that didn't relate to below the waist?' James said acidly. 'And you find my sexual problem funny, do you?'

'Not in the least, since it involves me, too.'

'Which of us were you thinking of when you tried to get me to a sex-therapist? I'm as capable of keeping a record of conversations as you are. And mentioning Myrna's theory was your second, if more subtle, attempt.'

'You're wrong about that. But I do think it's worth considering.' Anna finished her coffee and put down the cup. 'You were prepared to send me for analysis, may I remind you.'

'You already did! And it was no more true then than it is now.'

'Myrna said it was your current thinking.'

'Irving's current thinking, and Neil suggested I should give it some thought. When things get bandied about among a group of friends, Anna, they usually end up distorted. And there was a time when the word "analysis" had never cropped up in this house except when Kim needed help with her English-grammar homework. I'd like you to tell me one good thing that's come of all the delving we and our marriage have been subjected to.'

'We've begun airing our real thoughts.'

'And what has it led to but recriminations?'

'That's healthier than silent resentments.'

James flopped onto the sofa, smiled wearily, and said, 'Speaking for myself, I didn't know I had any. And we're back to happiness being a state of mind.'

'I was never under the illusion that it begins and ends in bed.'

'We're also back with my problem! You've bloody steered us back to it, haven't you? You're getting as crafty as Myrna – but you won't get me to a sex-therapist.'

'If you want the truth, it's for your sake, not mine.'

'Then let's leave well enough alone. Next time the beast in me emerges, I'll lock myself in the bathroom, and do what I did when I was a lad!'

He looked so forlorn, Anna wanted to take him in her arms and comfort him. But he would think it was pity, and rebuff her. They'd just said they still loved each other, hadn't they? – and meant it, but were no closer now than when the conversation began.

'If *you* want the truth, I felt like cutting my throat after brutalising you.'

'I didn't imagine you were pleased with yourself, James. That's why I want you to seek help. It wasn't you.'

James switched on the televison set, remarking that they hadn't watched any films or plays lately.

Anna said, 'There's enough *real* drama in our lives.'

'But it isn't going to include me lying on a couch learning why I've turned into the Bella Vista rapist. My balls're the

203

only bit of privacy I've got left – and I'm hanging on to 'em!'

He settled down to watch the nine o'clock news – over the top of his *Standard*, as usual. Anna felt as if a door had been slammed in her face, and picked up her knitting. She was making a shawl for Kim's baby, with love in every stitch. How would Kim fare on Easter Sunday, when there was sure to be a demonstration at the base, she was thinking when the telephone rang.

'If it's Myrna, don't bother giving her my regards!' James said as she went to answer it.

It was Kim.

'I was just thinking of you, love – but it was sometimes like that with my mam and me. Maternal telepathy. How are you, Kim?'

'Not too good. I've got cramps where I shouldn't have them.'

Why hadn't Anna stopped her from bashing in those tent pegs? 'Any blood?'

'A tiny spot.'

'Is there a doctor at the camp?'

'I haven't told anyone. I'd rather come home. If you wouldn't mind having me, Mum — '

'That's the daftest thing you've ever said to me.'

'But I can't call Harry to come and fetch me. He's on location in Holland. He won't be able to say he told me so until he gets back!'

Biologically, a woman was always beholden to her man, Anna thought. 'I'll be with you as soon as I can, Kim. Just sit yourself down, and don't worry.'

'Thanks, Mum.'

Anna put on her coat and went to tell James.

'What was it? An SOS from Julie? Or Maggie wanting to show you the latest damage her resident grandchild has done to the furniture with that horse-on-wheels Shirley bought him? I don't know how Mike stands it at his time of life.'

'You have got the grumps tonight – but it was an SOS. From Kim.'

The newspaper slipped from James's fingers.

'I'm coming with you,' he said, after Anna had told him.

'There's no need, love. And I got the feeling that right now it's just me she wants.'

'Well, you're her partner in crime, aren't you?' was the sole recrimination James made. 'And let's be practical about this, shall we? How would you go on, if Kim needed you for something and you were driving?' By then, they were in the hall and he was opening the front door.

'It'd be a laugh if this turned out to be the time some burglars decided to ignore our alarm box,' Anna said when they were on their way.

They hadn't paused to switch on the system. All but Kim had gone from their thoughts.

'You and your jokes!'

Apart from that brief exchange, neither spoke a word for the rest of the journey to Greenham.

When they arrived, Kim made a joke, though her accompanying smile was wan. 'I've brought you together, have I?'

'In a manner of speaking,' James replied. 'Now let's get you home.'

They were almost there, when Kim asked if Dr Kindersley was still doing night calls. 'He'll be getting a bit old for that now, won't he? But he might come, seeing it's me.'

Anna had to tell her that their old friend had retired from the practice. Kim's expression reminded Anna of her own feelings when the receptionist had told her that.

'I was banking on the man who told me the facts of life saving my baby. I met him in the park one day, it was just after I'd had my first period, and I was feeling very grown-up, so I told him — '

'Did you tell the park-keeper, too?' James said, to keep the smile on her face.

'*He* was a friend of mine, as well. He used to give lollipops to all the kids — '

'Now I know why your teeth had to have all those fillings,' said Anna.

James said, 'If you'd been to a private dentist, I could dig out all the bills and send them to the park-keeper.'

'Your dad's a great one for keeping bills and filing letters, love.'

Even when they were doing their best to keep their daughter cheerful, she still had to have a jab at him! Or was he doing what she kept accusing him of? Reading things she hadn't meant into what she said. She'd always found it amusing that he kept bills from way back, but had agreed that it wasn't a bad idea when the glass door of Maggie's oven blew out all over the kitchen, and Mike hadn't got the proof of where they'd bought it.

What the heck was he doing thinking about ovens with glass doors, when his daughter might be going to lose her baby? He didn't want to think about that, did he? 'So Dr Kindersley told you about the birds and the bees, did he, Kim?' he said, managing to laugh.

'It's as well he did, since neither of you two thought of filling me in. I'd've been left to make what I could of the words lads chalk on walls.'

What old-fashioned parents we were, Anna thought, and she wouldn't be if she had her time again.

'He was a lovely man, the sort you knew you could rely on,' Kim went on.

'But there's no guarantee of the outcome with you, love.' Anna thought it best to prepare her.

'And this could be curtains for Harry and me.'

Anna and James replied with one mind, 'Don't be daft, Kim.'

'It's my fault, isn't it?'

'Your Auntie Babs had a mis, love, before she had your cousins, and she's the sort who wraps herself in cotton-wool, and always was, wasn't she, James?'

'How my brother puts up with her beats me.'

'I expect he loves her.'

'That has to be it. And if Harry loves Kim as much as we all know he does — '

'Oh, it's love that's on trial, is it, Dad? I thought it was going to be me – with you, as well as Harry. And by the way, I've got another of those cramps, Mum — '

'We've only round the corner to go now, Kim. Your mother'll help you to bed, and I'll call the health centre the minute we get in.'

'And a lot of good either will probably do me!'

Anna held her hand. 'No guarantee isn't a reason to give up.'

'You're still my sensible mum, even though you don't look like her, aren't you?'

'I have to agree she still shows flashes of it,' said James as he pulled up in the drive.

Kim went directly to the cloakroom, and announced to them when she emerged, 'The bulletin on the blood front is still just one spot.'

Anna said, 'That's hopeful news,' and James said, 'The things these modern lasses say in front of their fathers!'

'Well, we're that kind of family, now, aren't we, Dad?'

'So it appears,' he said, watching Anna shepherd Kim upstairs. He thought the world of them both, and how sad it was that the grandchild who could have helped draw him and Anna close again might not now materialise.

The doctor on duty that night happened to be Dr Binns. Since James's call on the subject of Anna's tranquillisers had been one a young practitioner was unlikely to forget, he was relieved that it was Anna, not James, who let him in.

He managed not to gape when he saw her, and said with a smile, 'Over the menopause, are we?'

'I wouldn't know,' she replied. 'I seem to've stopped getting the physical symptoms, if that's what you mean. As for the particular anxiety I came to see you about, I finally dealt with it myself. I had my face lifted, and it's done me a lot more good than popping pills. But it's my daughter you're here to see.'

'That wouldn't be every woman's remedy,' he said as she led the way upstairs.

Anna thought of her companion in his waiting room. 'Every woman doesn't have the same kind of anxiety, does she? We all need our own special sort of reassurance, but all there's time for nowadays is to lump us all together for the *same* remedy. They should stop calling it a health service, and call it a machine.'

The doctor's reception from Kim was no more friendly.

'How are you feeling, young lady?'

'Spare me the bedside manner, Doctor. Camping in the mud has ruined my taste for the niceties. And you can cut out that "young lady" stuff – I'm not much younger than you.'

'It wasn't too wise of you to take the risk you did,' he told her, 'which isn't to say I don't admire you for it.'

'You can cut that out, too. And there were women more heavily pregnant than me there.'

'At your stage, the risk is much greater,' he replied, while taking her blood pressure. 'I shall have to wait for you to calm yourself, before I can get a correct reading,' he said with a smile.

'How calm d'you expect me to be, under the circumstances?' Kim retorted.

'As calm as possible wouldn't harm the circumstances, and I'm sure you know what I mean,' he said, perching himself at the end of the bed while he waited.

His patience and concern when dealing with a *physical* condition would, at any other time, have made Anna smile sardonically. But all that mattered right now was the careful examination he was giving her daughter.

'Am I going to miscarry or not?' Kim demanded as he was putting away his stethoscope.

'Provided you stay off your feet, there's always a chance. The only treatment is rest. And you're asking me to tell you what only God could.'

'We must keep our fingers crossed, love,' Anna said encouragingly.

'At the moment I'm wishing I'd kept my legs crossed!' Kim exclaimed as another bout of cramp gripped her. 'But I'd rather not go into hospital if I don't have to.'

'With your mother to take care of you, and the shortage of beds, I see no point in moving you. We could whip you in, in an ambulance, if it became necessary — '

'Terrific!'

Anna said to him on the way downstairs, 'I must apologise for my daughter's outbursts. It's the way she's feeling.'

'They're all in the day's work to me, Mrs Ridgeway, though I can't say the one I got from your husband on the phone was.' Nor the little lecture you gave me, he silently added.

208

He gave James, who was waiting in the hall, a curt nod, and warned him, before leaving, not to count on there being a family christening this year.

'That chap's got a prescription pad where his heart should be,' James exclaimed.

'He was telling you the truth, James.'

'But that was no way to tell it to an expectant grand-father.'

Anna followed James into the kitchen, and was moved to see that he had prepared a dainty supper for his daughter. 'I didn't know you could cook, James.'

'How do you suppose I managed while you were away having yourself beautified?'

'I didn't give it a thought,' she lied.

'I know you bloody didn't. And any fool can poach an egg and slap it on a slice of toast,' he added, glancing proudly at the small repast he had put in the centre of a large dinner-plate.

Anna refrained from saying that egg-on-toast ought not to be prepared in advance. It was the first time she had spared his feelings by not saying what she thought since she began not sparing them, and it stopped her short.

'Is something wrong with the egg?' James said aggressively.

'Of course not. I shouldn't think Kim's feeling hungry, but why don't you take it up to her?'

She had resisted the impulse to add, 'Before it gets even colder'. Not hurting James had been more important than speaking her mind, she registered after he had left the room. What was it Kim had said on the way from the airport? Something about there being a time to be diplomatic. But it had taken a soggy poached egg to show Anna that, in a different way from Myrna's, she had gone over the top – and was wounding those she would not wish to wound. Like the way she'd told Julie, while she was still licking the wound Neil gave her, 'I think you've been a fool.'

Anna washed the egg-poacher and gave herself a mental kick. Her new-found confidence had caused her to face people and life like a bull at a gate, and she'd have to be more careful, or she'd find herself like the one in the china shop, contemplating the damage.

A shout from James sent her rushing upstairs, all but her daughter gone from her mind.

It was to be that way for the anxious week that followed. Dr Binns called every day, and when the blood-spotting increased helped James raise the foot of Kim's bed on some bricks they found in the back garden.

Afterwards, he said to James and Anna, 'If I'd suggested hospital, since she'd rather stay here it could affect her emotionally, and when you're hoping to avoid a mis, everything counts. I got the tip about the bricks from my father.'

'One of the old school, is he?' said James.

'With a vengeance. He's in practice in Bournemouth, where I come from. But Father only takes private patients nowadays.'

James said, 'Bowed out of the system, has he?'

'And not for the money. He couldn't take the flak, and with fewer patients to see there isn't any.'

Reading between the lines, it was the nearest thing to an apologetic explanation for taking the easy way out with Anna that he could bring himself to offer.

'Would you like a cup of coffee before you leave?' James asked him.

'I'm surprised that you've offered me one!' he said with a grin. 'But no thanks. If I drank all the tea and coffee I get offered on my rounds, I'd have to get fixed up with an extra bladder. Some of my patients actually seem to like me.'

James said, 'I take folk as I find them, and at present you're doing all right. I'll nip back upstairs to Kim, and leave you to see Dr Binns out, love.'

'Why do I feel as if I've just received an accolade?' the doctor said to Anna. 'And by the way, if you need me during the night, don't hesitate to call me at home.'

'Even if it isn't you who's on call?'

'Kim's situation is traumatic enough, without a change of doctor at a crucial time.'

Anna watched him hurry away to his car. In looks, he reminded her of what her mother used to call a 'Brylcreem-boy' – slicked-back hair, with no parting, and a smile Anna had once thought too ready, as she'd thought his manner too polished. But he was really just an over-worked young man, who had to have his priorities.

Thankfully, Kim was one of them. But her independence had astounded James. She had refused to let him call the BBC to get Harry's hotel address in Holland and fetch him home. Anna was less sure that it was independence. Her daughter was riddled with guilt. Given that she'd gone against her husband's wishes, nobody was ever going to convince Kim that her plight hadn't resulted from that.

But James left a message on Harry's answerphone at the flat, and he was back in England and pacing the upstairs landing when Kim lost the baby.

Harry had arrived in the early evening, shortly after Anna recognised the inevitable and called Dr Binns. In the final stages, Kim sent her husband from the room, but clung to Anna's hand – as though her mother were the only one able to strengthen her.

It's her husband she'd want beside her now if their baby were going to live, Anna thought. But seeing her miscarry their child was something Kim would not want Harry to remember.

Nor was this a night Anna would easily forget. An unseasonable gale was threatening to blow off the roof, adding to the bleakness of what was happening under it. A friend who had experienced a miscarriage had said to Anna afterwards that it was like giving birth, but without the hope, or the joy that followed.

When it was over, Kim said, 'Harry can come in now. I'm out of the woods and must steel myself for the recriminations.'

But Anna doubted that there would be any. Her son-in-law had not reproached her for encouraging Kim to go to Greenham, which showed him to be a man who saw things in their true perspective. When she left with the doctor, Kim and Harry were comforting each other.

'This week has been like a year to me,' Anna said to James, after Dr Binns had driven off to his interrupted dinner.

'And what's gone on brings a person down to the basics,' he replied. 'Everything else goes by the board.'

'If you mean that all you and I've thought about is our daughter — '

'That's exactly what I mean. And what I'm trying to say is — '

'I know what you're trying to say.'

'But once Kim's gone off to her own life again, we'll be back where we were, I suppose. There has to be something to be learned from that.'

Anna mustered a weary smile. 'Let me know what it is when you've fathomed it out. Right now, I wouldn't mind a shoulder to lean on.'

'Me, neither.' James joined her on the sofa, and said when they were holding each other close. 'According to Myrna, love is a three-letter word. What price her theories now? It makes me wonder if the Sangers have ever spent a night just sleeping in each other's arms.'

'It's been a long time since we did.'

'It's time we resumed the habit.'

'Just so long as it doesn't bring out the beast in you.'

James was off the sofa in two seconds flat. 'It hasn't taken you long to revert.'

The step forward in their relationship had just been followed by two steps backward, Anna thought with chagrin, when he stalked from the room. But it was her fault. She should've bitten off her tongue instead of saying what she had – and had better stop congratulating herself for being diplomatic about a poached egg.

CHAPTER NINE

THE RIDGEWAYS' private interlude with their daughter had, as James implied when he referred to the 'basics', made the whirligig of events they had shared with their friends seem remote and unreal. It was as though everything else had been put on ice for a brief while.

Though Myrna and Julie kept in touch, they had limited their conversation to concerned inquiries about Kim. Irving, too, when he and James found time for a personal word at the office. It was as if the knowledge that the unborn child's life hung by a thread had given them pause.

'My commiserations about the outcome, boychik,' Irving said to James afterwards. 'But things will be back to normal before you know it.'

James was coming to think that Irving didn't know what 'normal' was. Nor was he any longer so sure himself. All he was sure of was that it was not the permutations and intrigues in which he had been ensnared since his wife threw a shoe at him – from which his daughter's miscarriage had allowed him some respite.

It was not to last.

'Myrna's throwing a surprise party for me,' Irving said gloomily.

'How can it be a surprise when you know about it?'

'She thinks I don't.'

Here we go again! thought James.

'And I'm not going to tell her I do. I found a proof of the invitations she's had printed. Guess what it said?'

'Myrna Sanger invites you to her husband's funeral – if she's received the watchdog's report,' said James facetiously.

'That wasn't the wording, but it describes my feeling when I read it. "This is your life, Irving Sanger", would you believe! Is she trying to tell me I'm finished at the age of forty-eight?'

'Nobody reads that into the show she's pinched the idea from.'

'Eamonn Andrews isn't Myrna, and his personality of the week isn't trembling in their shoes because they've been tailed — '

'And did something bloody stupid,' James cut in scathingly. 'People usually have to take the consequences of their actions, Irving.'

'Remind me to buy you a parson's collar.' Irving took off his glasses and polished them nervously. 'Who she intends to spring on me from the past, I shudder to think.'

'Is your past such a murky one?'

'Show me the guy who has nothing to hide. And don't say he's standing right beside me. Even you must have had your moments.'

'But they began and ended in my mind when a nice pair of legs flashed by.'

'When I was married to my ex, a few of mine went a little further,' said Irving with a reminiscent smile. 'We lived for a while in an apartment building in Manhattan where there was a wild crowd — '

'If this is going to be another of your sagas, I haven't time to listen to it. But I'm your captive audience, aren't I, Irving?'

'If I can't talk to you, who can I talk to, boychik? Since Neil jumped overboard, only the two of us are left in the boat.'

The only difference between the boat and the roundabout was the boat was 'men only', James thought wryly – and one was still rocking and the other still whizzing! 'I really do have to get back to my office, Irving. Can't this wait?'

'If you want me to blow a gasket, it can wait. Like Myrna and I once said to each other, it's better to release some steam *before* the gasket blows.'

'Then why the heck don't you have this out with each other? Instead of playing footsie, like you bloody do! About what you know that she thinks you don't, and probably vice versa.'

'The vice versa could land me in *schtuk*.'

'And where do you think you are now?'

Irving stared contemplatively at the picture of Myrna that adorned his desk. 'Once, when I was musing about marriage, it struck me that it's like a game of chess. How a move you think is never going to be made can enter the game at a later stage and be used against you.'

James recalled how Anna had waited until it suited her to reveal that she knew he'd stolen one of her tranks. Irving had a point.

'Getting back to the steam-releasing, it was your marriage we were talking about, James, when the gasket finally blew.'

'I don't get the "finally", Irving. Before then, there was nothing to let off steam about.'

'Your friends would have said the same, before it happened. But a gasket can't blow *without* steam building up to cause it. Figure that one out.'

James brushed aside a remembrance of Anna saying recriminations were better than storing up resentments. Was that what she'd been doing, while he blithely assumed she was happy and content? She wasn't that good an actress.

Irving resumed his interrupted story. 'When my ex and I got invited to one of that wild crowd's shindigs, she came looking for me to go home, and found me in the coat closet with a broad I thought it only polite to help strip off.'

'Why would she expect to find you in the coat closet?'

'It was during a game of "Sardines", which I thought was what kids played at birthday parties, until I met that crowd. The odd thing about them was they did everything respectably. Straight husband-and-wife swapping was out, but what you did while you played "Postman's Knock" or whatever, was allowable. Strip-poker was their favourite — '

'Can I return you to the coat closet? I've got work to do!'

'My ex just said, "Honey, we have to leave now." Myrna would have gone for me with a knife.'

'Then you're lucky Myrna's only giving you a surprise party.'

'Knives get used in the heat of the moment. When my loving babe takes time to plan something, it could turn out

215

to be a lot worse than a quick death. But I still think you can bet on her not knowing you were the guy in the pub.'

'You'd better be right. For a man who's got nothing to hide, who's a good husband, and wouldn't hurt a fly, I've already come in for enough that I don't deserve.'

'Since when was it the ones who deserve it who get it? And that inventory of your good qualities that you just supplied goes for me also.'

'Except for item one.'

James felt as if he was back in the school yard with another lad, trying to score one over each other. What a bloody puerile conversation, compared with the grim realities of the past week.

'Since Myrna's planned my execution for a week-night,' said Irving, 'it has to be because she intends conspiring with you to get me home from the office late, when her guests are assembled for the kill.'

'I'd be conspiring with *you*, too, wouldn't I? – since she doesn't know the surprise aspect has gone awry — '

'And the two of us would be conspiring against her,' Irving cut in, 'by not telling her until we're ready that all her plotting was for nothing. In front of her guests, that would sure teach her to think she can pull the wool over my eyes!'

'I don't want to be involved in your vendettas — '

'In this one, you already are.'

'Why has conspiracy suddenly entered my life!' James exclaimed. 'A year ago, I wouldn't have recognised a cloak and dagger if someone had approached me wrapped in one and brandishing the other.'

'Then you've learned something useful, haven't you, boychik?'

But James had been happier before he did.

'Which I hope includes that our young colleague is stalking you with a smile on his face and a stiletto hidden up his sleeve.'

And confirmation that he wasn't being paranoid about the pipsqueak was no comfort; nor from where it came. James's invisible hat did one of its quick changes to a vice. 'Your personal problems keep cutting into my working day, Irving.'

Irving gave him a warm smile, replaced his spectacles, and said, 'What would I do without you?'

James hoped he was referring to business, as well as to friendship. He was heading for the door when Irving stopped him short.

'Haven't you forgotten something?'

James turned to look at him. With his glasses back on, the bland look he had without them was distinctly missing.

'The folder you brought in to discuss with me is still on my desk.'

James went to get it.

'The whole of life is a conspiracy and forewarned is forearmed, is no reason to start getting forgetful,' Irving said with a chuckle that only someone in James's frame of mind could have found ominous.

Chapter Ten

Myrna was conspiring with more people than Irving supposed. She had mused long and hard about how she would handle the situation and had decided upon a devious approach.

Since deviousness was no stranger to her, she might even have enjoyed it had her marriage not been at stake, but she set that niggling anxiety aside and got on with her plan. To carry it through she required a broader canvas than a small get-together would provide, and Irving's 'surprise party' was thus destined to be one of those gatherings to which acquaintances are invited to swell the number, and those for whose benefit it was arranged are apt to wish themselves anywhere but where they are.

It was also Myrna's intention to use the occasion to strike a blow on Julie's behalf.

'How could you be so damned disloyal to me!' was Julie's reaction to hearing that Myrna had invited Neil and Mandy.

'Neil is Irving's friend, and it's his party. Also, I thought you might like to take a look at the opposition.'

'I would, as a matter of fact,' Julie reluctantly admitted.

'In a roomful of people, you can get lost if you feel blue.'

'All right, I'll come.'

'But instead of getting lost in the crowd, why don't you bring a guy, to give Neil something to think about?'

Julie's response was, 'If I don't get Neil back, I intend to put guys from my life. And who could I bring?'

'For a woman who works in a mainly male profession, that shouldn't be too difficult.'

'But when she's considered formidable — '

'She's in a position to make whoever she asks think it's

a big compliment, and could do him some good on his way up.'

'Maggie Thatcher could take lessons from you, Myrna!'

'Irving is going to think that Mata Hari could.'

Miserable though she was, Julie had to laugh. 'Is Irving's real surprise going to be you presenting him with the watchdog's report?'

'Not quite,' Myrna said enigmatically. 'I'm inviting your son Paul, by the way.'

'What the hell for?'

'I'd rather you didn't ask.'

This was the afternoon Myrna had set aside to make her necessary telephone calls. Her next one was to Paul Newton, who had to be fetched from his bed by whoever had answered the phone in his flat, and Myrna would have been happier if that person had been female, given her present preoccupation.

'I'm sorry to have kept you hanging on, Mrs Sanger — '

'Don't apologise. We all know a nightworker has to get his sleep.'

'That's the sort of thing my mother would say.'

'It's on her behalf I'm calling you.'

'Has my father shown up?'

'He sure has.' Myrna put Paul in the picture.

'In that case, I'm really sorry for my mother.'

'Would you like to try to help her?'

'If you mean, why don't I go and confront my old man at his chambers, I'd have a nerve, wouldn't I? I mean — well, when did I ever think *he* knew what was best for *me*?'

'There are other ways, Paul. Go get yourself a cup of coffee and call me back when your head's ready to put together with mine. If my line is busy, keep calling until you get me.'

Paul laughed. 'Brill. I'll do that. Father once said to me you were a bit of a girl. He was right.'

Myrna glanced at her watch — what time was it now in California? Eight in the morning. Her father would be sitting in his wheelchair on the patio, eating a lonely breakfast. Her mother never rose before noon and Myrna wanted a private chat with him. Though sickness had now put her father's dynamic working life, and most other things, behind him, he kept to his early-breakfast routine – as if shedding it would be like finally throwing in the towel, Myrna thought, while she dialled the number.

As always, since frailty overtook him, a lump rose to her throat when she heard his voice – it was evident vocally, too.

'How's my princess in exile doing?'

'Missing her pop.' It was true.

'So why don't I buy out an LA agency? All I need is the woid from you-know-who —'

'You're never going to get it, Pop. Quit asking and do yourself a favour. How've you been?'

'A roll in the hay would do more for me than that treatment I'm getting. My ass, it's like a pin-cushion —'

'What're they shooting into you now?'

'Vitamins. From A to Zee! When I said to your mom what I just did to you, she said one part of me isn't going to *need* rigor mortis to set in! How d'you like the noive of that old broad?' he demanded in the Brooklyn accent he had carried with him from poverty through to affluence. 'She can't wait for my will to be read.' The quavering voice softened. 'But I could never say that about my princess. Whatever I offer her, that piker she married makes her say no to!'

'I don't think it's true about Mom.'

'No? I wouldn't put it past her to be getting herself a quicky from my male nurse, the minute he gets through using the hypodoimic on me.'

Nor would Myrna. Her mother's need to prove she still had what it takes would be with her till they buried her. And caricature figures though they seemed to others, Myrna would not have had her parents any other way. Their fighting spirit was rare in old people, and that had to be due to the lustiness neither had let die in them.

'I guess when Mom said what she did, Pop, she was paying you a compliment.'

'What am I going to do with a compliment like that when I can't get out of my wheelchair and chase her around the pool? Is there something I can do for my princess?'

220

'I could use a little cash.'

'How much is a little? Tell me and I'll treble it, Moina. And this would be a good time to buy you a mansion over there. Not to use dollars to buy British real estate now is a waste of money. Sooner would have been better, when my neighbour here flew to London and bought himself an apartment block.'

'Irving couldn't maintain a mansion on his income, Pop — '

'And I would be wasting breath I no longer have to spare offering to pay the bills. My princess not only marries a piker, she chooses an independent one!'

'She happens to love him. Be happy for her.'

'Okay, you win.' A sigh that sounded like a dry leaf rustling drifted over the line. 'Happiness is not for sale.'

'And a guy who earns enough to rent a Park Lane penthouse isn't exactly a piker.'

'Why then does his wife have to come to her pop for cash?'

'I'm throwing a surprise party for my beloved. You told me not to touch the money you gave me to put in the safe deposit box that he doesn't know about.'

'The emoigency money you definitely leave where it is. Happiness can take a tumble overnight.'

The words had a chilling ring for Myrna. She was sparing neither effort nor expense to hold her marriage together — but if things went wrong, a possibility she had not until now let herself contemplate, her devious plan could have the opposite effect.

She had brushed that thought aside and was about to call Anna, when Anna called her.

'I'm still trying to fathom out your invitation, Myrna! What's it all about?'

'Can't a woman have a joke with her husband?'

'Bearing in mind what followed the little one I had with mine, I'd say the answer is no. And "This is your life, Irving Sanger"? What the heck are you up to?'

'I want you to make sure that James cooperates — all I need is for him to spill the beans to Irv. Apart from that, all I'm going to say is my intentions are good.'

221

'When are they not? But that doesn't mean the outcome will be appreciated. The very least that could happen is that Irving will have a lousy day at the office, come home and find the place full of people, and tell them all to leave.'

'Irv is too polite to do that.'

'Men can sometimes behave unpredictably.'

Myrna wished she could tell Anna that was the reason for the party.

'How's Kim?'

'Where does Kim come into this conversation?'

'I've thought of her a lot, but I couldn't bring myself to call her. When it was touch and go, I said a little prayer for the baby.'

'That was kind of you, Myrna.'

'And I know how she must be feeling now.'

Once again, the tiny ghost from Myrna's past was visible through a crack in the shutter, and with it the woman whom life had cheated of so much. A moment later the glimpse was gone.

'This is going to be one helluva party!'

When the night came around, James had trouble in persuading Irving not to anaesthetise himself with liquor before they arrived.

'My instructions were to delay you at the office, and then pretend I was off home. You go in first, and I'll follow a little later,' James said when they reached the apartment block.

Irving clutched his arm. 'Oh no!'

'What was the point of all this intrigue if we stop pretending now?'

'I am not going in there alone. You can tell Myrna that you told me Anna was out this evening, and you invited yourself to come and eat with us.'

James stood on the pavement with sagging shoulders and gazed across the road at the trees being whipped by a wind too cruel for spring. 'Did nobody ever tell you that one lie always leads to another, Irving? And a person can get caught up in their own web of deception? Some might say they deserve to – but it shouldn't bloody have to involve their friends! I'm starting to feel like a fly struggling to disentangle itself.'

'In friendship, you have to take the bad with the good,' Irving informed him unnecessarily. And added, when they were riding up in the lift, 'Me, I feel like Daniel must have, just before he entered the lion's den.'

'But you'd better enter with a smile on your face, as if it's only Myrna you're expecting to see.'

'She's the one who's waiting to eat me up. Did she tell Anna who the spectators were going to be?'

'Everyone she's acquainted with in London, apparently.'

'Then why didn't she just hire Wembley Stadium?'

As they entered the flat, Irving said, 'Where Myrna picks up all these people she thinks are her friends has remained a mystery to me. A fine thing, when a guy walks into his own home and nobody knows who he is!' he complained as they made their way past a noisy group who did no more than glance at him casually. 'Half the people who come here to drink my liquor I never set eyes on again — '

'You're not paying the bill for this, though. Myrna told Anna her father is.'

'In that case I don't drink and I don't eat,' Irving was declaring when he saw Myrna standing beside the bar. At first he wasn't sure it was her. She was wearing a tuxedo, and looked like a slender youth. He had never seen her before in that sort of outfit; her style was feminine with a capital F, as a rule. Nor did he like the way her hair seemed to be pinned back. He did a double-take. 'Am I seeing things, James? Or has my wife had her hair cut off?'

'In what used to be called an Eton crop.'

'You mean like a boy's? Could she be trying to tell us something?'

'Not us. You. If it isn't all in your mind!'

'I need to sit down,' Irving said weakly.

James glanced around and saw neither a vacant seat, nor a face that he recognised. 'You'll be lucky.'

'May I take your coats?' a butler hired for the evening said to them. 'And may I enquire how you got in, sir?' he asked James.

Irving glared at him. 'Why not ask me? I live here.'

'I do apologise, Mr Sanger. Shall I tell Mrs Sanger you've arrived?'

'I'd rather you didn't.'

'Shall I send the waiter to you, sir?'

'No thanks.'

'If I may just say a word in your ear, sir, lots of gentlemen react as you're doing when they first arrive at their own surprise party, but it doesn't take them too long to enter into the spirit.'

'Your words of consolation are lost on *me*.'

James managed to thrust his hands into his trouser pockets without elbowing the people on either side of him. 'Well, what do we do now?'

But Irving was staring at the huge basket of flowers on the coffee table. 'What kind of flowers are those, James? You're the gardener.'

'Pansies. Aren't they lovely? You remarked on the colours of the ones I put in our front flower bed, I remember — '

'I was just checking. Did you ever see them used in a floral arrangement before?'

'No, a florist wouldn't be likely to stock them – Myrna must have ordered them specially. Anna's not too keen on pansies.'

'Nor is Myrna. And I'm not referring to flowers. Stop being such a *schmuck*, will you, James? The first thing I see when I get here is my wife doing a *Victor-Victoria* number – for a minute, I thought Julie Andrews had dropped in at the party! Now, I'm standing staring at a basket of you-know-whats. It wouldn't surprise me to find my study strung with fairy lights and a fruit cake on the buffet!'

'Are you the chap who once told me not to build things up in my imagination?' James enjoyed saying. Then Paul Newton pushed his way through to them with a plate loaded with food and said, 'I haven't come face to face with a faggot since my schooldays.'

It took them a second to realise he was referring to something on the end of his fork.

They were doing their best to smile, when Paul added, 'I hope you're enjoying your "This is your life" party, Mr Sanger. Mrs Sanger has spared no effort — '

When did she ever? thought Irving. If the joke weren't at his expense, he'd have to hand it to her for ingenuity. Joke?

'The buffet is groaning,' Paul went on. 'Everything from pâté-de-foie to cold turkey. I've been looking around for my father, but he doesn't seem to've arrived yet. My mother has a gentleman friend with her, by the way – and good for her!'

'When your father gets here, you won't be able to miss his arrival,' Irving said cryptically.

'Mother's rival's as striking as that, is she? Hm . . .' Paul gave them a wink and drifted off.

'Can you see Anna anywhere?' James asked Irving. 'She said she'd come in by tube so we could go home together in my car, and I don't like her using public transport at night on her own — '

'She's over there, with Julie, and a tall silver-haired guy.'

'Over where?'

'Where else would Julie be but beside where the nosh is? And there could be a major collision when Neil's walking-talking-rainbow heads directly to feed her cute little face! Are you going to go with me to beard the lion, boychik?'

'Would you mind if I didn't?'

'Now I know what she's at — '

'What you think she's at,' James corrected.

'What I'm suffering from is anticlimax-itis.' Irving smiled grimly. 'Nothing's changed, has it? And the cold turkey has to be Myrna's way of telling me she's going to break me of a habit I haven't got. How do I convince her she's wrong without finishing up a human wreck?'

'You could try telling her.'

'Myrna only knows from sign language.' Irving eyed the basket of flowers. 'If I hadn't already known it, I'd have found out tonight. And how can I tell her something I'm not supposed to know she knows?'

If there'd been the space to do it in, James would have given him a bloody good shaking. 'Let me tell you something, Irving. When a chap starts getting messages from inanimate objects – including a dead turkey – what he's likely to finish up as is a head case.'

'If you walked through a dung heap and got shit all over your shoes, you'd kid yourself it was only mud, James.'

225

Not any more. But he was up to here with the way the Sangers behaved with each other. This party would cost a small fortune, Irving was lucky he wasn't paying for it, and what was it all for? So Myrna could let Irving know she knew what she thought she knew about him – in her usual ducks-and-drakes fashion! James would have to be daft not to have got the message, but he was damned if he'd say so to Irving. And the Sangers were now still further enmeshed in an episode of their crazy sparring that was all about nothing. The future possible complications were boundless.

The centre of the room had gradually cleared as people made their way to the buffet. Irving saw Myrna heading towards him, and felt as if he was waiting in the arena with only James for protection. 'The lion has sniffed out its prey, boychik.'

But attack was the best form of defence. 'Your fly's undone, babe!'

He had the satisfaction of seeing Myrna stop short and glance down at her groin – and of raising a laugh at *her* expense from those who heard him and saw her reaction.

Myrna joined in the laughter and came to kiss him. 'My resident zipper-up wasn't here to help me dress — '

'And the one thing you overlooked, babe, was I have a key to let myself in. What were you planning for my arrival? A fanfare of trumpets?'

'When did I ever overlook anything, Irv? I saw you and James come in and left you to get acclimatised.'

Yes, for what she was up to to sink in. Irving put a smile on his face and glanced at the assorted throng milling round the buffet. 'What did you do? Call up Rentacrowd?'

'All those young people are friends of Paul Newton's whom I said he could bring along. And I'm letting you off your diet tonight.'

'Since I'm not hungry, I'll take a rain check on that. But don't neglect your hostess duties on my account, babe. The guest of honour has had a hard day, and is going to his study to put up his feet and drink some of his own liquor with his buddy.'

Myrna pretended she had not got the message. Anna must have told James her father was footing the bill, but she'd've had to tell Irv anyways. Once he'd got some Scotch inside him, he'd relax and everything would be okay.

She mouthed him a kiss and went to join Julie, who had moved with her plate to a now deserted sofa.

'Much use it was Julie bringing that chap along,' said James. 'Where's he got to?'

'Probably relieving himself of a surfeit of free champagne! Do you think she brought him to make Neil think again? – if and when he shows up.'

'No, I think it's why Myrna told her to bring him. Your wife has a finger in everyone's pie, Irving, but I would've expected Julie to bite it off.'

Irving saw them laughing together. 'When the chips are down, boychik, all that matters is they're both women – and any guy who forgets there's a primitive bond between them does so at his peril. If the one in his life doesn't know how to go for his jugular, another will tell her. And who could be more qualified to do so than my wife? Let's go get that drink!'

'How am I doing?' Myrna asked Julie.

'If I knew what you were hoping to achieve, apart from letting the guilty parties know you've tumbled to them, I'd tell you.'

'I'm going to have to keep you guessing.'

Julie dabbed a splash of mayonnaise from her colourful caftan. 'These napkins are terribly small, Myrna.'

'To get one large enough to cover Julie Newton's lap it would have to be custom-made.'

'This whole evening is custom-made, by Myrna Sanger. But why go to all this expense and trouble? I would just have said to Neil, "The game's up, chum. You're out of the closet."'

Myrna replied, 'That's why you're where you're at. And if you get Neil back, you'd be wise to remember that,' she added as Neil came into the room with his new love.

Mandy had on an abbreviated, white, knitted tube and looked as if she was wearing nothing under it. But the rainbow effect was still there – the dress was just the foil for the rest of her. Around her throat was a vivid pink scarf, her tights were turquoise, and on her feet were purple suede shoes. An emerald-green girdle encircled her tiny waist, and her fiery hair completed the striking picture.

Anna was beside the bar, talking to a lady from Myrna's synagogue committee, and stopped in mid-sentence when she saw Mandy. Only the genuinely young could get away with an outfit like that, and the girl had a glow about her that couldn't be bought.

'I'll say one thing for her,' Myrna said to Julie, 'she has terrible taste.'

'Except in men, of course. And if that's what I'm up against, there's no chance.'

'Shall I go get you the paper-knife from Irv's study?'

'If you did, I'd probably use it.'

'And from you, that's quite an admission, isn't it?' Myrna said, before going to greet the latecomers.

Julie was left to consider this parting shot. Where now was her lofty, cerebral approach to everything? Elbowed aside by something she couldn't respect herself for, that put her squarely where she'd never expected to be – in the palm of a man's hand. It was a moment that Myrna would've said she had coming to her, she thought, watching her errant son join his equally errant father.

Julie's unhappiness was such that she had not allowed herself to view retrospectively her own contribution to the situation, nor that her success was achieved largely at their expense. She was one of those women with a masculine mind in a female body, and it had come as a shock to her that, in the end, biology held sway.

While his mother was engaged in a tug-o'-war with her human frailty, Paul Newton was appraising her usurper.

'Are you an invited guest?' his father asked him. 'Or doing your usual, Paul?'

'My father doesn't approve of gate-crashing,' Paul said with a wink, to Mandy. 'He can be a bit of a wet blanket at times.'

Mandy returned the wink. 'I'd like to see him try that with me. You wouldn't dare, would you, Neily?'

'I might,' Neil said with a laugh. 'But *you* won't have to gatecrash parties, pet.'

Mandy glanced around at the mainly middle-aged crowd. 'I wouldn't bother to gatecrash one like this.'

Paul gave her another wink. 'Don't you go insulting my father's generation! If you'd like to meet some of your own, there's a gang of them over there.'

'Now you mention it, I wouldn't mind.'

'Brill,' said Paul.

'Can we pick up a plate of something on our way, Paul?'

'I'll help you load it up.'

'Good-oh! Great! See you in a bit, Neily.'

'With your permission, Father — ' Paul took Mandy's hand and led her away.

Neil got his breath back, squared his shoulders, and went – with 'Good-oh' and 'Brill' whirling in his mind – to do the decent thing. Now was as good, or bad, a time as any.

'How've you been, Julie?'

She managed to smile. 'Do you care?'

'What sort of question is that?'

'A very fitting one from a wife whose husband walked out without a word, and reappeared with a teenage replacement.'

'The girl has nothing to do with it.'

'Then why was she hanging on to your arm when you came in?'

'That's just the way she is.'

'And I never was.'

A moment of silence followed.

Then Neil said, 'Hasn't it occurred to you, even now, that your self-sufficiency was responsible for my leaving you?'

'I thought it was my weight that broke the camel's back.'

'Then I have to tell you I'm a stronger camel than you thought me.'

The crisp exchange was a reminder to both that one of the pleasures of living together had been the quick ability of each to utilise a play on words – before the words turned sour.

'There was a time when our marriage was like a tennis match,' Neil said, 'and I enjoyed the volleying.'

'When did you stop enjoying it?'

'When you began aiming to kill, and I had no option but to retaliate in kind.'

Julie paused, then swallowed her pride. 'Then why not come back — and we'll call it a tie?'

Neil drank some champagne, and gazed at the glass reflectively. 'Do you really think things could be set right between us as easily as that?'

'We could give it a try.'

'You'd have to start seeing me in a different light from the way you always have, Julie. And put your money where your mouth is, as Irving would say. Where is he? I haven't yet set eyes on him or James.'

'Myrna said they're sulking in the study.'

And Mandy was enjoying herself with Paul and his friends: Neil could soon find himself joining in the sulking session.

Julie returned him to their marital problem. 'I think Irving would agree I would be showing willing if I tried to lose some pounds. When I look back, it seems to me that all our rows were about my girth. You really did get terribly nasty about it, Neil.'

'Perhaps because the more I urged you not to, the more you ate.'

'You seem to forget that my principles were at stake. Unlike Myrna — though in some ways I've come to admire her — I'm not interested in tailoring myself to fit the modern image of feminine loveliness. Nor, since I have my career, do I have to — '

'Why don't you just make a long-playing album of all this?' Neil cut in. 'Not that it's necessary for my sake, since I know the whole damned rigmarole off by heart, by now.'

'I'll ignore your sarcasm, Neil, though you don't deserve me to. And if you come back to me, I'll put myself in a health farm and stay there until I'm a sylph. I'm prepared to make a major concession to please you.'

Neil finished his drink, and put the glass on a handy table. 'And that about sums things up,' he replied. 'You see, it's people on high horses who make concessions, Julie. What I want is a wife who's on the ground, with me.'

'You're talking about equality, but that isn't what you mean,' she retorted. 'What you want is to have the edge over me, but my mind is the only one I've got – and the same goes for yours. I can't give you what you want.' If she could, she probably would.

Neil's response was brief and to the point. 'And what a pleasant change it is to make love to someone who isn't my superior.'

Julie watched him walk away and head for the bar. Then Anna and Myrna appeared one on either side of her.

'What would I do without my two staunch supporters!'

'You've blown it, haven't you?'

'But thanks for plotting with my son to give me the opportunity to.'

'Who, me? I just heard the viper get invited to go on from here with Paul's friends to a disco, by the way,' Myrna said with satisfaction. 'So hang in there, Julie. Tonight is not yet over, and tomorrow is another day.' She went to re-mingle with her other guests.

'Myrna's great strength is her eternal optimism!' Julie exclaimed.

'And I'd say the plotting you just mentioned is aimed at a little more than you thought.'

'Breaking it up, you mean? Neil will get bored with that kid in no time, Anna, if he isn't already. And I'm going to have to stop not being able to see the wood for the trees, except that it's too late.'

Julie smiled wanly. 'Before Neil arrived I was musing about marriage in general, wondering how many of the happy-looking married couples in this room are at logger-heads at home. People only stop putting up a front when they're with their intimates, don't they? – and not always then. Look how you and James used to be, even when you were just with Neil and me.'

'That wasn't putting up a front.'

'Then what the hell was it?'

'It would take too long to tell.'

'Maybe I should just tell myself I'm well out of it!' Julie saw Anna turn pale, and touch her brow. 'What's the matter?'

'I don't feel too good. The room's spinning round, let me hang on to you — '

But it was too late. One minute Anna was standing talking to Julie, the next she was lying at her feet.

Julie's escort chose that moment to rejoin her.

'Don't just stand there gawping, pick her up, Geoffrey!'

When Anna came to, she was lying on the leather Chesterfield in Irving's study, with Julie clamping a cold compress to her forehead, Myrna wafting a phial of something under her nose, and James rubbing her hands. Irving and Neil were gazing solemnly down at her.

'This has to be my deathbed,' she said, wanting to laugh, 'the way you lot are grouped around me.'

Myrna gave her a hug. 'We're relieved to know it isn't. You gave us all a fright.'

'Blame it on the champagne. I'm not used to it and I had two glasses.'

'You're still the suburban housewife, aren't you?' Julie said with a smile. 'Despite the out-of-character step you took.'

'This isn't the time to make cracks about Anna's face-lift!' Neil snapped.

'It wasn't a crack, it was just an observation. But one that strengthens my argument nevertheless.'

'How did I get here?' Anna asked, to divert the Newtons' attention.

'My friend scooped you up and carried you,' Julie told her.

'Lucky for him it wasn't you he was required to scoop up!' said Neil. 'Since he isn't Superman.'

'Is that what you're trying to prove you are, by laying a girl young enough to be your daughter?'

James emerged from his tongue-tied anxiety about his wife. 'A person can't even recover from a faint around you two, without your bloody cut and thrust going on over their limp body!'

'Maybe the rest of us should clear out of here, and leave James and Anna alone,' Irving said.

'A good idea, and talking of leaving us alone, why don't we all adopt that policy towards each other?'

Irving gave him a hurt glance. 'I'm going to forget you said that.'

'But I'd rather you didn't.'

'What a way for my lovely party to end,' Myrna said with chagrin.

Since, one way or another, the evening had been near-purgatory for the rest of them, a short silence followed.

Then Irving said, 'Your party is still going on, babe. Unfortunately, nobody has left yet. And since the only guests who matter to me are right here in this room, I don't mind saying to you in front of them that you went to a lot of unnecessary trouble on my account. Including with flowers I'm not partial to, and the way you've done yourself up.'

'But a change is as good as a rest,' said Myrna glibly. 'A person can get bored with roses all the way and variety is the spice of life. I'd be the first to admit it.'

Irving was flummoxed. What was she trying to tell him? That all was forgiven?

Julie said, 'You just used three clichés on the trot, Myrna!'

'If they say what I want to say, why shouldn't I?'

And that was probably as near as the Sangers would come to putting into words what was troubling them both, thought James. Instead, they'd continue the charades that Myrna dreamed up and Irving went along with. The Newtons were the other extreme. Did the style of a marriage have to be one way or the other? Manipulative machinations, or head-on confrontations? And oh, for the styleless marriage James hadn't realised he had when he had it.

Anna said from her still-supine position on the Chesterfield, 'Aren't you going to explain why you put "This is your life, Irving Sanger" on the invitations, Myrna?'

'I expected to find you'd had his parents flown in, at the very least,' said Neil.

Myrna smiled foxily. 'All I'm going to say is it doesn't have anything to do with the past; it refers to the future.'

Irving's expression was as though he had just heard the knell of doom.

'When everyone's gone home, our private party will begin,' Myrna added, 'and the mystery will be unravelled for my beloved.'

'Yuk!' thought Julie. But it had kept Irving tied to Myrna's hostess-apron strings.

CHAPTER ELEVEN

WHAT TRANSPIRED at the Sangers' private party is best left to the imagination. James had to hold his in check when Irving told him that Myrna's bedtime apparel that night was a pair of striped pyjamas, which she had said she would henceforth wear on Mondays and Wednesdays. It was apparently her intention on the remaining five nights to resume her fetchingly female nightwear and cover her Eton crop with a wig.

'Now we know what those three clichés were all about, boychik! And the mind boggles at my wife's ability to cater for all tastes.'

'Also at your inability to tell her she's barking up the wrong tree.'

'But only twice weekly,' Irving quipped.

He then surprised James by revealing that he found this particular example of his wife's deviousness somewhat touching. 'It proves she would go to any lengths to hold on to me, doesn't it? And if that isn't love, what is?'

But knowing that a woman loved you was no compensation for the way women in general behaved, thought James. Or Neil would still be with Julie, and Irving wouldn't be having to count himself lucky that Myrna still wanted him despite what she thought she knew. If a market research project was done on the subject, with a cross-section of the female population, the result would probably show them all to be variations of the same theme.

'You were so tensed up when I left you last night, Irving, I just looked in to see how you were. I'd better go and begin my day now — '

Irving stopped polishing his glasses and put them on. 'With my troubles and yours, James, it's remarkable that this agency hasn't ground to a halt. Do you have a luncheon appointment today?'

'No,' James said reluctantly.

'So we'll get together then.'

For more of the same. James had once thought Anna the exception to the rule, but the time when he'd sat back smugly listening to Irving, or Neil, or both, sounding off about their menopausal wives was long gone. And the way Anna kept remarking that they were communicating – on the odd occasions when she thought they were – was driving him daft. It was as if she'd only recently discovered the word and what it meant.

He was briefly delayed in the corridor by Ronnie, looking his usual spruced-up self and carrying a sheaf of papers with the air of having been hard at work for hours: he probably had.

'Morning, James. You're looking worried. Anything the matter?'

Only – among other things – another letter from the taxman that had made James put down his teacup with a trembling hand when he read:

I would draw your attention to the fact that it is a serious matter to omit any source of income from your tax return. Please give this matter your urgent attention.

James still had no idea what it was all about. He was honest-Joe personified in all his dealings, and always had been.

'You'll have to excuse me,' he snapped. 'I haven't the time to stand gossiping that you obviously have – and I'm probably not the only one who's noticed it.'

He had the satisfaction of seeing Ronnie's cocksure mask briefly slip. A little of the insecurity that kept executives on the boil, and stopped them from sleeping at night, was what he deserved.

Tracy had all the mail opened and was cooling her heels waiting for him – James always had to rush through his paperwork to keep up with her, which he hadn't with Marj.

'My brother and sister-in-law are splitting up,' she told him while he hung up his raincoat. 'The marriage-guidance counselling didn't work.'

'Perhaps because, in the end, it's up to the people themselves,' James answered cryptically. And it was going to take some kind of miracle to put him and Anna back where they belonged. Too much had gone wrong for them, in too many ways.

When he arrived home that evening, her first words to him were, 'You look terrible.'

Who wouldn't, with the taxman's threat in his pocket? 'I'm rehearsing my jailbird's pallor.'

She stopped stirring the soup – which James was coming to associate with some of his worst moments.

'Whatever do you mean, love?'

'Since the details are beyond me, they would certainly be beyond you. But Irving was right.'

'What about? I'll let the insult to my intelligence pass.'

'About a person probably being able to find themselves behind bars without knowing why – and for something they haven't done. And if all it took to sort out the mess I seem to be in was intelligence, I wouldn't be in it.'

'You're not making sense, James.'

'Nor do the letters I keep getting from the tax inspector. He seems to think I'm getting income from investments I haven't told them about. You haven't been dabbling in stocks and shares on the side, have you?' he said with a hollow laugh.

'Don't be daft.' Anna paused uneasily. 'Would a little nest-egg be looked on as an investment, James?'

'What little nest-egg?'

'A Post Office savings account, for instance.'

'Are you telling me you've got one? Oh my God!'

'Since when was it a crime to be thrifty?'

'The crime, love, is to keep it a secret from your husband, who then ends up the criminal for hiding its existence from the taxman.'

'How was I supposed to know it had to be mentioned on your tax return? I opened the account when I was a single girl, and I've just gone on doing what I've always done; whenever I had a bit to put by, that was where it went.'

She tasted the soup and added more seasoning.

'And what you're doing now, in the middle of this revelation — !'

'All that's left to tell, James, is that when I told Julie, some

237

years back, how much I'd saved, she advised me to transfer it from an ordinary account to the sort I'd get interest on.'

'Lord preserve me from all women,' James groaned. 'I was the one you should have told how much was in it – after you'd told me you'd *got* an account.'

'Would you like to know why I didn't?'

'If you insist.'

'My nest-egg's the only thing I've achieved entirely by myself. And it was going to be my contribution to the country cottage we had in mind for when you retire. I wanted it to be a nice surprise. Shall I tell you how much it's worth now?'

'I'd rather not know the worst till I sit down to write my excuses.' James needed a whisky! 'Not that the tax inspector's going to believe me. Who would?'

'Anyone who's married to a man who thinks it isn't necessary to explain to a mere woman how the tax system works,' Anna replied, 'just because her job is only keeping house. It struck me the other day, James, that if you pop off before I do, I wouldn't know a thing about your finances. What *you*'ve got invested, or where. I'd be a widow who'd got given the housekeeping money every week, and extra for clothes, but has never signed a cheque in her life – in company with a lot of women like me, I don't doubt.'

'If you'd asked me, I'd've told you.'

'But it never entered my head to – any more than it entered yours to involve me in matters men think wouldn't interest their wives. I'm sorry my nest-egg has landed you in a mess, James, but it's your fault as much as mine. Would you mind helping me into a chair? I feel a bit wonky again, though not as bad as I did last night — '

James was by her side in two strides. 'D'you think it's something to do with the menopause, love?' He settled her in the Windsor chair and eyed her anxiously.

'Well, I haven't been knocking back champagne this time, have I?'

'Can I get you anything? A cup of tea, maybe?'

'No. Just let me sit quietly for a minute – I feel better already.'

'I'm sorry I shouted at you.'

'We've had a lot of shouting matches lately, haven't we,' Anna said drily. 'Have you still got that tight feeling round your head?'

'What's that got to do with you getting dizzy spells, and fainting like you did last night?'

'I'm as entitled to my strain symptoms as you are,' Anna answered, keeping her tone light. 'And what went on with Kim probably put the tin lid on it. I haven't felt right since that terrible week.'

'Why didn't you tell me?'

'A year ago, I wouldn't have had to. You'd have known.'

James said after a silence fraught with feeling, 'Why can't we be like that again?'

'Too much has happened, James.'

'Including my bloody sexual problem.'

'If we could sort out the rest, I don't think you'd have one.' Anna paused reflectively. 'Of all the hundreds of things that seem to've been said to me by our friends, since all this began, it's something Julie said that I've come round to thinking makes the most sense — '

Just when James felt they had drawn a little closer, Anna was quoting Julie again. 'And what *was* this pearl of wisdom?'

'That you and I are having trouble establishing a relationship that's entirely dependent on ourselves, that doesn't include Kim. She could be right.'

James said, 'This may come as a surprise to you, love, but for me, marriage isn't something you can approach objectively. It might be a contract, but it shouldn't be one with the kind of clauses Julie insists on, or a wheel and deal set-up like Myrna enjoys. And much good your girlfriends' approach has done *their* marriages! Or their husbands.'

'If you're going to tell me that Myrna needs her bottom spanking — '

'I'm not. She'd probably enjoy it. You were talking about being left a widow, and if you'd like to know how to hasten the process, Myrna's the one to ask. What I *was* going to tell you, and you'd better accept it once and for all, is that approaches and tactics of any kind are not for me, nor

239

ever going to work with me. I'm just a simple
shire lad dressed up for the part I have to play in the
world. And you're supposed to be my helpmate.'

Anna had the last word. 'You'll be telling me I'm Adam's
rib, in a minute. But I don't have to believe it.'

PART THREE: And then . . .

ANNA WAS in the supermarket when the vertigo she had been trying not to worry about dizzied her again. She clung to her laden trolley with the smell of soap powder in her nostrils and the tower of toilet rolls ahead of her spinning like a huge top.

After a minute or two, the vertigo passed. It hadn't lasted as long as the last time, but if it happened when she was crossing the main road, with nothing to clutch at but a car or a bus — ? Time for a check-up, Anna. And this time her symptoms were all too physical.

She put her groceries in the car and went to the health centre there and then. Though it was surgery-time she expected to be fobbed off with an appointment, but the girl she still thought of as the 'squeezer-in' lived up to that name. Here and there, the Health Service still had some human touches.

Before Kim's miscarriage, Anna couldn't have envisaged ever consulting young Dr Binns again. With something like this, you wanted reassurance as well as whatever the treatment was. But they'd got to know each other, hadn't they? While Dr Binns was examining her she said, 'One of the troubles with the change of life is you never know if feeling off-colour is due to that, or not. If I told my husband I'd got earache, he'd suggest the menopause had caused it!'

'Apart from what brought you to see me, how have you been feeling?'

'I seem to be lacking in energy. And my appetite isn't what it was.'

'Any morning sickness?'

Anna almost fell off the examination-couch.

'Haven't you noticed that your waist has thickened, Mrs Ridgeway?'

'That happens to lots of women my age,' she said when she got her breath back.

'But it isn't why it's happened to you.'

'Are you sure, Doctor?'

'If I weren't, I'd have waited to get the results of the pregnancy test before sounding so sure. But you can wait till then, if you like, before telling your husband I was wrong when I said you might not have a family christening to look forward to.'

He smiled at Anna's stunned expression, and said kindly, 'You're a healthy lady – and not the first of my patients to find herself in your position and manage to cope with it.'

Anna was having difficulty coping with herself. Her mind was a-whirl with thoughts, and behind them she heard her mother's voice warning her on the telephone that a woman could 'get caught on the change'.

'I don't know whether to laugh or cry, Dr Binns.'

'That's the usual reaction.'

But no help to Anna. How was she going to tell James? He was always commiserating with Mike about his resident grandchild, and that wasn't a permanent disruption. And how could she break this to Kim, who'd just lost a baby?

It wouldn't be easy to tell Myrna, either – though Myrna would probably make one of the quips she used to hide her real feelings and keep the shutter firmly down.

The first person she told was Julie.

'I'd rather be in your shoes than mine,' was Julie's unexpected reply.

'But leaving how I feel out of it, it doesn't seem fair on the child. It will only be Kim's age when James and I are practically septuagenarians, and will have to suffer double the generation-gap problem we probably were to Kim in her teens. As for James, when he's in his fifties, having to chase a ball and a young kid on the Heath, instead of spending Sunday afternoon with his feet up – I don't see it!'

Julie laughed. 'Nor me. But you can't argue with God's will, Anna. I've never been religious, as you know, but it's struck me lately that there's a pattern to everyone's life. That things don't happen by accident.'

'You're talking to a woman who's just discovered otherwise!'

'But how do you *really* feel about it?'

'I'll tell you when I really know.'

Anna said nothing to James until the tests had proved positive. But by then, the onset of morning queasiness, if not sickness, was proof enough, and she relived how she had felt in the early stages of her first, long-ago pregnancy.

Memories she had filed away in a corner of her mind now dusty with the cobwebs of time had begun returning to her. James watching her breastfeed Kim. The two of them proudly pushing the pram. Herself pegging nappies on the line to dry, and gossiping with Julie who was doing the same on the other side of the privet hedge that divided their back gardens when they were young mothers.

Julie had often complained about wasting her brains on being a mum, and couldn't wait for the twins to start school, so she could resume her career. And how ironic it was that she had just said she'd prefer to be in Anna's shoes now. If Neil didn't return to Julie, Anna had no doubt that her friend would come to terms with it, and continue going from strength to strength in her profession. But something she wouldn't have expected was that Julie's sure step would falter, however briefly, when she found herself alone.

Anna's way of dropping her bombshell on James was to put it the way Dr Binns had suggested.

'A family christening after all?' James replied. 'Which of my nieces is in the pudding club?'

'Neither, so far as I know. I am.'

James, who had just poured himself a sherry, nearly spilled it as he sat down with a thump. 'This has to be a joke.'

'It is, in a way. An April Fools' one – on you and me.' Anna stopped herself from saying that April 1st was when the beast in him had last emerged, and said instead, because she wanted love to flower in the child she was carrying, 'The night I got back from Greenham, and we rushed over to Julie's was March 31st. I heard the hall clock strike midnight, before you made love to me, which means the deed was done on All Fools' Day.'

She smiled wryly. 'But Dr Binns and a rabbit – if that's still how they do the testing – have confirmed the joke, James. And you and I are going to have to take it seriously. We can't blame this on our friends!'

'I was thinking of blaming it on the milkman. And I'm just beginning to take it in.' James got up and paced the room with a dazed expression on his face.

Anna said, 'If you're practising for walking the floor with the baby, when it wakens at night, that's fine with me.'

'How are we going to cope with all that again!'

'Side by side. Unless you want me to have an abortion.'

'Over my dead body.'

'If I'd thought you'd say "yes please", I wouldn't have said it.'

'Do chemists' shops still sell that stuff called gripe-water we used to soothe Kim with?' James asked as his mind swooped backward to what seemed like another life. 'Or was it Milk of Magnesia?'

'I wouldn't know, but I'm going to have to find out. Can you see me sitting at the clinic, waiting for the baby to be weighed, with a crowd of young mums!'

'It's a good thing you had the face-lift, they'll think you're one of them. We used to give Kim something called Virol, too.'

'No, we didn't, it was Marmite. And *you* can learn to change a nappie, this time round.'

'It can't have been Marmite, I don't like the taste, and I used to dip my finger into the jar and have a lick before I put some on Kim's dummy.'

'Are dummies still in?'

'Probably not, in an age when they think hang-ups begin in the cradle!'

'I know potty-training is out.'

'It'll be back in again in this house,' James replied. 'The day anyone can prove to me that an adult's subconscious mind is linked to their infancy bowel movements, I'll eat my hat.'

James suddenly became aware that he was no longer wearing his *invisible* hat.

If he knew where it now was, he would risk putting it back on, in order to raise it to the son or daughter he hadn't yet met. Though the practical aspect of Anna's news had temporarily floored him, the aftermath was a feeling of ease and normality that he'd feared was gone for ever.

Anna was thinking that they had been talking happily for several minutes, but had the wisdom to refrain from saying so.

'So much for the peaceful retirement I was looking forward to,' James said, letting his mind leap ahead. 'A seventeen-year-old wouldn't take kindly to being removed from where everything's at to a country cottage.'

'Forget it, love. The picture's changed.' Anna patted her tummy. 'This kid isn't going to let us settle down to old age along with our friends.'

'Irving will laugh his head off when he hears what's happened to us. Myrna, too.'

'But their having no children might make them a little sad on their own account.'

James said, 'I couldn't imagine Myrna ever having wanted them.'

'You haven't known her all that long, have you? And I know her a lot better now than I did when she first befriended me — '

'In her own upside-down way.'

'What I've come to think about that, James, is it's just her way of dealing with herself.' It would be breaking Myrna's deepest confidences to say any more than that, but Anna wouldn't let her go undefended. She was a true friend.

'But I doubt that Irving has ever seen the side of her you seem to have,' James answered. 'And before we say goodbye to "analysis", which I hope we're going to, I'd also lay odds that Myrna doesn't know that under that brash exterior, her husband is the kind they call the salt of the earth. What bloody fools those two are! Like a pair of skaters skimming the surface of life, hand in hand — but as separate as strangers when it comes to what really matters.'

Anna said with a smile, 'It isn't like you to wax so lyrical. But I know what you mean.'

James poured himself another sherry. 'Because I'm

sometimes scathing about the Sangers doesn't mean I'm not fond of them. Sorry for them, too.'

'After the news you've just received, I'm surprised you can spare a moment to be sorry for anyone but yourself.'

'Then you've got me wrong, love.'

'I'm relieved to hear it.'

James went to kiss her, and they held each other close for a while, in the silent communion they had once known. 'What's happened to us, at a time when most people have no option but to put that kind of joy behind them, seems to me like a rare gift from God,' he said.

Was that what Julie had been trying to tell Anna, when she mentioned God's responsibility in the matter?

'Whether I'll still think so when my sleep is disturbed by infant teething-troubles is another matter,' he went on with a laugh.

'Neither of us has the stamina we once had.'

'But fathering a child, when I thought I was over the hill — '

'You never told me you thought that — '

'What husband would? And what it's given me to look forward to – well, it's made me feel a new man. It's going to be like you and me reliving the best years of our lives, Anna.'

'But with the benefit of hindsight,' she said enigmatically. 'Why do I have the feeling we've come full circle since the night I blacked your eye? Probably because what began with a joke has ended with one,' she answered her own question, with a laugh.

'Is that your womanly way of telling me there's now going to be peace between us?'

'If this doesn't do it for us, James, nothing will, since it's already begun to. It must have something to do with the sort of people we are.'

'I never lost sight of the sort of people we are. But let's not ruffle our feathers about it.'

'Just so long as you raise no objections to me being an "I", as well as half of our "we", everything will be fine. We can't give this baby young lovers for parents, like Kim had, but it's entitled to a mum and dad who are friends.'

'Am I getting any dinner tonight?'

'I'll go and serve it up – which is usually your cue to go to the loo.'

'And this isn't the time for me to prove you wrong,' James said, heading for the door.

Anna was wheeling the serving trolley from the kitchen to the dining-room, and imagining it was a pram, when she heard a resounding thud issue from the cloakroom. Who would have thought the plonk of plastic on porcelain could sound like sweet music?

ALSO AVAILABLE FROM
HODDER AND STOUGHTON PAPERBACKS